Praise for Vaughn R. Demont's *House of Stone*

"House of Stone is the first book by Vaughn R. Demont that I've read and I'll be looking for others in the future."

~ *Literary Nymphs*

"House of Stone is a humorous romp with some great characters and a fun plot."

~ *Whipped Cream Erotic Romance Reviews*

"...fun afternoon reading. ...I look forward to reading Richard's continuing adventures."

~ *The Good, The Bad, and the Unread*

"...ingenious. ...mixes savage romance with fairy tale with erotica, but manages to make it all a perfect melting pot."

~ *Elisa Rolle*

"Between Richard's accomplished characterization and the intriguing twists of the plot, this was an absorbing, entertaining read."

~ *Book Utopia*

Look for these titles by

Vaughn R. Demont

Now Available:

Coyote's Creed

House of Stone

Vaughn R. Demont

SAMHAIN
PUBLISHING

Samhain Publishing, Ltd.
577 Mulberry Street, Suite 1520
Macon, GA 31201
www.samhainpublishing.com

House of Stone

Print ISBN: 978-1-60928-091-8
Digital ISBN: 978-1-60928-061-1

Editing by Anne Scott

First Samhain Publishing, Ltd. electronic publication: June 2010
First Samhain Publishing, Ltd. print publication: May 2011

Dedication

For Heather McD, with all my thanks.

Acknowledgments

My deepest thanks to Anne Scott, my tireless editor who guided me through the revision process and helped me become a better writer. My thanks also go out to my dedicated beta readers Chris S., I.D. Locke, Scott G., Marc V., Jordan, Angie, Sophie, and Nicky, who kept me writing on nights I'd have much rather given up and watched TV. I'd also like to thank Pearl Jam, whose music I listened to so much while writing this book that their songs will likely provide the soundtrack to my dreams and nightmares for the rest of my life. And finally, my eternal gratitude to my Mom, who supports me without question despite knowing what I write.

Chapter One
I Am Mine

"Now that the foul beast is slain, gentle squire, wouldst thou allow me into your chamber so I might sheathe my blade?"

For the record, I don't actually talk like that.

The new guy is on his back, on a rock from props we used in the last one of these films. He has smooth skin, tight muscles, a sheen of sweat more from the lights burning overhead than actual excitement, and a decently sized erection twitching against his waist and leaking a little precome. He can't be more than twenty.

He stares at me with hungry brown eyes and shakes a lock of black hair away from his well-tanned face. I'm in costume, meaning I'm wearing about thirty pounds of ceremonial armor normally intended for formal events like a knighting or a celebration of the changing of the seasons or some other self-congratulatory circle jerk that we Fae are famous for among the denizens of the City.

Granted, my attitude would probably be different if I were ever invited to any of them.

I removed my codpiece about an hour ago, as I was busy slaying a dragon.

The "dragon" in question is a short human named Derrick

who only got this job because he had a high enough threshold of pain to have his penis (and a very impressive one at that) tattooed with green scales and the head of a dragon on the glans. The rest of him is covered in well-applied body paint to give him a decent dragonish look. I "slew" him by weaving an enchantment that rendered him helpless. In plain English I took off my codpiece and told him to suck me off, which contradicts the faux-high diction I'm expected to use, but hell, I didn't write the script, and it's a general rule that you don't tell the writer or the director how to do their job.

Ye gods, kid, stop staring at my dick and just say your one line.

"Yes, my lord," he says quickly. "Please break the dragon's enchantment on me with your mighty blade?"

I fight the urge to roll my eyes. The way he emoted, I'm tempted to ask if he'd like an order of fries with that.

Granted, he's probably staring because in his eyes I'm the most attractive man he's ever seen. People aren't able to tell that I'm a sidhe, one of the Fae (we're just stories and superstitions, after all), but they can still recognize my unearthly beauty (as I'm not really from the Earth most people know). My skin is flawless and fashionably tanned, smooth, devoid of hair save my shoulder-length auburn locks (which never need brushing) and perfectly groomed beard (which I don't even have to shave or trim). I'm decently muscled, more lithe than bulky, definitely strong enough to wear thirty pounds of armor while I'm either fighting a duel for my honor or getting a hummer from a guy with inked equipment. Regardless, I'm pretty enough that he's a bit stupefied. I hate working with new guys.

The irony is that among Fae, I'm actually quite homely.

I lift his legs and nudge him to pull his knees back to his

chest. Not comfortable for him but it'll be easier for the camera to see me push my fingers into him and pump them slow. He's already moaning rather loudly, overselling it. Rookie mistake. If he's this intense, it won't be all that impressive when I finally put my dick in him. Not doing that yet, though. Not until Will, the director, tells me to. They need to get the shot first, so I'll probably be fingering the kid for the next five or ten minutes.

While I'll make sure he's plenty loose for me, I could have my share of fun with the kid. Hell, I could tickle his prostate and see if he climaxes, slip in a third finger, even use a little magic if I really want to be cruel. I smile at him with the side of my mouth currently away from the cameras and start poking around his secret spot. I see him close his eyes and moan, his hands gripping his legs now, holding them in place.

"Rein him in, would ya, Dick?" The director's *sotto voce* even though this is the part where the music is turned up during editing and we could converse normally if needed.

"If he can't handle my fingers," I say *sotto voce* out of deference to Will. "How's he going to handle the rest of me?" I don't actually have magic fingers, I was exaggerating. I'm just Fae. When it comes to humans, we do damned near everything perfectly. I'm doing a cold read of this kid's erogenous zones, but I know the look in his eyes, the pitch of his moans. Sure, he wants the job, but at the moment he's far more interested in me screwing him. And, well, that really isn't all that professional.

So I wriggle my fingers against his prostate, poke it, rub it, pump my fingers in and out of him, and then it's only a matter of time before...

"Uhhhnnnnnnnnnn!"

And the rookie finishes about an hour before he's supposed to. Without Will's okay. Maybe they'll bring in someone who can actually attempt to deliver a line.

I pull my fingers out of him quickly, making him gasp. He's grinning stupidly up at me, and I smile in return as I look down at the puddle of seed he's made on his chest, a bit of it having reached his chin.

"Nice volume, kid," I say and give him the smile that usually goes on the DVD covers. "You just got fired."

For the record, the three most important words in working in adult films are not *location, location, location*, they're *endurance, endurance, endurance.* You have to hold off shooting your spunk until your scene is done, which often takes more than an hour, and you usually have to remain erect through all of that, and then come on command. If you can't do that, don't bother applying. It's a simple rule.

Off the record? He probably could've lasted the hour. Probably.

"Damn it!" Will storms over to me, wearing his you-just-cost-me-money face. I hold up my hands in surrender. One of the interns brings over a robe, but I wave it off. "Dick, I told you to rein him in. We just lost an hour of shooting time 'cause of this."

"You honestly think I'm *that* good? It was my fingers. And he wasn't touching himself at all. Kid's got a hair trigger up his ass and it slipped by." I won't ask who the kid slept with to get the job. Will doesn't do that. "Kid wasn't ready for the pros, simple as that," I say. "Send him back to the farm team making the amateur shit."

"Oh, right, yeah," Will says and fakes a look of contemplation. "The farm team." He's about five inches shorter than me and not nearly as well built, but he does hold my current career in his hands. "I told you to rein him in, you didn't. We're going again after lunch and the kid gets another shot." He shakes a finger in my face before I can complain. I haven't earned enough fame to play at being a prima donna.

Will walks off and then stops, looking over his shoulder at me. "Can you do that with your cock?" If there's any reason I like my boss, it's because he's helped me learn the joys of low diction.

"What, get him off whenever I want?" I check the kid, who's peeling himself off the rock, a grin still plastered on his face. "I don't know, probably." Never tried with just the one longer thicker "finger" before, but it should be the same principle. I can bash away at a guy's prostate all I want, but making him finish on command? What am I going to be, his training wheels?

"Good, then do that on the next run-through." Before I can tell Will that it's not a sure thing, he whistles sharply to no one in particular.

And, well, that's lunch. End of conversation. We get an hour because we're usually recovering from a scene. And I need an hour anyway because I've been wearing my armor all day and I need a break.

Blue Line Productions (named for the train line, not because we do blue films) is set up in a warehouse about a hundred yards from Destry Bay (the actual bay, not the suburb), which would be pretty damned impressive if we weren't surrounded by closed factories, rusted piers and a pervasive smell coming from the sewage-treatment plant. As a result, we don't have trailers for the actors, just partitioned spaces that serve as dressing rooms. Since we're doing moderately well now, we were finally able to get ceilings for our rooms last week.

My dressing room is rather simple, just a table and mirror and a padded chair, as well as a cot for the rare occasions there's enough time between scenes for a nap.

"Did your scene go as expected, Your Excellency?" I'm greeted as always by Simaron, my manservant. Sim's father served my father, his grandfather served my grandfather, you can probably see where this is going. He's a couple inches shorter than I at six flat, and built more solidly than I as well, and dressed impeccably in a butler's uniform. Short black hair, bright blue eyes, his skin a bit lighter than mine. You'd never guess there was sidhe blood in him.

"Well as can be expected, Sim. We're on lunch for the next hour. The new kid came too fast so he needs time to recover."

"Very well, my lord." He motions to a platter of fresh fruit and a goblet of poured wine. "I have prepared a small meal, sir. I apologize for the limited selection. May I assist you with your armor?"

I nod, primarily because he's the one who put it on me in the first place. His fingers work the straps and catches, and within minutes I'm wearing naught but a padded vest and my armor is on a stand. I'm still exposed from the waist down, but Sim sees me naked every day when he dresses me. (He has made comments about my usual taste in attire. "T-shirts and jeans are not proper for a man of your station, good sir.")

"You seem a bit tense, Your Excellency. Is there anything amiss?" I see his eyes dart down to my groin for the barest of seconds, and realize I'm still rather erect. I shake my head once.

"Everything is fine. Any tension is from wearing that armor all day." I stretch my back and grab an apple, biting out a hunk of it. I have no idea where he finds fresh fruit and good wine in St. Benedict (or just the Benedict as the locals say), but I'm not about to ask. "I didn't get to finish the scene, so I'm afraid I'm still a bit eager in that regard."

"Would you like me to attend to it, Your Excellency? My skills are as always at your disposal."

"More than anything I'd like a shoulder rub. My back is full of knots." Cool air slides over my body as I take off my vest. After I hand it to Sim, he dutifully folds the vest and places it on the table. I toss out the apple after taking another big bite and lie down on the cot, which Sim has furnished with satin sheets. My boots are still on. But considering how long it takes to get them off with all the laces, it's best to leave them where they are. While on my stomach, I hear the bed creak as Sim straddles my thighs, the fabric of his slacks rubbing against my skin.

I put my face in a pillow so I won't moan too loud when he works his magic on my shoulders. He isn't professionally trained or anything, but after doing this for fifteen years he's rather well-acquainted with my musculature and knows how to work out anything he'll encounter.

"Harder, Sim, I've got less than an hour." I wriggle a bit to get comfortable, sandwiching my penis between my stomach and the mattress. His fingers press harder, changing their positioning, aiming for deep tissue to find the tension and work it out as his hands travel my shoulders and spine.

"As you wish, my lord." I can already feel the stress and tension melting away, he's that damned good at his job. "A message arrived for you by courier this morning, sir."

"Was it an actual courier," I say, well, half-moan. Like I said, he's good at this. "Or are you talking about the mailman again?"

"The post arrives in early afternoon, sir. The message was from a courier of Her Grace, Duchess Cadwyn." His hands immediately move to the knots that just bunched up in my shoulders. There's a bit of tension in them, now.

The City has many counties. Not counties you might think of. I mean actual counties with counts and viscounts, baronies with real barons, as well as two duchies, all part of the Kingdom of Rainbows (because when my ancestors first arrived here, there was, you guessed it, a rainbow overhead). I'm the viscount of a small part of St. Benedict that no one among my people really cares about. Duchess Cadwyn is the Duchess of Tolon Wood, right in the middle of Allora, surrounded by the rich, the famous and the cultured, which *everyone* among my people cares about.

And since the Queen has other areas of her kingdom that require her attention, most of the responsibilities fall to the most powerful and favored noble, who is Duchess Cadwyn. And if she sent her courier, it means one of two things, which I can discern by asking one question.

"How was it addressed, Sim?"

"To His Excellency." His voice immediately takes a formal tone. "Count Pembroke Kendrick Llewellyn Richard Firemane, Lord of the House of Stone, Knight of the Realm, Viscount of the Benedict Shores, and Custodian of the Azure Blade."

Fuck.

"Nice calligraphy?" I ask, but it's a given.

"And in silver ink, sir," he says, putting some accent on silver. His hands gently inspect my shoulders, my spine. I'm not tense, it's just...I really don't want to go. When you get an invitation written in silver ink from the Duchess of Tolon Park, to your full formal title, though, you go, lest you gravely insult her and humiliate yourself, your father, your grandfather... "Shall I continue the deep-tissue massage, my lord?"

"When is it?" Might as well find out so I can get it over with. I know that he opened the message, it's his job to. It's probably why he didn't drop it on me until he was already giving me a rub down.

"Tomorrow, sir. Your presence is requested at dusk, formal

attire of course, so your armor will need to be properly cleansed." I hear the soft sigh, and I know what's going through his mind: *Thank the gods that Count Kendrick and Countess Regina are not alive to see their son treating family heirlooms in such a fashion.*

Hey, I could be doing worse, like using the hilt of the family blade in a rather vulgar fashion in these films.

Still, tomorrow?

"Sim." I try to keep the grumbling out of my voice. "Right now I believe I will need a much deeper massage to lift my spirits."

"If you feel it necessary, my lord." He gets off the cot and begins disrobing, quickly, efficiently, everything neatly gathered and folded and immaculate for the moment he needs it.

Simaron stands to the side, *au naturel.* His body hair is sparse and short, and he'd gladly shave it off every day if I allowed him to. Even his pubes are groomed, shorn close to his skin. His eyes are cast downward toward his feet, embarrassed, bordering on shame. This has nothing to do with the fact that he's standing nude before His Excellency. This has to do with the fact that I can see he has body hair.

For the record, Simaron is what is called in the Fae community a "tainted dream". What's so tainted about body hair? Mostly the fact that the only way a Fae can ever grow hair anywhere other than their face, head and groin is if the still and glorious dream of Fae perfection was tainted by base human waste. In other words, Simaron's mother was a talented and gifted pianist with a wonderful personality, a beautiful face and a magnificent soul, who made the dreadful mistake of being human and having a sidhe's bastard son. Granted, it'd have been considered a mistake even if she'd had the son of a pooka or a brownie, but a sidhe? Most revolting, apparently.

I refuse to allow him to shave off any of his body hair because I'm not about to let him forget that he's half-human, or that his mother was human. I figure that my family owes his mother that much, at least.

Besides, thanks to his "tainted" blood, Simaron could easily get a job here as an actor if he "ever allowed himself to stoop to such depraved acts of public debauchery." (Though my working here is "an unfortunate but ultimately noble sacrifice of my dignity to preserve the solvency of my county.") He's hung like a satyr. Twelve and a half inches, uncut, straddling the line of too thick and just right, it's...well...

It's bigger than mine, that's for sure.

"Your Excellency, may I remind you again that this is *quite* improper?" His eyes plead me but I'm not letting him out of this.

"You may not. Now, His Excellency will need some preparation first. Fetch some oil, Simaron."

Despite all his protestations about protocol and how my father must be rolling in his grave and my mother must be wailing in shame, he never fails to stand erect when I ask him for this. And the shame isn't because I'm asking another man to slicken his fingers with oil and tenderly slip them inside me, considering that my mother and father probably only slept together a few times to conceive me.

It's not even that I'm asking a *servant* to please me sexually, considering that my father's preferred lover was apparently Simaron's father, who was Dad's manservant since he was ten, much like with Simaron has been with me. Mother had a few handmaidens as well. Both of them were happy, got along, produced an heir, and there were no bastard children. That's how it usually is with the Fae here. Sex and love don't necessarily go hand and hand with us. Love is a beautiful emotional bond between souls. Sex is a base desire that has no greater importance than brushing one's teeth, as far as romance is concerned. Granted, that doesn't mean we don't enjoy doing it.

So why is Simaron so convinced that my parents are being humiliated as we speak? I'm on *bottom* in this scenario. A noble? Taking it in the ass from a mere servant? And a tainted one at that? Oh! The scandal!

"Am I ready yet, Simaron?" I've lost a bit of authority in my tone, mostly because that kid recovering from my own ministrations isn't the only one in this building with a hair trigger up his ass. I can tell Sim's got three fingers in, and considering I've had plenty of practice with his endowment, I should be getting close enough for him.

"Your Excellency, I *beg* you, let me please you another way. If anyone were to see what you are asking me to do—"

"The longer you try to convince me not to," I interrupt him, but I'm sounding more like that kid out there with each passing minute, "the more time there is for someone to see you with a prominent erection and three of your fingers in my ass."

"Four, my Lord."

I glance at him over my shoulder and then motion at his groin with my eyes a few times, hoping he'll get the idea. He looks at his feet, or probably tries to, considering that big piece of meat that's in the way of his view, and then sighs in resignation.

"Please get on your hands and knees, sir." He removes his fingers and applies more oil as I lift myself into the proper position. He glides his reslickened fingers over his shaft, keeping his breathing steady as he brings it to an oiled sheen.

Once satisfied, he gets onto the cot, taking position behind me on his knees, his hand guiding his penis into my cleft, the tip gently kissing my entrance, rubbing it slowly.

"You will not reconsider, Your Excellency?"

I don't answer him, I don't want to give him any excuses to stall. Once he enters he'll eventually let himself enjoy it. He doesn't make any noise as he starts pushing in, the broad head of his shaft spreading me wide, my mouth parting in response, silent as well. It hurts, it always does when he's just getting in. The only way around it would be for him to spend much longer preparing me or take me from behind every day of the week. I'd be happy with either, and Sim is thrilled with neither.

I hear him inhale sharply as he holds my hip in one hand, his other hand still guiding his behemoth into me. I try to relax but I'm still a bit tight despite having had four fingers wriggling around in there painting my walls with oil. Besides, a part of me *likes* that he's almost too big for me. I want to work to get as much of him into me as I can. I want there to be some effort because everything in my life comes too damned easy.

"How am I doing?" My brow is furrowed because relaxing takes a concentrated effort.

"Three inches so far, Your Excellency. You're tighter than usual, but you're warm. My phallus is being taken at the normal pace."

I chew my bottom lip a second, my fists gathering up wads of satin in their grasp.

"Sim, this isn't a medical exam. How am I doing? How do I feel? How do I make you feel? I'll go first. We don't do this nearly as often as we should."

I hear his breath halt in his throat as he pushes himself again, and I let out a slow moan, feeling him creep deeper inside. His hand strokes once over my thigh, his fingers grazing the skin. I can feel my own shaft twitching now, leaking a fair bit onto the cot.

"I'm afraid I have no point of reference, my lord." I can hear some strain in his voice as he speaks, his body sending pleasure and warmth and tightness to war against his nigh-unassailable composure. "I have not done this with anyone save you, so I have no point of comparison. But I am confident that if I were able to compare, you would be a superior lover, Your Excellency."

"Sim, I must admit you amaze me. I had no idea you were so flexible as to be able to kiss my ass whilst you were fucking it." I receive an almost rough insertion of another couple inches in reply. He doesn't like when I mock him, but I've got more than half of him inside me now, so I'll just rule myself the winner here, okay?

"Are you permitted to crest, sir? Or are you required to save your seed for your...film?" He's started thrusting now, and it feels like a battering ram against my prostate, bashing the county gates to my climax. Boom. Boom. Boom.

"I should probably save it." Boom. Boom. "But I can recover much quicker than that kid out there." Boom. *Boom.* "And I am rather stressed." *Boom. Boom. Boom!* "So perhaps it would be best for my state of mind if I climaxed. Calmed myself down about the whole thing."

I can't do what I want to do, which is to look back at him and yell, *By the gods, Sim, fuck me as hard and fast as you want!* I'd probably scare him off and he'd never do this again no matter how much I exerted my authority. When I do look at him, he's sweating, his chest heaving a bit faster, his eyes half-closed, and he's gritting his teeth with an intense fortitude.

"Sim? Are you going to come?" He'll pull out, of course, and catch it in his hand, and ensure that nary of drop of his tainted seed fouls my noble body. He's never done anything different, and honestly, I've never felt him come inside me. Never with any other guy, really. I'm a strict top in the films. I've had Sim pumping in and out and in and out of me many times, when I've been tight and loose and...I've never felt him let go.

"Y-yes, Your Excellency, I am afraid that it is approaching quickly."

"Stay in, Simaron."

"But, my lord! I...I *couldn't possibly* do such a thing! Please, I will help you reach your crest and once you have been pleased, I will remove myself and attend to what I spill." I glare back at him. I am not backing down on this. Sim whimpers softly, continuing his rhythm. "Please, Your Excellency. I beg you, release your seed, I cannot hold myself back much longer."

I shake my head emphatically.

"Simaron, remember your place and do as your master commands. Or, forget your place and enjoy what you're doing with me. Either way, you are going to finish inside me. Every drop. I want to feel every twitch, every flex, every pulse of you, do you understand?" *By the gods, Sim, please, just enjoy this as much as I do for a change. For a moment I want you to feel how good you make me feel.*

A moan escapes him, followed by another at higher pitch, his thrusting slowing, and the cot creaks loudly as he wraps his arms about my chest, hugging me closely to him. Heat bursts inside me as Sim trembles, his chest hair tickling my back as his lips ravenously kiss the back of my neck. My eyes go wide.

This...is *quite* improper behavior on his part. He's...*touching* me. *Kissing* me. Simaron is showing actual passion and directing it at *me* whilst he floods my insides with his come. Inside me. His superior. His lord.

Quite understandably, I'm doing my impression of the proverbial fire hose, and vocally at that.

And a little too loudly, I believe, as someone's banging away at my door.

“Dick! Lunch is getting cut short, the kid’s ready.” Oh damn it all.

It’s enough to break the spell though, and Sim quickly but carefully removes himself from me and sets to wiping me down before it registers that maybe I should respond.

“Yeah, I’ll be out in a couple minutes, Will!” Right, I still have a scene to shoot today.

When I roll off the cot to get all suited up again, Sim isn’t making eye contact.

“I need help with my armor, Sim.”

That’s enough to rattle him back to reality. We’ll act like it didn’t happen. He’ll be grateful for that. My armor gets put back on with the speed and ease in which he took it off me. We don’t say a word through it, he doesn’t meet my eyes at all, and he still hasn’t dressed himself, as my needs are supposed to come first.

“The disarray will be taken care of before you return, Your Excellency.” His voice is small, afraid.

“Thank you, Simaron.”

“Are you prepared, sir?” I lift his chin with my finger, make him meet my eyes. “I offer my deepest regrets for my actions, Your Excellency, as any apology I could offer would never suffice.”

“Are you under the impression that I’m angry with you?” I smirk slightly. “Or do you regret it for a different reason? Was I *that* bad, Sim?”

I can tell he’s fighting the desire to be rather cross with me. “My lord, you mustn’t indulge in such activities, especially with one such as I, the damage to your House would be irreparable and—”

Holy shit, am I kissing Sim? Lips pressed to his, head tilted, tongue pushing into his mouth slowly, light fluttery feeling in my chest... Yeah, I'm kissing Sim.

And...I like it.

It takes another aggravated series of bangs on the door to make me pull back. I put my finger to Sim's mouth before he can launch another protest.

"Simaron, the reputation of my House is not your concern, nor is how I choose to 'indulge' as you put it. I am the viscount of these shores, and His Excellency will exercise his prerogative as he sees fit, do you understand?" I don't allow him to answer, I just head out to the set before Will pitches a fit and threatens me with my job. Luckily for me, I'm ready again, thanks to Sim. That kid won't know what hit him this time.

"What the hell took you so long?" Will is focused on his PDA, considering we're still half an hour behind schedule. "It's looking like we're going to go long on this one, so I need you to come in tomorrow night to reshoot the dragonslayer scene. I didn't like the angles."

I'm about to agree when I wince and remember I'm otherwise booked.

"Sorry, I can't make it tomorrow night. Day after, definitely. I've got a wedding to go to. I've been trying to get out of it for, gods, seems like forever, but I'm in the wedding party as it turns out. You know how family can be, right?"

"You're killing me here, Dick. Absolutely killing me." He grumbles, tapping away at his PDA. "No way you can get out of it, huh?"

"I'd much rather be here."

Because let's face it, spending my Thursday night getting my knob polished by a guy with a tattooed penis is a hell of a lot better than marrying some woman I've never met.

Chapter Two
Not For You

The ride that comes to pick me up the following evening is, I shit you not, a formal carriage with six white horses pulling it. To the rest of the world, it'll be a white stretch limo. I am related to the current ruling line, no matter how many people there are between me and the throne, and this *is* my wedding day, so I guess I have to expect a certain degree of formality.

The kiss hasn't been mentioned since it happened, despite my best efforts, because I'd really like to find out how I became inspired to do that. I mean, I care about Sim, sure, and he and I have a lot of fun together, but...I think I crossed a line yesterday. I can't really get an answer out of Sim now because he's been avoiding... Rather, he's been preparing.

Simaron spent most of last night and the better part of today making sure that my armor was cleansed, that I had a suitable cloak, that the Azure Blade was cleaned, polished and peace-knotted (making me question the point of the previous steps if I won't be taking it out at all). My hair has been washed, brushed, my skin scrubbed clean, teeth brushed, and about twenty different variations on formal attire have been placed on me in the previous three hours. (I said that the *humans* see me as hot and perfect. Other Fae? Yeah, I need to go all out there.) I honestly don't know where he gets the energy, and he has already vehemently refused any assistance.

To be honest, I'd just as soon sell off my ceremonial clothes and pay my property taxes for the next two years, but Sim won't have any of that. I might need them for nights such as these, he'll say. I don't really understand, though. How hard is it to find gray formal clothes for men?

Regardless, I have to admit I'm looking pretty good. Black knee-boots with silver trim, charcoal hose, and a gleaming silver breastplate with the coat of arms—a gray mountain with the roots of a tree embedded in the peak, the rest of the trunk not in view, all against a field of royal blue. The coat of arms is obviously not affixed while I'm in front of the camera. My parents probably will return from the dead if I do that. Perfectly fine to embarrass myself, that's my problem to live with. The House, on the other hand? Big no-no.

My escort has already been let into the foyer. I'm allowed to be a little late. I'm a noble, after all. Perfection's supposed to take time and all that. He'll be waiting patiently while Simaron comes to fetch me.

Even though Sim's been handling it all day, I have to be the one who takes up the Azure Blade this evening, because a knight should require no assistance retrieving his weapon. At least that's the way it is with us. The family blade is one of those swords you read about in the fantasy novels or see in the movies. It's a longsword, one-handed variety, three sapphires set in the cross-guard (the Tears of the Sky is what Dad called them), the coat of arms in the pommel, the grip never slipping no matter how wet it gets, made from the leather of some long-dead and forgotten beast. The blade has a broad fuller, with scenes of great battles and duels engraved in it, all exploits of my forebears. My father's engraving shows him defeating a warrior demon in single combat.

We're supposed to ignore the nick on the blade that came from him almost blocking the strike that killed him two days later. I miss him, yeah, that's a given, and yes, killing a demon is always a good thing, but I still don't understand why he did it. Sim says he did it because he had to, and accepts it at that. I wish I could understand the world the way Sim does sometimes. Must be nice for things to be that cut and dry.

It's called the Azure Blade because when a member of the line is holding it, such as myself, the blade is sheathed in a deep blue flame that does a fair bit of damage should I take a swipe at someone. An honestly magical sword, one of maybe five in the City and only two of those swords are held by the Fae. The other is held by Duke Tremaine who rules over Destry Bay, the *really* rich part of the City. When it comes down to it, the Azure Blade is the lone reason any noble woman would look at me twice. There are far better fish in the sea, even with the blade. Seriously, I work in gay porn. Is that a quality any woman would look for in a husband?

Actually, I'll withdraw that question. I might not like the answer.

"Your Excellency, your escort has arrived." Sim is dressed in his butler's uniform as always. I finish tying the blade to my belt and turn to face him.

"How do I look, Sim?" I use my practiced "noble smile", the one you see members of the royal family do on TV in parades, that utterly photogenic and ultimately fake grin. Most times when I do this it's to mock it openly.

"As His Excellency should, sir." He retrieves a lint brush from his pocket and removes the tiny little fuzzies that I can't even see, but I trust his judgment. "Will my services be required when you return with the lady of the House?"

"Well, it'll probably make conceiving an heir a hell of a lot easier if you're helping me out, yeah."

Sim takes a deep breath, keeping his composure. "My lord, will you still be requiring my services?"

I quirk a brow at him. "What, am I firing you? Of course not. Granted, the viscountess-to-be might have a few handmaidens you'll have to show the ropes around here and get along with. No gossiping about my prowess, though." I wink at him.

"I am certain that His Excellency's reputation will far precede him without any assistance from me, sir." He then produces a golden box from his pocket with many jewels set in it, and presents it to me. "For your bride, my lord."

It starts sinking in that this is serious, this is actually happening tonight, and most importantly, I'm not getting out of it. In case you're curious, that's my mother's ring. My father gave it to her, my grandfather gave it to my grandmother... You're seeing the trend here. When I open the box, well...

It's not gold, there are no diamonds or anything like that. It's a polished band enchanted with Fae magic so it'll fit any finger it's put on, and imbued with the strength of my House. And it's made of stone, no precious metals. Elegance in simplicity, you know? Granted, it's the viscountess's ring for the House of Stone, so it's about as strong as aircraft-grade titanium. You could take a jackhammer to the thing and it wouldn't scratch or dent. Not that I'd do something like that to my blushing bride or her wedding ring.

I remove the ring and put it in my pocket, stretch a bit, and then figure I've made the escort wait long enough. "All right, lead me downstairs." He bows deeply and proceeds to the door. "And Sim?" He stops, turning to face me.

"Yes, Your Excellency?"

"You will always be part of this House."

"Very well, sir. Thank you, sir." He bows again and exits to the hall leading to the stairs. I follow afterward but don't show myself. I need to wait after all. "Presenting His Excellency, Count Firemane." Thank the gods he went with the abridged introduction. I'm probably running late. I begin my descent of the staircase, keeping it graceful and elegant and too damned slow.

The escort is female, about my height and looks to be sidhe. It might seem odd, but in these interesting times there are even sidhe among the commonfolk. The nobility is comprised wholly of sidhe, while the pooka and brownies and knockers and goblins and trolls and all the rest make up the commoner class.

She stands at attention, dressed in coachman's blacks, and bows deeply as opposed to curtseying, and there's a saber at her side. Clear pale skin, vibrant blonde hair tied back into a braided tail, violet eyes. Six one, athletic build, she could get some work at Blue Line, even more if her breasts were bigger. (Still, she'd probably make more than me.)

"How are we doing on time?" I haven't been practicing my snooty voice so I don't sound all that uppity like I'm supposed to. I'm talking to the help after all. "I can only get us green lights until we're out of the county, then we'll have to deal with the evening rush."

"We *are* proceeding to a noble wedding, sir. Duchess Cadwyn sent missives to the counties between here and Tolon Park to allow us all possible haste. And a wedding does require the bride *and* the groom to go forward as planned." Her façade falls with a smirk. "So would you mind picking up the pace to something more than a leisurely stroll so I don't get my ass chewed out for being late?"

I want a camera. Right now. I want the look that I know is

on Simaron's face captured on film forever.

I smile genuinely. "Would you like a job?"

"I have a job, get your fancy ass in the wagon." She winks at me, and I have to laugh. I guess my rep does precede me a bit. I head out to the carriage and accept Simaron's assistance in getting into it. He won't be riding with me, he'll be preparing the house for when I return. I wish he could be there, however. It'd be nice not to have to do this alone.

In some ways, I'd prefer the carriage actually was a limo. For starters, a limo would have seat belts and could go faster than twenty miles an hour. It's going to be a long ride across the City. I should be arriving at Tolon Park just after dusk, which will earn no small share of finger-wagging from Duchess Cadwyn. Hopefully she, and my wife-to-be, will be understanding of my tardiness. It'd be nice if I could at least open the shutters, but as this is currently a wedding coach, I'm not to be seen until I'm exiting it.

I do have to wonder who they dug up to marry me. Probably an elevated commoner, or the daughter of one, which I certainly wouldn't mind. I'm all for tossing my seed into a gene pool as opposed to a stagnant gene puddle. So what if my son or daughter doesn't have perfect skin? At least I'll be confident there won't be any webbed feet or a second head.

"Stay in the coach." Wait, when did we stop? The driver's voice is stern and I hear the metallic sound of a sword being drawn.

"What's going on, uh..." Shit, I forgot to ask her name. "Driver?" No answer.

Aw damn it, don't tell me I'm being kidnapped. This is *not* how I planned to spend my wedding night. Excuse my calm, but we nobles aren't supposed to be frazzled, especially sidhe. I'm already undoing the peace knot on the Azure Blade. Whoever is about to give me trouble is going to find out how much of a badass I can be.

I hear the sounds of battle outside, steel against steel, so this isn't a carjacking. I'm still working the peace knot rather than opening the shutters to check, because it's better to make sure I'm armed before I let my attackers know I'm in the coach. It sounds like there's at least three, not including my escort, which makes me hurry all the more because three-on-one doesn't give fantastic odds, even for a sidhe.

Finally the knot comes free and I pull the sword, kicking the door of the coach open and jumping out with the Azure Blade held high.

Holy shit.

We're stopped in the middle of an intersection in Beckettsville, with cars carefully driving around the carriage and horses, and avoiding the four people locked in combat. I should probably add that to you humans it looks like the limo broke down, and there's a quite animated discussion about whose fault it is, but nothing to actually worry about. Humans can't handle the sight of a sidhe woman standing on the hood of a taxi cab fighting off three goblins with swords (which is a pity, 'cause it's a damned sight to behold), so they come up with something more mundane to see instead.

You heard me right, I said goblins.

Goblins for the most part look like short humans with green skin and big noses and long pointy ears and big yellow eyes. They also have slightly longer arms and tend to go shoeless as their feet have claws. All three of them have swords and are wearing black studded leather like they just left a renaissance fair.

And contradictory to the fantasy novels, goblins aren't the wusses they're made out to be who die by the dozen. Mostly because there aren't thousands of them around, they have to be pretty damned good at what they do if they want to keep goblins in the world.

I bring down the sword in front of me, getting into an offensive stance, about to deliver a nice little one-liner relating to their parentage, when I notice something is dreadfully wrong in this situation: The blade isn't on fire.

I'm a member of the line. I am my father's son. I've held the blade before and it's gained a sheath of azure flame like it's supposed to. But it isn't now. I sheathe it and draw it again. Nothing. All the while my driver is practically giving a clinic on blocking and countering and the perfect riposte. I feel the edge with my finger, as the blade will also be of preternatural sharpness when held by a member of the House of Stone.

Nothing. I probably couldn't cut butter with this thing.

This is a big problem.

"It's an impostor!" Right, I probably should have kept it in mind that I'm standing exposed in the middle of the street. I probably also shouldn't have assumed there were only three enemies. Two goblins emerge from inside a large black windowless van, one of whom just shouted and pointed at me. The three getting nicks and cuts from the warrior coachwoman back off and chance a look at me, seeing me and my not-so-magic sword. My driver leaps off the hood of the cab and takes a hard slash at the goblin nearest her, a spray of red visible in the air for a moment before they all break off running for the van.

I sheathe the sword as it's not going to do me much good, and my escort gives chase toward the van before the goblins all pile in and haul ass out of the intersection. She comes over to me, checking my face and my clothing.

"Are you hurt, Count Firemane?"

I blink at her. “Are *you*?”

She smiles cockily in reply. It would appear not.

“That was amazing,” I say. “There were three of them. Goblins.”

“You sound surprised, sir.” She cleans her blade and slides it back into her scabbard.

“Well, you’re a coachman. Seriously, the offer stands if you want a job.” What the hell did they mean by impostor anyway? “You probably saved my life though, thank you... Gods, what’s your name, anyway? I’m sorry, I forgot to ask.”

She shakes her head slightly, but she’s still smiling as she escorts me back to the wagon.

“Lady Delia Isolde Jennifer Heartwood, Daughter of Countess Isolde of the Emerald Shores.” She smirks and bows gracefully. “As well as Sir Reece Demonbane. And as I said, I have a job.”

“So uh, what *is* your job, Jen?” The last name before the family name is what we go by, usually.

“Well, *Dick*, yesterday my job was training to be a proper sidhe knight. Tonight my job is getting you to Tolon Park. Tomorrow, my job will be...” She chuckles as she helps me into the coach. “Love, honor, cherish, you know the whole spiel.” And then she closes the door.

Chapter Three
Man of the Hour

For all that the Fae influence the stories, our weddings are hardly like a fairy tale. Granted, every now and then you get a marriage where the bride and groom actually do love each other and will have the kind of marriage they write greeting cards about, but it's about as common for us as it is for regular humans. And it's a little frowned on because such marriages are rarely the marriages that were arranged to begin with. It's one of the reasons there are sidhe among the commoner class now; those unions always result in loss of title. Victory for romance but not great for bolstering the noble class.

And among the Fae, bolstering the noble class is important to supporting our continued existence. Kind of tough to be the Noble Fae when everyone's a commoner. Just the way things are, really, I don't set the rules. If I did, I'd probably knight a pooka or two to shake things up. And I'd certainly change the kingdom's stance on people like Simaron.

Jen leaves when we're a block away from Tolon Park, letting a proper coachman take me the rest of the way. Can't have a viscountess-to-be driving the groom's wagon, after all. Wouldn't be proper. Besides, I doubt she's getting married in coachman's blacks.

I redo the peace knot on the Azure Blade, firstly because

it's supposed to be knotted for a formal occasion and secondly because I don't want anyone to know about my little problem. I can only hope that Sim had an elaborate copy made of the Azure Blade and replaced it, and currently has it at home for safekeeping in the unlikely event that I'm accosted by goblins. Granted, if he actually *did* do that he'll be in a heap of steaming trouble, but it's a hell of a lot better than the alternative.

Namely that the Azure Blade isn't magical anymore. I don't even want to consider how something like that could happen. So I'll just go with the "it's really a fake" scenario for now.

That the goblins would call out "it's an impostor", though, implies that this was *not* a random event. Someone is after me or, much more likely, after the sword. Let's face it, it's not like people are lining up to marry me for the lovely tract of land I lord over, but a true magical sword is worth anyone's attention.

And you'd think that I'd be more focused on my imminent nuptials, but considering that I at least got to meet Jen, I have to say I could've ended up with a lot worse. Though I do have to wonder just how badly she fucked up to get paired off with me. This is not an elevated commoner. Her mother is Countess of the Emerald Shores, namely the coast of the bay over in Grunstadt, which is between the Benedict and Destry Bay. So yeah, rich important family. Her father's a Demonbane (three guesses what they do for a living), a highly respected line of non-landed knights and warriors, and she's being trained for the same job.

Allow me to underline this for you: She's too good for barely noble trash like me. Either I did something really good, which I doubt, or she fucked up royally. (Which could be a very literal possibility.)

But right now it's time to walk down the aisle.

The wedding is being held at a hotel on Park Street, in the

Grand Ballroom, and to any human lucky enough to poke their head in, it's a high-society wedding. Flowers, silk bunting, an orchestra to play the wedding march, high ceilings and a packed house on both sides of the aisle, even though my immediate family is pretty much dead. This is a sidhe-only event (the few commoners allowed in will be the brownies who clean it all up afterward), with every noble in the City and a few from outside attending. Not to wish anyone well, it's just expected of us.

The orchestra does its best to play my family's theme, the Requiem of Stone, a slow piece that relies primarily on percussion, as the rhythm is closer to primal, reflecting my House's connection to the earth. It's not being done all that impressively considering they don't have the right drums for it, using kettledrums instead of what's required. I carry myself well enough, putting one foot in front of the other. I nod to the various counts and viscounts and barons and baronesses and knights and ladies (and ye gods, there are a lot of people here) as I make my way to the man and woman at the end of the aisle—the Duchess of Tolon Wood and the Duke of Destry Bay.

The duke is dressed in deep blues and greens, his shoulder-length hair black as the void, his eyes a bright and near-white shade of gray, his complexion pale, flawless and perfectly smooth. He's wearing a finely tailored suit, which is a slight dig against me, his own little way of saying I'm not noble enough for his formal attire.

The duchess on the other hand is wearing a gown woven from leaves and flowering buds, her skin a creamy white, eyes a verdant green, her hair a loose and barely tamed mass of locks, a deep brown and gray, like tree bark. It isn't how she looks all the time. It is more symbolic of Tolon Wood's alliance with the local forest god, which was quite a coup for Duchess Cadwyn that helped cement her duchy's prestige. As I draw near, I catch the slightest of nods from her, which I do my best to return with all the subtlety I can manage.

Ever have something happen in your family that everyone knows but no one's supposed to talk about? Most of the Fae nobility is built on that. Take Duchess Cadwyn and Duke Tremaine. Both of them are married to trophies, both are perfect and beautiful and smiling up there on the dais, waiting for me to finish my stroll to the end of my bachelor days. Everyone knows that and freely talks about it.

What we don't talk about? They were betrothed to each other once (for maybe a month), an excellent bit of politicking by His Grace, the Late Duke Rowan of Destry Bay, to finally link his House to the royal line. Everything was set to go, all favors were cashed in, influence was exhausted, the wedding was given the reluctant blessing of the Queen, and then? The at-the-time Lady Cadwyn, well, we're not supposed to talk about it. But regardless, the wedding was called off, Cadwyn married a weaker noble, Duke Madoc, and asserted control of his House, and the Duchy of Tolon Wood became a matrilineal line. It's whispered that it was a rather emasculating experience for Duke Tremaine.

Sure, they're all smiles up there, but trust me, they hate each other. You can see it in the subtle glances, the slightly narrowed eyes, fingers that yearn to make a fist, the way that Duchess Cadwyn is a step beyond Duke Tremaine, to make it perfectly clear that the point of my little walk down the aisle was to reach *her*, and Duke Tremaine is just there to bear witness. This is why I tend to avoid noble functions if I can. Well, I would if I were invited. This wedding really isn't about me or Jen, it's about the two of them getting their digs in ever-so-delicately.

But I'm still bowing deeply to both of them. I'm not stupid.

When Heartwood's Minuet begins to play, I don't turn to face the congregation behind me to watch Jen walk down the aisle, because that would mean turning my back on the duke and duchess, and well, that just isn't done. Jen and I are here for the honor of being wed by Duchess Cadwyn, after all. I don't need to see her, though. She's a proper lady Knight of the Realm. She'll be wearing a full ceremonial armor, including leg plates, pauldrons and a hunter green cloak emblazoned with the Heartwood crest. Her family blade will be at her side, her hair tied into a warrior's braid. Her mother will be seated in the front row, probably for the only time in her life, her father perhaps afforded the grand honor of guarding the door outside, a feather in the cap of a non-landed knight, no matter what his family's name is. Duke Tremaine will be the one to give her away.

Father would definitely have approved of her. Mother would have appreciated her wit.

Gods, I wish they could have been here.

When Jen reaches my side we both kneel, bowing our heads to the duke and duchess as Knights of the Realm are expected to do. I sneak a glance over at Jen, and she's staring intently at Duke Tremaine, nearly a glare, but she looks at me with her eyes only and chances a slight smile.

I was right about her attire, by the way.

Another reason that our servants and handmaidens are not allowed to be anywhere near our noble weddings is that sometimes they forget their place and profess their undying affection in the middle of the ceremony. I doubt Sim has those kind of feelings for me, no matter how passionately he might've kissed me yesterday while riding on top of me. But only for the moment, I feel a bit relieved that he's not here.

I'd feel bad if he had to see me marrying Jen, I don't really know why. Hell, Jen probably has her share of handmaidens or, given that she's a knight, squires. After tonight it'll be pretty much business as usual save the rare social event where Jen and I pose as the happy couple and gab about how many heirs we're in the midst of producing.

Yeah, that's another thing that we Fae don't talk about. Just because we encourage our offspring to be same-sex oriented doesn't mean we admit to doing it. As far as the world is officially concerned, we're all straight as a quiver of highly conservative arrows.

Our vows are exchanged in an ancient language called...I can never remember the name. Sigil, I think. Is that what it's called? Anyway, it's a language of power, and to swear an oath in Sigil is to completely bind yourself to a task, person, whatever. There's no getting out of it. At all. This is why there's no divorce for the Fae. When we say "'til death do us part" we aren't kidding. Unless you want to be an Oathbreaker, and trust me, *nobody* wants to be an Oathbreaker.

Still I feel like I'm forgetting something.

Once I've finished my vow to serve as her husband, to accept her into my House as my equal (a recent addition to the vows in the last hundred years), I take the ring from my pocket and, in accordance with protocol, present it to Duchess Cadwyn. This is really it. I'm really going to be married. I'll be leaving here with a wife.

I wonder if said wife will be okay with my early-morning shoot tomorrow. No, that's not what I'm forgetting.

The duchess takes the ring from my hands, opens it, inspects it and shows it to Duke Tremaine for a similar once-over. The duke nods curtly, and Cadwyn nods once to me, handing it back.

It wasn't the ring, it was something else about this

ceremony, particularly for my family. Mother had to do something when Father gave her the ring, though.

Duchess Cadwyn looks to me. "It is acceptable." Only I really catch the slight smile on her face. Warm. With Their Graces' leave, I turn to Lady Delia Isolde Jennifer Heartwood, take her left hand, and slide the Ring of Stone onto her finger.

"Count Firemane, Lady Heartwood, you may seal your vows. May the House of Stone flourish in fertile earth." In other words, you may kiss the bride, don't waste any time in knocking her up.

I lean in closer to her and she does the same, our eyes remaining open as our lips press to each other's. I hear a soft and immediately muffled sob from somewhere in the front row, probably my new mother-in-law. A neighborhood in Grunstadt will find itself giving a damn about a shitty little part of St. Benedict because of this alliance. I can only guess this means Blue Line Productions will see an upswing in sales. This of course means bigger residuals for me, so I'm not complaining.

Damn, this is going to drive me crazy, what am I forgetting?

When I pull back from Jen, the colors of her armor have changed to muted grays, her cloak the color of slate and bearing the crest of the House of Stone, the viscountess's ring having accepted her as a suitable wife.

"The Ring of Stone has accepted her." The duke speaks with all the enthusiasm of a dog-show announcer. "Let it be known that Lady Delia Isolde Jennifer Heartwood has been granted the title of Viscountess of the Benedict Shores. May the alliance with the Emerald Shores stand longer than the mountains." The duke then sighs expectantly.

Jen is looking at me, motioning to my waist with her eyes. Damn, she doesn't want to waste any time, does she?

"The Azure Blade." Duchess Cadwyn steps toward me. "If

you would, Count Firemane."

Fuck.

I *knew* I was forgetting something. Jen has to draw the Azure Blade to show that she's fully accepted by the House, that the bloodline of my forebears finds her of sufficient virtue to wield the blade. She'll draw it, it'll burst into a brilliant blue flame to impress the congregation and maybe rub it into Duke Tremaine that despite his prestige I have the more impressive sword, and then it's pretty much dancing and cake.

"Count Firemane." Cadwyn's tone is a bit firmer. "*If you please.*"

Gods, it's supposed to just be a symbolic show that the House has accepted her. She doesn't *need* to hold the sword. I undo the peace knot deftly and unbind the scabbard from my belt, keeping my expression as calm as I can. I present the blade to Cadwyn, who looks it over once before handing it to Jen. My new wife wraps her fingers around the hilt and pulls the blade.

This will end badly, in one of three ways.

One, Jen pulls the blade and it doesn't go ablaze with blue fire, and it's assumed that the sword is a fake. Consequence? Either I have to publicly execute Sim for replacing the sword, or my family blade was somehow stolen from my home. Both of these scenarios? An embarrassment for myself, my family and my House.

Two, Jen pulls the blade and it doesn't go ablaze with blue fire, and it's assumed that the House has rejected her. Consequence? Well, the humiliation is a bit more immediate for starters, but mainly for her. None of the blame would fall on me. This was an arranged marriage, after all. I didn't pick her (not that I probably could've picked better), so the shame would fall on her shoulders. This is all assuming that I keep my mouth shut that the sword didn't burn for me either. Only I would know, really, and I could probably live with the guilt. Doesn't mean I'd want to, though.

Three, Jen pulls the blade and it doesn't go ablaze with blue fire, and the sword isn't a fake and the Azure Blade is no longer a magical blade. Consequence? Well, the family blade would be about as useful as a paperweight. How do you think something like that would go in front of *every noble in the City*?

Plus there's the tiny problem of a magical sword, one of less than a hundred in existence, suddenly being just a regular sword. Besides the embarrassment to my house, it would also mean that a little more of magic and wonder has passed from the world. And to the Fae, that's never a good thing.

All shitty potential outcomes.

Jen pulls the blade.

I can't watch.

Duchess Cadwyn's voice echoes throughout the ballroom. "The Azure Blade has shown its favor."

Wait, what?

I look over to Jen who is gazing at the blade, which burns with a brilliant flame, reminiscent of a cloudless sky. Her eyes are filled with wonder, humility, her hands almost straining to hold the blade aloft as a tear slides down her face. She nods once to no one in particular and replaces the sword in its scabbard. Jen turns to me, the barest hint of a smile, her eyes almost sad. Cadwyn takes the blade from her and hands it to me. I accept and tie it back to my belt, speechless.

The sword is real, why didn't it light for me?

"It is my honor and privilege to introduce the Count and Countess of the House of Stone. You both may rise and face your peers."

With that, Jen and I stand and turn to face the congregation, where we're treated to a sea of fake smiles and the dull roar of polite applause. It's not like we're hated or anything. It's just that we're a couple of low-level nobles who watch over a crappy part of St. Benedict. This is not exactly the social event of the season.

"Richard." I can barely hear the duchess's words in my ear, which is more than likely the intent, as she follows my name with the four words all men dread to hear. "We need to talk."

Chapter Four
I've Got a Feeling

"Have a seat, please."

I've been escorted to the duchess's private chambers, which amounts to the elaborate penthouse suite that she lives in, which has its own greenhouse, aviary, and probably the best view of Tolon Park in the City. The meeting is not out in her rose gardens, where she holds the majority of her clandestine-but-not-really dealings (because let's face it, anyone can pay off a couple of ravens to snoop), but rather in her kitchen, which is actually one of her most secure rooms. I have no idea why, but judging from the sacred marks on her doors leading in, there's no way in hell anyone could eavesdrop on her.

It's not like the kitchen's all that great. Sure, there are modern appliances, an island in the center, plenty of counters and cupboards done in rich woods, but it's what you'd expect to see at any upper-class person's apartment, should they not be a fan of granite. No real point in keeping it locked off from the rest of the world if necessary.

Maybe she's got some kickass cookie recipes or something.

"What did I do now, Aunt Cadwyn?"

I mentioned that I'm her nephew, didn't I?

"Absolutely nothing. Can't I have a private word with a

family member to congratulate him on his nuptials?" She has a problem with the word "nephew", makes her feel old, I guess. A plate is set in front of me, then a glass. Milk and brownies.

"You know, as far as the humans are concerned, I've been old enough to drink for over ten years. It's also my wedding day. You think I could get a nip of the Arcadian Reserve?" Don't look for it in stores. My aunt gets it from the fine vintners at the Palace of Wisdom. One of the perks of her alliance with the local forest god. "And the last time we had a private talk in your kitchen," I say, motioning back to the archway, "with the doors closed and the wards active, I might add, it was to tell me about Dad." To tell me he hadn't made it through his battle with the demon unscathed. "What's going on?"

"The sword, Ricky." I wince more than a little. I...hate being called Ricky. She's the only one who can get away with it. "Why didn't you watch when your wife unsheathed it?"

I had to figure she'd notice that. I open my mouth, but she places a finger over it.

"Uh-uh. No bullshit." Another source of my fondness for low diction, though Aunt Cadwyn has much more tact about it than my boss. She removes her finger and I take a long, deep breath, look down at the plate of brownies. Little bits of golden yellow in the fudgy brown. Cookie dough. Obviously this requires my utmost attention. I hear an exasperated sigh from her. "Ricky."

"The sword is fine, Aunt Cadwyn. Jen pulled it, it lit up, everything seems to be peachy."

"Jen already, is it?"

I nod sheepishly.

"Rather familiar nickname for someone you're supposed to have only just met."

"What, you didn't send her to pick me up?" Judging from

her reaction, I can guess I slipped up there. Apparently Jen playing coachman was not Aunt Cadwyn's idea. "She drove the coach when we got attacked by the goblins—"

"You were *attacked*?" She rubs her temples a few seconds. "Ricky, when my sister informed me she planned to follow your father, I promised her I would look after you." In other words, when Mom was too distraught to continue on without Dad, she conducted a long and elaborate ritual that's solemn and beautiful and eloquently worded and perfectly explains why at the end of the ritual my mother had a cold-iron dagger deep in her heart. Children, thankfully, are often requested to not be present, otherwise I'd probably be all kinds of fucked up.

"Well, Jen made pretty damned sure that I didn't get hurt. I'm guessing that's why you matched me up with the daughter of a Demonbane, right?"

"The attack, Ricky. Tell me about the attack." She takes a breath and leans against the counter.

"A few goblins jumped the wagon, Jen fought them off, no biggie."

"When a member of the royal line is attacked, it is, indeed, a 'biggie'. What happened?"

"I'm hardly royal, Aunt Cadwyn." I take a bite of the brownie, trying not to overreact to the taste of it. Perfect balance of chewiness, taste, and even mortals could eat these without starving to death later. "There are so many people between me and the throne I've lost count."

"Don't change the subject. The goblins. You were attacked. Where did it happen?" I look up, and her arms are folded. Mother would do that shortly before my full name was invoked.

"Beckettsville." I sigh in defeat. "Middle of an intersection. I didn't get the street names, so I don't know if I was in a barony or a county or what, or even whose it was. The goblins were in a van, an actual van. They could've come from anywhere. They ran off because they thought we were decoys, so they were after me or the sword."

"A contingent of guards will be dispatched to your county then."

"I can handle some goblins." I smile weakly. "And if I can't I'm pretty sure my blushing bride can."

She shakes her head in reply. "There could easily be more, and it would not look well for me to limit protection to one who shares blood with me when I've been made aware of an attempt on his life."

"Nothing says they were trying to kill me, Aunt Cadwyn. And I'm perfectly able to defend my county. So are Jen and Sim."

"Despite your faith in your wife and your...servant..." As derogatory terms go among the Fae regarding tainted dreams, that's probably the most tolerant one she could've picked. I have to be thankful that Aunt Cadwyn's a bit more accepting of people like Sim (and there's a growing number), but as far as the sidhe, pookas, brownies, trolls, and all else of the Fae are concerned, breeding with humans will only lead to the death of our noble race. "I cannot accommodate your judgment. I will send a contingent."

I grumble under my breath.

She relents. "A *small* contingent. There is another matter we still need to discuss."

"That being?"

"The sword," she says. "Draw it, now."

I need to stall. "It's certainly not proper to draw a weapon in the presence of an unarmed lady, especially one of your stature, Your Grace, unless of course I were acting as your champion."

"*Pembroke.*"

I swear under my breath. I can feel the weight of her authority in the air, on my shoulders, in my heart, not just her title, but the blood as well. Very slowly, I draw the Azure Blade, the sword dull and thoroughly unspectacular.

Her gloved hand runs along the fuller of the blade, her eyes closing a second. "Oh, Ricky, what have you done?"

"I didn't do anything, that's the truth. And it lights up for Jen, so maybe I've been cursed?" Aunt Cadwyn gives me an indulgent look in reply. Of course, she would probably sense if I were cursed, we are family after all.

"The crest on your breastplate, remove it."

I stand stock still for a moment. "Please, Aunt Cadwyn, don't." She smiles, reassuring. After a few seconds I whisper the charm that keeps the crest adhered to my armor, and hand her the Crest of Stone.

She inspects it and places it on the counter. "Hold out your hand."

I do so, feeling a little better, but still nervous. She's not dissolving my title, thank the gods, but she is testing to see if the House of Stone still considers me among its membership.

Something to know about the Fae nobility is that there are Houses and there are bloodlines. The difference?

The bloodline is what makes me noble, it's the notable Fae ancestor that I'm descended from. You'll always be part of your bloodline, unless you truly fuck up and get rejected. It's a lot like being disowned by your family.

My bloodline is that of Mercia the Firemane, who slew the Ra'Keth Deathsinger of the Northern Wastes with his own sword and kept it for herself as a trophy. The same sword is currently on the wooden counter next to a plate of brownies, repurposed for Fae use. The sword, not the brownies.

The Azure Blade has been synonymous with the Firemanes for ages, it's *our* sword. It's why we're granted the title of being the sword's custodians.

The sword isn't reacting to me though, which obviously means there is a problem with the bloodline. There's nothing else I can see it meaning. And the House! While it has accepted Jen, what about me? What if—

"Ow." My palm has been cut, my azure blood drizzling down onto the crest. Fae, unlike most creatures of magic, don't have silver blood, but rather have blue, which is still a very easy way to tell that we're not human, if you didn't already see the pointed ears and such. I hold my breath, staring into the heraldry of my House, watch my lifeblood slowly coat the mountain peak, and then I see the roots eagerly drink it up, the crest starting to glow softly. I breathe a loud sigh of relief.

"Thank the gods." I won't go into what happens if the crest doesn't take my blood, but it's safe to say I'm still a Stone, at least.

To explain Houses, they're like bloodlines, but not. The House of Stone has been controlled by the Firemanes since it was founded, at least as far as we know. This doesn't mean another line can't take over the House. Currently, I have no heirs and I'm married to a Heartwood, namely Jen. If I die, the House, having accepted her, will be controlled by the Heartwoods and become a matrilineal line. Every noble House has a bloodline, but not every bloodline has a House.

"Normally," Aunt Cadwyn says, "I would assume that the blade had faded from wonder, but the viscountess, it..."

"Damn near made a conflagration for her."

"An exaggeration, but only slightly. Obviously it recognizes her valor as a Demonbane. Perhaps it simply prefers a proper sidhe knight to act as its custodian." I can feel her reining in her judgement. "And you." She pushes the crest back toward me. "You have done little in the way of adventurous deeds."

"So what, I have to go on a quest or something? Prove myself worthy of the blade? It's lit up for me before, why would it stop now? I needed it tonight when the goblins attacked." I'd drawn it last week to practice my swordplay, and it had been burning with righteous fire the whole time.

"Ricky..." She goes to the doors of the kitchen and double-checks the charms that seal the room and make it secure from magical prying. "Have you done anything to shame yourself?" Even with the room essentially soundproofed, her voice is hushed low.

"Do you mean have I knocked anyone up?" She nods, and I do my best not to roll my eyes. "No, I have not. I've slept with some humans, but they've all been male, and it's been safe. And of course, I've been having plenty of sex with Sim, but he and I have been doing that since we both figured out what sex was."

Yes, I am perfectly comfortable talking about the guys I fuck in front of my aunt who happens to be the Duchess of Tolon Wood. Unless you're doing it purely for procreation, same-sex sex is generally an idle pastime among the sidhe. Not that we'd ever admit that we do it in public. Quiver of arrows, remember?

She sighs, shaking her head. "You know I have no problems with who you spend your time with, but..." A couple of seconds pass. "You are aware of the consequences of your affair with your...servant?"

"This is about him being tainted, isn't it?"

Aunt Cadwyn doesn't make eye contact. "I bear him no ill will, but his nature cannot be ignored, Ricky. We are not meant to couple with..."

"Filthy mortals?" My arms are folded. "Or the children we're responsible for that we treat like shit because one of their parents made the mistake of loving our kind?"

"You *know* I don't approve of that, the way they are treated, but coming out to support them would ruin my House. Ricky, your family's blade has rejected you. Have you even considered what might have caused it?"

"I have done *nothing* wrong, Aunt Cadwyn." I take the sword from the counter and sheathe it, turn away from her and instantly wince. I just turned my back to a greater noble than I. *Without* her leave. Big no-no. I face her, her expression hurt, angry. "I apologize. I forgot my place. Forgive me, Your Grace." I bow my head, drop to one knee. "How might I mend the insult of my disrespect?"

I feel her hand on my shoulder. "Find your wife, Count Stone, and return to your lands. And do not return until the Azure Blade has deemed you worthy once more to wield it." A slight pause before she continues. "As for your disrespect, considering this is your wedding night, I could outright forgive such actions, but instead I will merely be lenient with your punishment. As your actions have shamed your line, I see no reason you should be allowed the privilege of brandishing the Azure Blade until the solstice. Obviously, the restriction will be lifted in time for the tournament."

I breathe a sigh of relief. Sure, it's a hit to my reputation, but if I can't draw it, then no one will know it's rejected me. Always looking out for me, just like she promised. And with the deadline, I have a little over a week until the tournament.

"I am grateful for your leniency, Your Grace."

"You may rise." I do so, and she takes my face in her hands and gently kisses my forehead. "I have one more request, Count

Stone." I wait patiently, her hands still on my face. "Despite your title and station, you are still my family." She smiles warmly. "So please, do me a favor and stop by every now and again? You're the only Fae in the City who allows me to bake for them."

"Does this mean I have a box of those brownies to take home?" I see her nod, and I smile. "Don't worry, I'll tell people they're probably from a bakery or something." Because a duchess should never have to bake for herself. Granted, she hasn't actually *said* that she baked them, that's why I can say otherwise without lying.

"Just a bakery?"

"A gourmet bakery, then."

She places her hand on her chest, sounding almost hurt at the suggestion. "A local gourmet bakery?"

"So I'd assume they were flown in? From, like, San Francisco or something?"

"Or Germany."

I laugh a little, easing my mind of the stress that is waiting for me outside those sealed doors. "They're that good, huh?"

"You'll still be able to eat other brownies, of course." She grins, but it's a very Fae smile. "Not that you'd want to."

Chapter Five
State of Love and Trust

Despite the fact that it's my wedding night, the party really doesn't have anything to do with me or Jen. It's not like a human wedding with a reception and beautiful toasts and a flower grenade thrown into a crowd of desperate women. Once we're hitched we're free to go. So after I leave my aunt with my box of brownies and my eight days to figure out how to prove myself to the line, I find Jen outside, already out of her finery and tending to a Harley Softail. She's wearing a black leather jacket, jeans, sneakers, a pair of black gloves, her saber off her waist and holstered on the bike. Her hair is tied back in a simple braid, the tail sticking out from under her helmet.

"Nice bike." I look around, not seeing any other cars, the carriage and horses from earlier more than likely having been on loan. I glance at the tiny seat behind hers on the motorcycle, and sigh softly. "Let me guess, I have to ride bitch?"

"That's right, fancy-man." She pats it twice with her hand and looks me over. "What's in the box?"

"Brownies. You *could* say they've been flown in from the finest bakery in Europe, quite possibly the greatest known to humanity." My tone doesn't match my words at all.

"Trying to ply me with chocolate?"

"Hell no, get your own. These are mine."

"I am your wife, I'm entitled to half."

"Considering divorcing me already, huh?" I make a show of checking an imaginary watch. "Sorry, you've already lasted longer than an hour, you won't make any money off the pool. Betting closed at twenty minutes."

You might wonder why I'm not freaking out about the fact that I'm probably rejected by my bloodline. Or talking about it. Or begging for help. I'm standing out in public, with my wife. Such conversations and behavior are best left for private, where no one will see. For now, we keep up appearances. And it seems the appearance that we're going to keep up is that Jen wears the pants in this marriage.

Like I give a damn, really. Better all eyes be on her instead of me while I'm figuring everything out. Besides, once the tourney rolls around, I'll be able to show I can hold my own in this marriage.

I get on the bike after she mounts up, and I place the sheathed Azure Blade into one of the holsters, the brownies in one of the side bags. I then put my hands on her hips to keep steady while she starts up the bike, the Harley tuned to be a bit louder than average. She revs it more than a couple of times, letting the engine roar. I lean forward while some of the assembled nobles look our way. I give them all a wave and a smile, and knock gently on the side of Jen's helmet.

"Yes, yes, I'm sure they all know your dick is far larger than theirs. May we go now?"

Her response is to peel out from the parking space and enter traffic at high speed. I'm sure she's smirking.

Considering conversation isn't all that possible with the volume of the engine and her wearing a helmet, I decide to muddle through the problem at hand.

And it is a *big* problem. That the sword rejected me is a sign there's a problem concerning my standing with the bloodline. The Firemanes rule the House of Stone. Period. It's been that way since the beginning and I'm not about to change that. If I'm not a Firemane, any little tykes Jen and I manage to produce won't be truly part of the line, have no claim to the county. Because their father will be a lowly commoner. And I'm not going to relinquish the House to the Heartwoods to duck this. To hell with that. No offense to Jen, her blood is as blue as mine literally, but not figuratively.

And that's not just an expression. Not red, not silver, blue. One of the side effects of your ancestors blending blood with god-killers. On the upside though, we can use Sigil to make our oaths all the more binding. Despite my previous joke, there's no divorcing Jen. That would mean breaking an oath, and I certainly don't plan to do that. I've never seen an Oathbreaker, but I've heard you'll know when you see one, and you shouldn't even trust the treacherous bastard to pick up your dry-cleaning.

Granted, I have to ensure I don't get myself killed first from this whole rejection thing. Dad didn't have to deal with this, but according to him, he married Mom pretty young and went right out to prove his claim to the line. He recorded several kills of demons, weres, a couple of vampyr, even placed well in a Solstice Tournament, and somewhere in all that managed to knock up Mom with me.

You know, the kind of good example that a normal person can never live up to.

I haven't been paying attention, figuring we were just heading back to the Benedict. Instead, Jen pulls the bike off the avenue we were on, into a parking lot for a barbecue place. She parks, takes off her helmet and checks back at me, probably to make sure I haven't fallen off.

"You hungry? I'll treat, seeing as I doubt you brought a wallet in that get-up of yours."

I look at the establishment, one of those franchised places with its own line of sauces. I'm not much for the many methods of eating pork products, but I hardly have much choice, it seems.

"You like barbecue?"

She nods once, getting off the bike and stowing her helmet. "I figure since we're going to be spending the rest of our lives together, we can at least get through those first-date questions before you carry me over the threshold."

"Can't argue with that." I get off the bike as well, stretching a bit and retrieving the sword from its holster. Something I'm thankful for is that humans will largely ignore it, because I'm not about to leave the family blade out in the parking lot. I offer her my arm, and she pauses a moment before accepting it.

It doesn't take all that long to find an open table. We're both sidhe, after all, the beautiful people. You humans fall all over yourselves to impress us. And no, it never gets old. We skip appetizers, instead starting with mixed drinks, rum and coke for me, Long Island iced tea for her.

"Didn't really see you ordering that." I take my glass and have a sip. Eh. Okay. She picks her own up and gives me a look.

"What? I went to college. Guys bought these for me all the time, either that or zombies." I arch a brow. She takes a gulp of it before giving me a dubious look. "Yes, Dick, I went to college. What about you?"

I down another sip of my drink. "Tutors, mostly. Enough to get me a diploma, do the tests with all the varied letters. I'm afraid the majority of my study was on modern popular music of the Pacific Northwest in the early to mid-nineties."

She smirks. “Nirvana or Pearl Jam?”

“Seattle’s favorite sons, all the way. Mike McCready is a living god. You?”

She takes a long swig of her drink, letting an ice cube roll around on her tongue before she crushes it in her teeth. “We’ll agree to disagree there. I think Cobain was more influential, but I’d have to go with Bikini Kill for that area.” She laughs lightly, and it’s a bit big for her size, definitely a warrior’s laugh. This is a woman who’s probably drank trolls under the table on many occasions. “I prefer harder stuff, actually. Even split between Judas Priest and Iron Maiden. Lacuna Coil if I’m in the mood.” She then does the goat horns, the “I’m metal” gesture, with her free hand as the server returns. We order. Well, she orders, actually.

More than a few minutes pass in relative silence, false starts at reengaging the conversation. There is something that I do need to know if Jen and I are going to live together.

“So when is your girlfriend moving in?”

She practically does a spit-take. “Excuse me?”

“Sorry, I mean, when should we expect your handmaiden to be joining the staff?” I get an incredulous look from her. “Okay...I take it you call her your ‘squire’ then?” Still no response. “Ye gods, lady, when is the chick you’ll be fucking in your spare time going to move into our house?”

Of course this is when the server stops by the table to refresh our drinks. Gods bless him, he keeps it under control, and takes our now-empty glasses and departs without comment. He earned his tip right there.

“I don’t have a girlfriend.”

I roll my eyes slightly, looking around the family-friendly eatery that I just made a little less so. “Jen, there’s little chance of other sidhe being here. I’ve got a guy at home I sleep with. I would think there'll be a girl moving in within the next few days, so I want to know what I should refer to her as."

"I know what you're talking about. I don't have a girlfriend, and no one will be moving in."

This could be bad.

"Okay…this next question has the potential to be very awkward then…"

"Yeah, Dick, I eat pussy." My eyes go wide as once again the server has perfect timing. She takes a long drink of her refilled Long Island iced tea and winks at me. "You know you had that coming, right?" She waves off the server, who probably earned himself a bigger tip. "So you've got a guy stashed at the manor, I take it?"

"You've met him already. Simaron." Gods, how is he going to handle her? "He's my manservant. His family's been in service to mine for about six generations now."

"Simaron? The…" I can tell she's looking for a term. "The purple?" She could've picked worse.

Purple is a reference to their blood. Mix blue and red and what do you get? As racial epithets go, it's definitely tame, but still.

"I'd prefer it if you never use any of those words to describe him. Ever. It's not his fault his mother made a mistake and fell for one of us."

Jen studies me for a few seconds.

"Seriously," I say. "It's a very touchy subject with me, so it's best you know about this now."

"All right, I can deal with that." She takes another drink. "Not like you can knock him up, right? So what's wrong with your sword?"

My turn to do a spit-take. "Beg pardon?"

"I had three goblins on me earlier tonight and three more itching to join in, and when I looked over at you, your sword wasn't burning with flame. And at the ceremony, you were a little hesitant to hand it over. It lit up for me though, which is the confusing thing." She leans forward, resting her elbow on the table, her chin in her hand and an intrigued smile on her face. "So c'mon, spill it. What exactly am I getting into here?"

Those are the kinds of questions Fae usually love to be asked. Direct questions are great tests of our skill of talking without saying anything and still telling the truth. Fae can't lie, we're unable, it's the way we were made, but there are ways around it. It's just harder with Fae. You can't bullshit a bullshitter, as my director Will is fond of saying. If I try something, I'll be sending a message I don't want to send.

"It's something I need to take care of, that doesn't really affect you." I see her give me a look. "I'm working my way up to it, okay? This is kind of a big deal and I don't want you to freak out or anything." I take a deep breath. "I've been rejected by my sword and I've got about eight days to make up for it or every noble in the City will think I'm not a Firemane anymore when I draw the Azure Blade at the Solstice Tournament and it's not all that azure."

"Whoa, dude, lay off the ren-fair talk, man." I look up to find the up-till-now silent server who has our orders and places them in front of us. He leans down to mention in my ear, conspiratorially, "Girls don't go for that nerdy stuff."

I give him an exasperated glare as he hurries off. Someone just lost his tip.

Jen, in the meantime, is staring at me. "All right, you have to explain how you managed that."

I shrug. "Dad taught me how to say 'fuck off' with naught but a look."

“Not the waiter, Dick, the *sword*. What did you do?” Her face is serious now, no more witty banter, because this affects her just as much as me.

“Want me to be honest? I don’t know. This thing is kind of unprecedented in my family. I mean, I haven’t filled the house with trophies of conquest, but it’s not like my forebears were all warriors. Hell, my grandfather was a patron of the local arts, back when there was more in the Benedict than—”

“A porn studio.” She gives a light chuckle and shakes her head as I wince. “Yeah, I’ve heard about it. You realize you’re going to have to quit doing that? Can’t exactly convince the other ladies of the court that my husband’s committed to knocking me up when you can see him starring in *Ass Commando 7* for thirty-nine ninety-five.”

“How else do you see us paying our property taxes? You’re new to being a viscountess, so I’ll lay it out for you.” I see her fold her arms, and I show my hands in preemptive surrender. “I’m not patronizing, okay? You’re a knight, you can go on quests anywhere in the City, wherever your liege commands, and collect tribute or rewards or boons no matter where you do it, right?” She nods once before I continue. “Well, I can’t. My county is my responsibility, so I need to uphold and support art, music, culture, however a creative person chooses to pursue their dreams in there.”

She motions for me to keep going. “Haven’t sold me yet.”

“Jen, we’re Fae. We need them, okay? It’s hard to be a living dream when there’s no one around to dream for you.”

It’s a rather poetic way of putting it, but yes, the Fae are essentially living dreams, or at least we were in the beginning. We thrive on creativity, wonder, wild imagination, racing emotions, all of that good stuff. You people supply all that to us, so it really is in our best interest to nurture that in humanity.

I lean toward her. "Currently? Blue Line's the only game in town as far as the Benedict Shores are concerned. Urban renewal would be nice, sure, but it's the Benedict and the place isn't exactly bohemian. While my family owns the land the manor's on, as well as the manor itself, there are still property taxes to pay on it and gods know what else. So yeah, it may be a little embarrassing for you to admit that your husband stars in those movies, but it's a dramatic pursuit, and I'm acting as a patron of the arts, which is more than a lot of sidhe can say about their baronies and counties."

I take a sip of my drink. "And I'll have you know *Ass Commando 7* is selling rather well at *twenty*-nine ninety-five."

Our food arrives not long after that, and we eat in silence, again, the conversation hitting a dead patch. I really wish I knew more to tell her. I wouldn't mind knowing someone had my back in this.

Jen runs her tongue along her teeth for a few seconds, apparently thinking. "Is there any way to discern what you did? Some sort of divination or scrying? Something one of the..." She stops. I figure she was going to mention that a Ra'keth, a human sorcerer, could probably find an answer, but they're no one you ever get involved with. Ever. "We'd need someone discreet."

I smile slightly at the mention of "we". Maybe she does have my back. "We'll figure it out. So... That little remark about convincing the other noble ladies I'm trying to knock you up... I take it you're already planning on kids, huh?"

She shakes her head. "I figure we've got about a year, maybe two before the whispered comments start. Another year after that before they become subtle hints. If I'm off questing it'll make that period even longer. You in any hurry?"

I shake my head as well. "An heir will be nice, take the

pressure off. I'm worried about Sim, though, his line's pretty much done. Too bad, really, his mother brought a lot of life to the house before..." Another thing we Fae don't talk about. Let's just say for all intents and purposes that Sim's mother is now in a place where she can't hurt herself anymore. If you need clarification on that, it was what it sounds like at first, but now it's the more tragic interpretation. Humans are very good at loving us. Unfortunately it's not the two-way street it needs to be.

"He's important to you," she says, her tone softer, eyes cast to the side. "Isn't he?"

I lean back, a little nostalgic. "He's been part of my life as long as I can remember. I give him a fair share of flak, but I can't imagine getting through the day without him, really. I depend on him for a lot." Even though Jen can probably guess some of the things I depend on him for, I keep it quiet. "So, want to just get out of here? Pack this stuff up and head off to your new home? I promise your room will be immaculate, considering Sim's been alone in the house all this time. He tends to clean when he's got nothing else to do."

After a second or two of surveying the table, she says, "Yeah, let's go." She then motions over the server to ask for take-home boxes. I have no idea how we'll carry home five pounds of barbecue on a motorcycle, but I've no doubt she's done this before. After paying, we head out to the parking lot.

"So, what about a mystic?" It takes me a couple of seconds to respond to her because it's completely out of left field.

"Beg pardon?" Mystics, as far as the Fae are concerned, are Fae with a little more magical blood in their veins than average. While they can hardly work magic, they often just have a knack for something, a singular remarkable talent. Some have inexhaustible stamina, some can work more complex bindings, some have a special affinity for the gods and can beseech them for special favors. They're rare though, and mystics keep themselves on the down low, more often than not because they would overshadow the local noble, which is nothing you want to do.

"I know of one. Fate-blooded." She's not meeting my eyes. "I can arrange it."

"Jen, how the hell do you know a mystic? How did you even get him to reveal himself?"

She mounts the bike. "It can be tomorrow. Considering the timeframe you have..."

I exhale hard, getting on the bike behind her. "Eventually you'll have to tell me how you know this person, but you're right, eight days isn't all that much time." I wince slightly, remembering something. "Could it be tomorrow evening? My morning's a tad booked."

She turns on the seat to look at me incredulously. "Are you kidding?"

"I gave my word that I'd be somewhere, Jen."

She grumbles under her breath, as for Fae that is a very legitimate excuse. "Fine, fine. I'll arrange it for dusk. I'll tell you the meeting place in the afternoon." She starts up the bike, not revving it this time. There's no need. "What the hell is it that you're doing anyway?"

"Probably? Derrick."

Chapter Six
Get Right

"Did your...film go as well as expected, Your Excellency?"

I can only shrug. I honestly have to admit that I pretty much phoned it in today. Sure, we got the shot, it'll be good and keep the arousal rate high for the people watching at home, but it took a bit longer than expected mostly because I was preoccupied with the fact that I'd be meeting a mystic after work. Will isn't too happy with me, but the work is done, and I'm off for a few days. Another film to shore up the paycheck.

Sim helps me out of my armor while I remain quiet, putting my street clothes on as soon as I'm free of it.

Let's just say my wedding night didn't go the way most people would expect.

Sometime around one in the morning it hit me that I was really married and there was no getting out of it. I was in bed, Sim on top of me, riding my shaft slow and easy, helping my tension considering the day I'd had. I was into it, looking at Sim's body as he pumped his hips back and forth, his eyes closed, his skin gaining a sheen of his sweat, small moans escaping him whenever he took me to the hilt. Sim has no reservations about being the "catcher", after all.

And then there was a knock on the door, and within a

minute Simaron had hopped off me, dressed, and opened it. Jen was there, asking where she could find the kitchen for a late-night meal. Simaron quickly obeyed, and that was it. I have to accept that it is going to be a regular occurrence, more likely than not. My life is different now, less freedom, more changes, having to maneuver the delicate net of social reputation. Even though Jen *knows* I am sleeping with Sim, she still can't *see* it. Plausible deniability is one of the greatest assets we Fae have. As long as she doesn't *see* me pounding our butler's ass, she won't be lying when she says that as far as she's seen, there's nothing between us.

Just like I would be telling the truth if I said that as far as I had seen, Jen wasn't a lesbian. Sure, she said flat out that she "eats pussy", but that she prefers the exclusive company of women in her bedchamber? Nope.

"Is there anything the matter, my lord?" I shake my head once as I lace up my sneakers. "Shall I take your equipment to the car then, sir?"

"Yeah, I'm running late, so you might have to come along with me on my next errand, Sim."

He lowers his head deferentially. "But of course, sir." He then leaves my dressing room, wheeling a dolly with the cases containing my armor and the Azure Blade to my car outside. I take the moment to stretch, check myself in the mirror to make sure I got off all the face makeup they pile on me every morning I'm here.

My hair's tied back simply, my skin fashionably pale save some fading red areas where I scrubbed myself a bit mercilessly in the men's room. My eyes are a bit baggy. I feel like hell, really, which let's face it, is not a good sign among the Fae. The rejection is already starting. I'm probably going to look practically human by the end of the week. It's a good thing I won't be doing any shooting with Blue Line, no one will want to fuck me by then.

All the more reason to go meet the mystic and find out how the hell I make things up to my storied ancestor.

I head out to the parking lot to find that Sim has already loaded up the car, a 1981 Pontiac Trans-Am that used to be Dad's. His definition of the "noble steed" was changed by Burt Reynolds, but I'm hardly complaining. Dad called her Lilah, I didn't see any reason to change it.

Sim's already in the passenger seat, the trunk and backseats filled with the various cases. He looks to me after I get in, expectantly, his eyes motioning to my seat belt, and I chuckle as I put it on. "Don't trust my driving, Sim?"

"I trust your driving skill implicitly, Your Excellency. Other motorists, I'm afraid, do not share that honor."

I start the car and peel out of the parking lot. Sim is relatively unfazed by this action, as I do this a lot. He turns on the radio to the rock station before I think to, and returns to his near-statue pose in the seat next to me as I shift gears, merging with traffic. I glance over at him. "Did Jen call?"

"Yes, Your Excellency, the Countess Stone contacted you on your mobile while you were busy with your...film. She allowed me to relay a message to you, directions which I took the liberty of inputting into your mobile's GPS. I hope I did not overstep my bounds, my lord."

I shake my head, fighting off a yawn. "No, you didn't. Thank you, Sim. You put the directions in the what, now?"

"Your mobile is equipped with the ability to show where you are anywhere on the planet, sir, and use maps of the area to direct you to your various destinations." He holds up my phone and I look at it, seeing a miniature map of the Benedict and a green line drawn on the streets, as well as directions for me to continue on for a couple more miles before my next turn.

"Thank the gods for humans and their unending obsession with technology." I turn my eyes back to the road. "So where am I going?"

"The intersection of 107th and R Street, my lord." A second passes. "The..."

"The Tomb of Keres." I take a deep breath and exhale. If I'm meeting a mystic, it makes sense to go there. The land was never claimed by a barony or county, which means it is outside the eyes and the concern of the noble class. The tomb was named as such because a death god was murdered there. A Ra'keth met his end there as well, but they aren't the kind of people you memorialize. According to local legend, humans can never find the intersection, only the Ra'keth can find their way. Lucky for me, I'm Fae, so way the hell back in my family tree, there's a god-killer perched on a very high branch. Doesn't matter how thin that blood is, it's there. So while I'm not a Ra'keth *per se*, as far as the tomb is concerned I'm close enough.

I'm still a bit nervous though. This would be a marvelous place to kill me and have no one know about it, but that's the sort of thing you have to worry about when you're going for maximum discretion.

It doesn't take all that long to get there, and I park the car in front of the tomb, a three-story building with a storefront and a collapsed wall on the first floor. I get out of the car, leaving Sim to guard it.

I climb through the hole in the wall, seeing the dusty remains of what was once a clothing store. Pieces of brick and dirt are strewn on the hardwood floors, the clothing racks are knocked over, still filled, though all the suits are dirty and worn from a lengthy exposure to the elements. Sigil is written in the door and window frames from the inside, meant to seal them shut, deny any entry, but it apparently didn't apply to the hole in the wall. Someone either came in here forcefully or had to leave in a hurry.

Regardless, I don't sense any other magic.

"Hello?" I don't know what else to say, other than ask myself why I didn't just bring *another* sword that I'm not forbidden to use.

No response.

"Great." I stretch a bit and survey the room, seeing a long counter/display case, the goods inside intact and preserved, an unmolested old-fashioned brass cash register, and a staircase leading up. Upstairs is where the death goddess and Ra'keth were killed, supposedly, but I've never been one for haunted houses, so I'm not too keen on poking around. "Is anyone here? I was sent here by Countess Stone?"

"I know."

My hand goes on instinct to a sword that isn't there as I turn in the direction of the voice. A woman about my height cloaked in blue, a hood obscuring her features, but what's visible is very impressive, a perfectly shaped chin, lips that form every word like the language is only meant to be delivered by them. Definitely sidhe.

"You're the mystic, I take it?" I drop my hand to my side as I look ridiculous trying to draw a weapon I don't have.

"And you are the shamed one." Her voice is strong, confident, but softer than I expected. I'd always imagined mystics were a little...touched, so I'm put off-guard by her apparent lucidity.

"How did you know about—"

"The Fates can see much and I am privy to their secrets,

Richard of the Line of Mercia, Last Scion of the Deathsinger."

My eyes go wide. *No one* is supposed to know about that. Not a soul, not Simaron, not Jen, nor Aunt Cadwyn knows that. Even Mother didn't know. It's a secret known only to the lord of a House. Dad told me before he died what his own father had told him and so forth—that the Azure Blade was taken by my illustrious ancestor, Mercia the Firemane, from the Ra'Keth Deathsinger. Her husband.

The father of her children.

Sure, the Fae generally (and grudgingly) accept that we have sorcerer blood in our veins, but not which ones. *Which* sorcerers we're descended from, well...considering the sort of atrocities they were guilty of, it's not something you want to compare at dinner parties.

Regardless, the mystic possesses my complete and undivided attention.

"What do I need to do?"

She walks slowly toward the counter, running her fingertips along the glass. "You speak as if there were a simple list of procedures to be followed, Stone."

I take a deep breath. "How do I prove myself worthy of Mercia's blade?"

"It is not just the sword of Mercia that you have shamed, Richard. Your worth must also be proved to—"

I stop her, standing in front of her now. "I have to prove myself to that fucking butcher? Do you know why he was called Deathsinger of the Northern Wastes? You think they were *wastes* before he came along?"

"And yet, your forebear became his mate, bore his heirs, took up his blade." Her hand takes mine, and it's smooth, perfectly manicured, her skin slightly cool against mine.

"Perhaps all is not as your House would believe."

I yank my hand away. "No, that I won't buy. The Firemanes are a proud line of warriors, poets, artists. We would *never...*" Turning away from her, I clench my fists tightly. "If I have to prove myself to a *god-killer* then perhaps it's better if the House..."

I can't finish that sentence. Despite my feelings on the matter, I can't just let my House fall. I can't. I can't. I—

"*Fuck!*" I kick the display case hard, the glass shattering from the impact. I lean heavily on the counter, gripping the edge in my hands while the mystic stands silently nearby. The throbbing in my foot starts a few seconds later. Damn it. "What do I need to do?"

Chapter Seven
Nothing As It Seems

There might be a bit of confusion on the point concerning my ancestors. Allow me to explain. Remember how I told you that pretty much all of the Fae have affairs but as far as the world is concerned, we're all monogamous and straight? Quiver of arrows? It's the same with our sorcerer blood, no matter how thin and weak it may be. We all *know* it's there but if it's all the same to us, we'd prefer to hate it and distance ourselves as much as possible, thank you very much.

To not only insinuate that you're descended from a Ra'keth, from a *god-killer* of all things, but name the *specific one* who's sneering down at you from the upper boughs of your family tree...

Criminals and traitors to the Fae are often addressed as scions of Ra'Keth before they're put to the chopping block.

So I'm apparently in some very deep shit.

"Please, just...tell me what I have to do."

The mystic steps away from the scatter of broken glass on the floor. I can almost feel fear coming from her, but it fades. She waits a few seconds before breaking the silence. "Again, you speak as if there were some series of tasks to perform. Who is to say what your ancestors desire of you? I am not of your blood, they speak little to me. What have you done to earn their shame?"

"I don't know." I grit my teeth, kicking away a larger shard of glass. "Mercia was a warrior, the sword was handed down from her, that's really all I know."

"And what valorous deeds have you committed?" There's a pause. "Tell me about Count Kendrick, Richard."

I stop and look at her. "My dad? He never shamed himself. Ever. He was a hero out here. He killed demons, supported the arts, everything."

Another longer-than-expected pause. I swear I hear whispering on the wind outside. "The demons. He hunted them. Why?"

"*Why*? You need a reason to hunt them? They're evil, they rape and kill and pillage, and you need to keep the numbers down."

"But there is an entire line of Fae who have devoted themselves to their destruction. Why would a Firemane devote himself as well?" She steps closer, her voice gaining an older, ethereal quality. "Was it all demons your father hunted, or just one in particular?"

"It was... There was a demon who killed my grandfather."

"And the son sought to avenge the father."

"Well yeah, but..." And it begins to sink in. "The demon who killed Dad. But, Dad killed him. Dad swore he was gone with his dying breath. It's not like I can kill him again."

"Are you certain of that? As you said, he swore the demon was gone, not that it was dead. Mercia was known as a vengeful knight, Count Stone. Despite her name, none of her quarry were spared her wrath. Her passion and zeal are part of what made her the founder of your bloodline. If the demon that took your father's life still walks this earth, perhaps it is business your sword considers unfinished."

I can't mention it, but if that's true, I am well and truly fucked, considering that even with the Azure Blade my father had a hell of a time (no pun intended) taking down that demon, and all the sword is for me is a conversation piece. A conversation piece that I can't draw from its scabbard.

And yes, Mercia the Firemane was exactly as described. We are living dreams, after all, that can just as quickly become nightmares.

"And the other ancestor? How do you suppose I prove myself to him? Lay the countryside to waste? Murder a god or two?" I shudder to think what Dad might have done should he have had to prove himself to the Deathsinger as well.

"The Ra'keth have always been beyond the reach of Fate and pride themselves on being mysteries. They do not return to the dreams of the living upon their death, as the Fae do. Perhaps the answer will come to you on its own, or perhaps you will have to find your own method." Her voice gains a harder edge, her face looking older, wrinkled. "But you will soon become well aware of what you have done to shame your people, Scion of Deathsinger. Only betrayal will avail you of your betrayal."

"What...the hell does that mean?"

Her voice returns to its previous tone. Young, stronger, confident, and slightly hushed. "I apologize, I am unaware of what you have been told, but I ask you not repeat it to me. It is not for me to know."

"Wait, what? Run this by me again? You don't know what you just said?"

She nods. "It is the price of carrying Fate itself in my blood, Richard. The Three may speak through me as they wish. The

Maiden, Mother and Crone... They told you what you sought to know?"

"So what, you were possessed?"

She shakes her head. "There are old pacts that bind our people to the gods, the sorcerers and humanity. They all are part of us. We are a people forever in between. I channel the Fates, but I may never keep any information granted by them for myself, as it is not for me alone to know."

I couldn't help but wonder if I'd met her before. "How shall I show my gratitude for the service you have done me, my lady?"

"Your silence will be payment enough. An oath that you will speak not of this meeting or of my burden to anyone." She looks around. "Swear it now. Here."

I blink once. This woman seriously doesn't want anyone knowing she's a mystic. This is the tomb of a death god, supposedly where a Ra'keth met his end as well. To swear an oath here... If I break it, the consequences will be severe. My entire House would be branded as Oathbreakers and betrayers, particularly to anyone associated with death. So I damn well better watch my tongue.

I kneel on the floor before her and swear the oath. The rhythms of Sigil leave my mouth, my skin wrapped in tight chain as I finish it, a phantom weight there. I'm in deep now.

I remain kneeling. "May I ask you something? Don't worry, I won't ask who you are—"

She drops her hood, and I'm given the sight of a beautiful Fae woman. Everything about her is perfect, the shape of her mouth, her elegantly upswept cerulean hair, the light powder-blue of her skin. Her eyes are the most striking, though, an ocean-blue. (I understand that the ocean is many different shades of blue, but she's sidhe, her eyes are all of those colors, shimmering and glorious.) Any mortal who gazes on her will weep and never find anything to compare to her beauty.

See why I said earlier that among the Fae I'm kind of homely?

"You are bound, Count Stone, I see no reason to conceal my identity further."

I was going to ask her why she wanted to meet here of all places, but this has answered my question.

I seriously doubt that the wife of Tremaine, the Duke of Destry Bay, wants it known that she is a mystic. As I said there is nothing wrong with it. Openly, that is. But it would be a bit of an embarrassment privately for it to be known that the bearer of the duke's children has a bit more Ra'keth blood in her than usual, enough for her to make use of. It would explain why she hasn't borne the duke's children yet.

"I will keep my oath, worry not, Duchess Catrin. I am curious how my new bride knows you though, Your Grace."

"Countess Stone squired under my husband for a time, until her marriage to you was arranged." That...is odd. If she was squiring for the Duke of Destry Bay, it made sense that she was being groomed to either be one of his knights, or possibly even arranged to marry one of his lesser counts or barons, maybe an older knight. Instead she was put with me.

"Perhaps you know, Your Grace. I'm not ungrateful for my bride, but why was she betrothed to me?"

She responds with a sad smile. "I am afraid such matters are not a concern for one of your title, Richard." This is another way Fae can get out of telling the truth: We're afraid that information is above your paygrade. Despite the fact that Duchess Catrin is only a duchess because she married into it, she's still above me in station, and therefore doesn't have to share the information with me. Hell, with a bit of maneuvering, she wouldn't even have to tell Aunt Cadwyn. Only Duke

Tremaine demanding as her husband, or the Queen Herself, could get a straight, honest answer out of her. Fuck.

"Well, I have some idea how to set things right. I still have no idea what I did, other than letting the demon who killed Dad stay alive, even though as far as I know it's dead, or at least gone..."

She places her finger on my mouth. "Stop. Please. This is information that was meant only for you. While you are bound to not repeat anything you have heard here, I am under no such obligation, and one of your title cannot demand an oath of me. I shall go and offer you good fortune on your endeavor. There is little else I can do." She starts toward the stairs. "I will depart after you have gone. I do not wish anyone to see me leave this terrible place."

"My lady?"

She stops and looks at me expectantly.

"Being a mystic," I say. "What's it like?"

"You should be thankful, Scion of Deathsinger, that the blood of your sorcerous forebear remains silent in your veins. To be mystic... It is a harrowing experience that I would not wish on any kith, kin or foe."

And with that, she proceeds up the stairs, rounding a landing that takes her out of my sight, her steps so light that I barely hear her. I stay a few more minutes, leaning against the broken display case, before I exit through the hole in the wall into the air outside. The weight of the oath is there already, hanging around my throat whenever I consider everything I've learned in the Tomb of Keres, reminding me to keep it to myself.

I only have a vague idea of what to do, and I've paid a heavy price for it. As I go to join Simaron back at the car, I have to wonder if I'm even going to be alive to see the Solstice Tournament. To be honest, all I want to do is just go home and go to bed with Simaron.

"Sim?" I fasten my seat belt after getting in the car, him still in the passenger seat. "I believe that we'll be returning home, and His Excellency will be requiring a deep massage."

"As you wish, my lord." A second passes. "You won't be requiring..." He looks down, blushing deeply, biting his lip. "Any specialized services on my part?"

Meaning he's hoping I won't be asking him to fuck me in the ass again. Granted, he doesn't *sound* as adamant against it as he usually does, probably because of how much he enjoyed it last time, finally releasing inside me, kissing the back of my neck like a lover. I still find it humorous that he was so terrified that I would bring shame to myself and my family—

"Oh gods, no."

Chapter Eight
Dissident

The ride home is understandably quiet. I want to say it's just a coincidence that within forty-eight hours of me telling Sim to go all the way with me my family blade casts me aside. These are not the kind of problems you expect to have at the end of the day when your morning is spent being fellated on camera.

Sim is silent, mostly because I haven't said anything since "Oh gods, no", which he undoubtedly took as a harsh rejection of his very ginger advance. He'll probably never want to do that with me again. The scary thing is that it's probably for the best.

Considering I live in the Benedict, it doesn't take all that long to get home, but the drive seems like hours anyway. Too much to deal with, too much information and too many damned questions. How can I kill a demon and avenge my father when the demon's supposed to be dead? If it's alive, how do I kill it without the Azure Blade? Why do I have to prove myself to some long-dead butcher ancestor, much less wonder what he'll require of me? What more is there to Jen's arranged marriage to me? And Sim...

Gods, Sim.

I can't tell anyone about this. Especially not him, he'll be all too ready to take all the blame onto himself and possibly do something incredibly foolish. I won't have that. Maybe I catch some heat over my acceptance of Sim's "mixed blood" but I refuse to let that be the reason I've brought shame to myself. The thing is, I have no idea what else I've done.

Just about that time the car stereo starts emanating the opening riffs to "Yellow Ledbetter". I look over to see Sim withdrawing his hand from the console. I'd replaced the original mostly because I wanted more than an FM radio.

"I have noticed that you tend to choose this music to improve your mood, Your Excellency. Forgive me for taking the liberty, but it seemed your mood at present could use some lightening." He leaves it at that, not pressing further. It's not his place to, after all.

"Thank you, Simaron." I—I want to tell him that I—

"You are quite welcome, my lord. Are there any special requests from you or the viscountess about tonight's dinner?" Right. The noble life.

"Anything you prepare I'm certain will be more than adequate, Simaron." Because I can't tell him his cooking is rather good, it would embarrass him. However, so many years of practice making my favorite foods, he was bound to perfect them sooner or later. Here's hoping Jen and I have the same tastes.

"Thank you, sir." A few more moments pass, the song going into the solo. Usually Simaron would be right, I'd hear Mike McCready's fingers plucking over the strings and not help but feel better, Vedder's voice like a warm blanket to wrap myself in. Not tonight though. There's too much on my mind, but it's still a small comfort. Maybe because Sim thought of it.

"I'm going on a hunting trip this week, Simaron." Might as well let him know I won't be around.

"I have figured as such, Your Excellency."

I pull the car over a few blocks from the manor and look at him. "Oh?"

"Yes, my lord." He motions to the backseat. "I would suppose it has something to do with the Azure Blade." I blink once. Simaron smiles knowingly. "Sir, I have been in your service as long as I can remember. I can read your moods. There is little reason you would visit such a terrible place as the Tomb of Keres unless something dire was afoot. Also, when I was cleaning the Azure Blade for your ceremony, I noticed it had lost some of its luster."

"You knew? And you didn't tell me?"

"I was not certain yet, Your Excellency. I did not wish to trouble you with idle musings and worries. You have often chided me for seeing problems where there were in fact none. I wanted to be certain before I brought it to your attention, though I would imagine you are already aware." He looks away from me. "Would I be correct in assuming I am responsible for this difficult situation you find yourself in?"

I take his chin in my hand and turn his face back toward me. "This isn't your fault, Sim. I'm—" I wince, feeling the weight of the oath digging into my neck. Why did I have to swear it in the tomb of a death god? "I can't discuss it, but what I can say is that I'm fixing it, and the first step is finding the demon that killed Dad."

"Count Kendrick?" He doesn't remove my hand from his face. "You seek to avenge him?"

I lean back in the seat, taking my hand from his face so I can rub my temples a few seconds. "I don't know how exactly I'm going to do it, though. I mean, the demon's supposed to be dead. Dad died killing him, after all. If he didn't kill him, then..." Then I've been assuming the wrong thing since he died.

I exhale softly. “Going to be a bitch pulling it off without the blade.”

“Luckily, you have someone who will accompany you on your quest, Your Excellency.”

“Jen would be the logical choice, being a Demonbane, but she’s a viscountess now.” I place my hands back on the steering wheel. “And if I’m going off on an adventure, she unfortunately has to watch over the county. The manor can’t be left alone. I’ll have to do the same in the future should she go off on some knightly quest, but for now—”

“I am aware of Her Excellency’s responsibilities, my lord.” He looks down, humbly.

Oh.

“You, Sim?”

“Only if you would have me, sir. However, forgive me for reminding you, but I am in your service, as my father was in your father’s, and my grandfather before him, and so forth. It would dishonor both me and my family greatly were I to stand idly by while you put yourself in danger. I shall accompany you on your quest, if you will have me.” He seems to blush slightly. “I ask you forgive my outburst, sir. It was uncalled for.” This is something Sim will say even while sounding like he reads the news for the BBC. Still, that he would put himself into danger, just to ensure that I wouldn’t have to face it alone.

“You don’t even have to ask, Sim. It would mean a lot to me. I’m worried, this is a demon I might be hunting, and—”

“Worry not about my martial prowess, my lord. As your father taught you, so my father taught me. While my skill certainly doesn’t rival yours, my father’s blood runs in my veins, and with it his innate expertise.” Meaning despite being “tainted”, he retains the Fae knack for, well, everything. His father had been a commoner, of course, but a commoner sidhe, and that counted for something.

"Let's not forget your mother's intelligence, Sim. I'd like to think a lot of her creativity rubbed off on you." He looks away, but I continue. "Trust me, it'll come in handy, don't discount it."

"If you insist, sir." He sets his jaw. "I'm sure Her Excellency is growing curious why we are yet to return, my lord."

More than likely not. Jen doesn't seem like the type who'd sit up and wait for her dinner. It's obvious Sim doesn't want to talk about his mother. Someday I'll crack that but obviously not today.

I take the car out of park and proceed the last few blocks to the manor. Once we're inside the garage, I head to the dining room. I would help Sim with the armor cases and the sword, but he will insist on doing it himself. I'm a viscount, after all, manual labor is beneath me. After he's done he'll go to the kitchen and make something for me and Jen, our first official meal together. We both kept the barbecue place secret, not wanting to hurt his feelings, not to mention the fact that he'd have considered it "hardly a meal worthy of a noble wedding's repast".

To my surprise, Jen is in the dining room, dressed in jeans and a T-shirt (for Judas Priest at that) much like me (except my shirt is Pearl Jam). She looks up when I enter, and waves before returning her attention to a book in front of her. "How'd it go?"

"Can't say. Oath. What are you reading?"

"Your family's history. I figured I might as well familiarize myself, since I'm part of the House now." She closes the book as I approach, giving me her attention. "Any leads yet?"

"Like I said, oath, so I can't say much. I'll probably be hunting a demon though."

She closes her eyes and curses under her breath. "And I can't go along. Fucking noble law. You couldn't have figured this out last night *before* I became Mrs. Fancy-Pants?"

I shrug. "I didn't know I was shamed until last night. And by that point we were already married."

"Married to the daughter of Sir Reece Demonbane. I would've been perfect to have along." She grumbles, rubbing her forehead. "I'm still allowed to go off on hunts myself, right? You're not going to forbid me?"

I laugh lightly. "Yeah, sure, I'd love to see that fight. Go off and hunt all the demons and whatever you want. Going to rethink bringing on a squire?"

She shakes her head. "No need for a squire, not in the way you're thinking." Personal harem, that's the way I was thinking. Jen takes a moment to stretch and shrugs. "I might look among the commoner sidhe though. A squire's never a bad idea. Might help out the House, build a reputation that we're reestablishing ourselves as a warrior line." I smirk, and she arches a brow. "What?"

"Dad would've loved you."

Her mouth opens for a second, and she smiles, taking the compliment. "So, your parents..."

"You know about my dad, demon got him. Mom, well, broken mirror." She nods solemnly, not saying anything, but I know that look. "Broken mirror" is what the ritual's called when a spouse chooses death over spending the rest of their lives without the one they love.

Sure, Dad had been sleeping with Simaron's father quite a bit, but according to Dad at least, that's all it was. Hell, Simaron's father couldn't have seen much in it either if he was willing to have a child with a human. Mom and Dad did love each other, one of those greeting-card kind of loves, only in an open marriage.

Jen places her hand on mine and squeezes it gently. "I

suppose you'll be meeting mine. Mother will approve of you eventually, but Father..."

"Typical dad? Disapproving? And I work in porn. Gods, he's going to *love* me." I take my hand from hers as I sit at the table. "Duchess Cadwyn's dispatching a small contingent of guards here to keep an eye on you while I'm gone."

"I hardly think I'm the one who needs protection, Dick. She won't change her mind about the guards?"

"I'm her nephew, what do you think?"

She gives a silent nod, but it implies *I see.*

I look at the generally empty table. "You eat yet? I think Sim's making something."

"What about him, by the way? He's hardly said three words to me. I mean, he's not ignoring me or anything, but I get the feeling he isn't all that happy about me being here."

"It's a change for Sim. It's just been him and me for the last couple decades, since Mom. You also didn't bring any of your own staff, so we've doubled his workload. I'd seriously consider that squire, maybe a handmaiden or two, even if you aren't going to sleep with them. There's plenty of room in the servants' quarters."

She rolls her eyes light-heartedly. "Fine, I'll think about it. I wasn't expecting to end up in the ruling class. My job was supposed to be hunting demons."

"It still can be, just wait for me to get back from my own little hunt, fix everything with the sword."

This is why being a noble sidhe is a pain in the ass. She can't risk her life if I'm knowingly risking mine, even though she's much more qualified to do so, because someone has to be alive to carry on the House. It'll change once we conceive an heir, but now is hardly the time to knock her up.

Jen rubs her temples slowly. “This is starting to get too complicated.”

“Hey, if it’s too rough then you never should’ve done whatever the hell it was you did to get stuck with me.” I grin a bit and wink, but the humor is apparently lost on her as she gets up from the table to leave the dining room. “Jen, I’m sorry, I didn’t mean to tease, really. Come back, have dinner.”

“It’s fine, Dick. I already ate. I’m going to check around the house, make sure everything’s secure and safe. Get the lay of the land.” She leaves the room as Simaron enters with dinner.

“Will Her Excellency not be dining with us this evening, my lord?”

“It would appear not, Simaron.” I turn my attention from the door to Sim. “I’m plenty hungry though, so please, feel free to serve.” I check the door leading to the foyer, half-expecting her to come back, explain everything, but it’s not in the cards. My guess is that I struck a nerve, something she doesn’t want to talk about. Granted, I could make her answer, as I’m her husband and gained my title by birth, but I have the sneaking suspicion she’d tell me she’s under oath, more than likely to the Duke and Duchess of Destry Bay. “Join me, Sim?”

“It wouldn’t be proper, Your Excellency.”

“Sim, considering what I imagine we’ll be going through over the next few days, if we both survive, it would surprise me if you didn’t come out of this with an appointment to be knighted. With that in mind, I suggest we both eat our fill this night, for tomorrow we hunt a demon.”

Chapter Nine
Blood

Despite the fact that I'm descended from a bloodline of warriors, my family's armory isn't all that impressive. As far as swords are concerned, there's only the Azure Blade and a few practice sabers. No firearms, as Fae tend to stay away from those. Something complicated and mechanical that fires projectiles of forged or alloyed iron? No fucking way, thank you very much.

"Ye gods, Dick, how did your family ever get by?" Jen is inspecting the rather pathetic (in her eyes) collection of arms hanging on the wall in my father's armory. I've never really considered it mine. "Maybe a bow?" She lifts a recurve off the wall and strings it with relative ease. "It's a pretty good one. The bowyer did a good job on it."

"That was my mother's." I rub my forehead, having had a headache since breakfast that I try not to call a sense of foreboding. "I've never been a good shot. I didn't take after her family in that regard."

"What line was your mother?"

"Sunleaves." She stares at me a moment, and I manage a slight smile through the headache. "Don't worry, I'm rather far down the line. So many people have to die before I'll matter." As

I've mentioned, I'm related to the ruling line through my mother, but it's still impressive to some Fae when they first hear it.

"A Sunleaf who can't shoot a bow." She chuckles lightly. "Gods, that would be like..."

"A Demonbane who shits himself at the sight of a succubus. I know. I know." I appraise the weapon collection and sigh softly. My father hunted demons, but it was done with the Azure Blade. Little reason to have another sword when you've got one of only a few magical swords in the City. "I don't suppose I can borrow anything from your dad?"

She shakes her head. "Sir Reece is out of the City right now, the Queen requested his services. He wasn't even there for the wedding."

So I was wrong about that at the ceremony. I'm not infallible. I give her a look, though, at calling her father by his title.

Her tone is a bit indulgent when she answers. "We're a tad more formal by the Emerald Shores, Dick. Wouldn't be proper to refer to him by an informal title." She shrugs once. "Anyway, I can't use any of his weapons, much less lend them out. Period. If I could come along, I could probably wield the Azure Blade, but that's academic right now."

"So I hunt a demon unarmed? I doubt I can parry a blow with my rapier wit." I rub my temples again slowly. The headache's getting worse. "No time to commission a blade, and I doubt anything made by man would suffice. I'm really fucked with this time limit." I sit in one of the wooden chairs, resting my head against the back. It does little for the throbbing. "Do me a favor? Ask Sim to get me some aspirin?" Because I can hardly ask a viscountess to fetch it. Can't get it myself either. Wouldn't be proper. Much more noble to suffer from an impending migraine for an extra ten minutes instead of disgracing myself by getting my own damned headache relief.

"Yeah, no problem." She heads for the door and turns back for a second. "You really need an aspirin or just need to be alone for a bit?" I look at her, my fingers still massaging my head. She gets the message. "Right. I'll ask for the extra-strength." Jen closes the door behind her, bless her, as quietly as she can.

I've never had one this bad before, not without getting clocked pretty hard, and that's happened maybe once. "What the hell am I going to do?"

"Hell's never a good answer." I look up at a man I've never seen before sitting behind my father's desk. A human. Light brown hair, blue eyes, pale skin, dressed in dark green robes. "I should know, I've been there once. Those Christians turned out to be a bunch of masochists."

I swallow hard. "Who are you?" Like that's a tough one to figure out. A human magically appears and starts talking about hell?

"I'm not a demon." What the? Does he know what— "Yes. I know what you're thinking."

"What are you?" I say. "What are you doing here? How did you get in here? No, that doesn't fucking matter, get the fuck out!"

He shakes his head and rises from the chair, walking over. The human appraises me. "Maybe the chin, definitely not the eyes."

"What the hell are you talking about?"

"Let's start simple." He starts counting on his fingers. "How did I get in here? I'm not here. What am I doing here? You need me. What am I? Well... Why is your blood blue and not silver?"

I blink at him a couple of times. “I don’t get it.” The first two answers I dismiss out of hand. The last question? Well, Fae mixed their blood with Ra’Keth—

“And when a Fae has a little too much of that blood in their heritage?” I stare at him, and he smirks. “Mystics. Charming little term you came up with. In some cultures that’s a term of respect, whereas in yours it’s shameful.” He kneels to meet me eye to eye. “Now, can you guess my name?”

“Deathsinger of the Northern Wastes.” The words trickle from my lips. I am terrified. “You’re supposed to be dead.”

He snickers. “I am. Been a long time. But my kind, we never planned on dying. We found ways to immortality. Some made their undead servants, some bound their souls to gods, to demons, some swapped blood with who knows what...” He runs his hand along my face, or seems to. I don’t feel any pressure there. “While some of us preferred bloodlines. There’s no certainty that my sons or daughters by a human would carry a whit of my talent, but my Fae...” He smiles with no small amount of pride. “What better refuge for blood that surpasses reality itself than a living dream?”

I pull away from him, hitting my head on the back of the chair. “Get away from me.”

“I’m in your blood, Richard, I’m not going anywhere. And if anyone should be considered repugnant it’s you. You’re the betrayer after all. You’ve always known you were of my blood, why act so surprised now?” He leans in close to me. “And you don’t know my name.”

“I’m not descended from Deathsinger?”

He shakes his head slowly, dismissively. “That’s one of the things they called me, but it’s not my name.” The apparition studies me for a moment and stands to drop his robes, wearing a simple T-shirt and jeans underneath, similar to mine, his shirt even having the Pearl Jam logo. After appraising himself and appearing satisfied, he continues. “I see fashions have changed again.”

“How am I a betrayer? What did I do? What do I need to do to prove myself?”

“If I just tell you it won’t mean anything. Don’t worry, it’ll happen in time. In the meantime I suggest you chase that quest of yours.” He doesn’t sound too interested, looking at a small mirror hung on the wall. He runs his hands through his hair, lengthening it, letting it hang simply.

“Hunt a demon,” I say dubiously. “How? I don’t know how to track the one who killed Dad, and even if I could, what the hell do I fight it with?”

“It’s an odd name, don’t you think?”

“What?”

He walks over to the rack of weapons and inspects them. “Deathsinger. Of the Northern Wastes.”

I finally get up from the chair, my headache subsiding for the moment. “What does that have to do with anything? They were the Northern Wastes after you were through with them.”

“Truly?” He faces me. “You were there to witness it? When I supposedly sang the song that unmade the world and began it again in my image?” He chuckles to himself. “Or did I lay a nation to waste because they refused me a simple courtesy? Perhaps I slaughtered the local gods and drank their souls? Made the Fae themselves my weapon and perversion? Tell me, descendent, what atrocities have been attributed to me this century?”

“I suppose you’re innocent of all they say about you?”

He appears to think about it for a moment. “I destroyed a god who was demanding unreasonable sacrifices, and I used the power I drew from his corpse to establish a bloodline with my favored concubine, who I'm certain you've heard of. You have her hair, after all. All the rest was grown in the telling, which I cared little about. It enabled me to concentrate on my plans, until Mercia decided she didn't need me anymore. I'm not saying I was pure as the driven snow, but Mercia was hardly the same either." He looks around the room. "I'm glad to see your people have grown more civilized."

"Why are you here? What, to change my mind about you? That's the betrayal, I don't see you as a noble ancestor?"

"Richard, I care little for what you think of me. What matters is that my blood is strong in you, and that may be all the weapon you need."

"I'm...a mystic?" He makes no move to refute me. I shake my head quickly. "No, my House has already suffered enough. This would ruin us. They're already starting to address me as a Scion of Deathsinger!"

"Rem." He smirks. "My mother named me Rem. It does little for my reputation in your eyes, I'm certain. Sing. In..." The next word doesn't make any sense to me. It's in a language I've never heard before.

"In what? And what do I have to sing?"

"Ah, yes, you call it something different now...Sigil. And you have to sing because if I worked my magic through flapping my arms about and waving a stick at my problems, I wouldn't have been called Death*singer*."

"Are you telling me I can work magic? Just sing up whatever I want?"

Rem shakes his head. "You're not Ra'Keth, Richard, no matter how potent my blood might be. And since I was never foolish enough to become any god's *pet*, you won't have any access to the little favors some of your kind can acquire."

"So how the hell do I fight a demon then?"

He points to one of the practice sabers.

"That doesn't even have an edge!"

"Take it," he says expectantly. "Draw it and sing."

I fight the urge to roll my eyes and take the saber off the walls. The blade is thin, dull as I pull it from its sheath, having seen only limited use. I feel stupid. Very, very stupid. I hum a couple bars, but nothing happens.

Rem sighs loudly. "Sing *something.*"

"I only know oaths, okay? And I don't want to bind myself to anything, I'm not a moron." I lunge suddenly, sticking the blade through Rem, who looks down at it, unimpressed, as all I've done is prove he's incorporeal. I shrug with a slight grin. "Worth a shot, right?"

"Is your voice truly that bad? You must have a passing vocabulary in Sigil." He walks away from the blade, which seamlessly passes out of his body. "Just sing something that draws out your passion. Anything that has meaning for you."

"Why are you doing this? Really?" I turn away. Ra'keth are always working an angle. Always. They use us, that's what they do. It's why their blood is in our veins, to control us, force us to work their bidding, even from millennia ago.

"Because you're the last of my line and I'm not all that happy with that prospect. I'd much prefer you live long enough to have children so they can continue the line. I'm sure there's some ulterior motive I can come up with to make this benefit an incorporeal hallucination of your forebear, if that will set your mind to ease." Rem walks around in front of me. "Though I do believe you're simply afraid of singing and having something happen. You're hoping I'll go away, and you're not actually a mystic. The wishes of a desperate man with nowhere to turn."

"Stop that."

"There are some demons you can traffic with. They're hardly a unified front. Getting one to betray the other should be easy. Your fellows would prefer that to your being a mystic, I take it?"

"Shut up!" I keep him at sword's length. He walks toward me, the blade sliding through his chest, emerging quickly and bloodlessly from his back.

"Sing, that is all I ask, and I will leave you for a time. I give you my word." He smiles slightly. "For all it will be worth to you."

I take a long breath. He's right. I am afraid of what will happen. Mystics are accepted, but only grudgingly at that. Depending on how strong Deathsinger's blood is in me, I could risk private embarrassment all the way up to avoiding "tragic accidents" for the rest of my life. Regardless, I seriously doubt I would be permitted to have children. Did Dad know about this? Did he see he had a mystic for a son and that's why I have no brothers, no sisters?

As long as I don't sing, it won't be true. But if I don't, I'll still be left with little means to find a demon, kill it, and somehow prove myself to Deathsinger. Well...Rem.

"Anything I want?"

Rem nods once, and I think through my vocabulary and clear my throat. I'm Fae, like I've mentioned once or twice, so singing comes naturally to me. I let my mouth shape the words as they emerge, closing my eyes, hearing a guitar riff and drumbeat in my head as I begin to sing the opening lines to "Yellow Ledbetter", which might as well be in a different language considering how unintelligible the lyrics are.

My headache vanishes, my body feeling oddly warm, comforted. I can literally *feel* the music inside me, pulsing through my veins, enlivened by my lungs when I draw breath. I become aware of the sword in my hand, like an empty staff seeking notes to fill it. The Sigil weaves through the metal, the music flowing with it. When I open my eyes, the practice saber is sheathed in a soft silver flame, which understandably startles me. I break off the song halfway through the chorus and the flame immediately vanishes.

Rem is gone.

“Your Excellency…” I turn toward the door to see Simaron, who is holding a goblet and a small tray with two white pills on it. His expression is that of shock. He saw.

“Simaron, you’re not to tell anyone about this.” Perhaps I sound a little more intense than I intend, because he almost backs away a step. “Please, you’re aware of what it means for a noble to be revealed as…” Ye gods, I can’t even say it.

“I hardly see the embarrassment, my lord.” Sim smiles knowingly. “After all, the Firemanes have long been respected as artists as well as warriors. It is little surprise that you have a lovely singing voice as part of your repertoire.”

Chapter Ten
½ Full

Understandably it took me a little while to accept that I'm a mystic. A couple bottles of wine as well. Okay, three. And the rest of Aunt Cadwyn's brownies.

I'm not really feeling any better about it, but after confirming in private that I could light the saber with the silver fire using nothing more than a sung Sigil translation of "Do The Evolution", I had to accept that I'm not really like other Fae, and not in a good way. It fills me with a lot of questions that I never wanted to ask, and certain things make sense that shouldn't. I haven't told Jen. I probably won't if I can help it. Even though Jen knows that Duchess Catrin is a mystic, it's difficult to say if she'll be as accepting of her husband being one.

Thank the gods Sim's been cool about it, but given his own status in Fae society, he's probably in a position to be far more accepting than most. He hasn't said a word, but I know that he knows, that he knows what it means, and he's been discreet.

"Your Excellency?" Sim's outside my door. I've been getting myself ready, dressing in a brown leather jacket, jeans, sneakers, driving gloves, and a fresh Pearl Jam T-shirt. You'd think that since I'm going demon-hunting, I'd go with the ceremonial armor. But that's all it is: ceremonial.

The Crest of Stone, which thankfully hasn't abandoned me yet, however…

I've mentioned that magical swords are a definite rarity in the City, but other magical items, well, we Fae are famous for collecting them. It's one of the reasons Fae are more likely to play dragonslayer than the Knights of St. George, as dragons tend to keep plenty of pretties and shinies in their hoards. There's only one dragon in the City, though, and his hoard isn't worth stealing, so he's left alone for the most part. The head of the Sunleaf line has a magical bow that can bring the sun even on the darkest winter night when one of its arrows is fired into the air. The Matriarch of the Heartwoods has a set of panpipes that can summon every dryad in a five-mile radius. And the Crest of Stone?

I hold the cool disc in my hand, the emblem taking up most of the space there. Softly, I whisper the words my father taught me. "*Our heart is the mountain, our blood is the land, our minds are the wind, our bodies a house of stone.*" I press the emblem to my chest, the stone vanishing, my T-shirt shimmering as the crest appears on it in a deep gray against the white cotton. Unless a real fan looks at it, it'll appear to be part of an album design. I breathe a soft sigh of relief, then take a knife from nearby in my hand, get a good grip, and stab down hard at my leather-covered forearm.

There are sparks, and I find myself holding a hilt with a broken blade, my jacket completely unblemished.

I grin a bit bigger than I probably should. "I will never get tired of seeing that."

There's another knock at the door. "Come in, Sim."

Simaron opens the door and enters, looking me over and sighing softly. "To utilize the crest in such a way, my lord." He then appraises his own clothing, outfitted more like a SWAT team member than anything else. “I would imagine your quest will require more...” He actually winces. “Casual attire?”

“I’m hoping to not stick out, Sim. And you look like we’re going on a drug bust. Where the hell did you get that, anyway?” He doesn’t answer, just starts shedding his clothes in a quick and efficient manner. It’s not like I’m complaining. He closes the door soon afterward, and I understandably stare. “Uh, Sim? Just confirm this for me. Are you coming onto me right now?”

His eyes go wide in disbelief, and he folds his arms, getting a huffy look on his face. “My lord, I might remind you that not everyone is as...blessed with a libido such as yours. Please forgive me for not finding now to be a suitable time to satisfy your urges, but I would remind you that there is little time to—”

“Sim, while you chew me out in a proper and respectful manner, you’re still standing naked in front of me with a growing erection. Would you like to borrow some of my clothes so you’ll blend in better?” He looks down at his groin and sets his jaw, probably more angry at himself than at me for pointing it out. Still, it’s not hard to discern where my attention is at the moment. “Simaron.”

He takes a long breath and looks at me. “Yes, Your Excellency?” I walk to him, kneel before him, lean my head forward. I can hear the shock in his voice. “My lord, please!”

I know he means otherwise, but I open my mouth and lean farther forward anyway. Hey, I could die today. I’m not letting a perfectly good opportunity like this pass me by. I take him in, a few inches, nothing freaky, it’s not like I’m a satyr with a bottomless and elastic throat, you know. I taste his musky sweat on my tongue though, the jewel of precome that has leaked from the tip, salty and sweet. I really have little experience in doing this.

I tried fellating Sim when I was younger but his father

caught us and quickly punished Sim for "forgetting his place" even though it had been my idea. However, I have been attended to by many an eager mouth, so I understand the principles and procedures involved. Bob your head up and down, suck a little, use your tongue, remember to breathe through your nose, and accept that your jaw is going to get tired. Hand/mouth hybrid technique is best, especially for the "big boys", which Sim certainly is.

I wrap my fingers around the base, pumping slow, letting my teeth brush along the ridge of his glans. I notice that the skin's nice and smooth on the underside as I slather it with my tongue. I also notice that he's yet to push my head away.

Working in porn has taught me that there are two types of guys when it comes to fellatio: guys who get off in two minutes and guys who won't get close until your jaw is practically falling off your face. Guess which one a person realistically wants to be with?

I'm aware that it's something like this that very well could have shamed me, but if that's true, I'm already shamed. It's just a matter of degree now. What's one more bit of intimate time with Sim?

"Please, Your Excellency..." His voice is starting to sputter, his hips starting to move against my rhythm, taking the lead which I follow. I'm more going off theory at this point, but I think I'm doing rather well. My director Will told me that first timers tend to have the best enthusiasm, which can make up for a lack of skill.

Sim's breathing grows more shallow, the pitch of his moans sliding upward as my hands grip his hips. His voice goes into more of a babbling than anything else. I'm rather grateful that Jen is out schooling the regiment (the *small* regiment) of guards that arrived this morning. Otherwise she'd probably hear the noises Sim is making. As I've said before, she doesn't mind what Sim and I do, as long as she can keep up that plausible deniability. Still, at least I know he's enjoying the ride for a change.

"Oh gods, Richard!"

I stop dead. Simaron just addressed me. By my *name.* My mouth quickly floods with his seed, which dribbles a bit down my chin before I come to my senses, kind of, and swallow the rest of the warm thick liquid, feeling it trickle down my throat. He continues a few more seconds before pulling himself free, my hands already limp at my sides as he kneels, his eyes filled with fear. There aren't any words.

I've really fucked up now. I'm supposed to feel bad about that, right? Why don't I?

"Sim?" I'm sure my tone conveys my confusion. This is the second time I've done this, essentially serviced my servant, taken his seed into me. Each time I've charged toward it so eagerly. I don't quite understand.

"Yes, my lord?" His voice is small, afraid. I honestly couldn't say why I don't sound the same.

I reach up to my face and wipe off the excess fluid that was still stuck to my lips and chin, and then slowly rise to my feet. "Why did…" I look away from him, toward a window. "Why did I do that?"

A few seconds pass before he answers. "I can only offer my apologies, Your Excellency. I shall go and fetch more appropriate attire for your quest." I don't hear him leave, but I know that he's gone, and there was something in his voice, a hint of anger, pain.

I just fucked up again, didn't I?

Chapter Eleven
Off He Goes

There's a saying in the City: The Benedict isn't on the wrong side of the tracks, the tracks are on the right side of the Benedict. This part of the City isn't where people live for the most part. There's just rusted waterfront and empty warehouses and closed factories and a whole lot of boarded-up storefronts. What few tenements we have mostly aren't up to code, and those that are won't be for long. The Benedict is mostly considered to be the diseased part of the City that most people are hoping will fall off on its own. Hell, the whole reason we don't call it St. Benedict out here is that you could hardly imagine a saint watching over it.

My county isn't the whole Benedict, the "Benedict Shores" comprise some rusted-out shoreline of Destry Bay and a whole lot of closed factories, as well as the warehouse that Blue Line is based out of. The Houses here were weak, they died out, and their land fell under the jurisdiction of Her Majesty. And I believe I mentioned earlier what Her Majesty's level of concern about St. Benedict is.

I'm mostly a vestige of a once-respectable duchy. Look at it now though. Weres, giant spiders, vamps, the rare demon popping up every decade or so, even a damned Ra'keth at one point. It's probably why Jen will have a time of it finding a squire. The few Fae that were here? Mostly brownies and knockers, and they fled into the better counties and baronies as soon as they could. All that's left in the area is a sidhe. And where's that guy?

Well, I'm at a gas station, filling up the Trans-Am with premium at a disgusting price while Sim is inside paying for it. This is one of the few stations in the Benedict, maybe three total. The only reason I'm at this one is because there's a small attachment of wonder to it. During the blizzard that nearly ended the world not too long ago, the sign for this station was struck by lightning. During a blizzard. That doesn't happen.

As a result a couple people occasionally come out to examine the evidence of the "phenomenon", which the owner left intact, at first because he couldn't afford to fix the damage, and now because it's a small boost to business. Regardless, there's some wonder here, some questioning at how the impossible could happen. It's the stuff of dreams, those questions, that keep my people existing.

"Everything set, Sim?" He's returned carrying a small bag with bottles of water inside, nothing else. He holds up a receipt.

"The expenses have been taken care of, my lord." He hands me a bottle, which I open and take a long swig off. Ugh, it's warm. He puts the rest of the water in the car. "Might I ask how we will track our quarry?" Sim's wearing jeans as well, dark blue, hiking boots, a heavy leather jacket and a buttoned dress shirt underneath. He doesn't look too happy about it.

Still, he's asked the $64,000 question (as Sim's mother would say, it was an odd expression but I liked the sound of it), and the only clue I have is to be a good little mystic and let my Ra'Keth blood solve all my problems. I can't help but wonder if I ever would've had to deal with this if I'd simply gone the warrior route after I became the Viscount of the Benedict Shores upon my mother's... When she abdicated in her way.

"I'm going to have to do something I don't want to do, Sim."

"Sir?"

I take a second, drink some more water. "I'm a mystic, Simaron."

"And?" He sounds expectant.

"And? That's all you have to say?" Sure, I was expecting him to take it better than most, but I wasn't expecting blasé.

"Your Excellency, you are still, as you are aware, the lord of the House of Stone. Whatever other responsibilities are demanded of you will not change my service to you. As for your reluctance, the quarry is difficult to find, yes?" He doesn't give me time to answer. "It has also been revealed that you possess a latent ability. Perhaps you also possess the power to track the creature? Why resist such a possibility? Because you are wary because of potential embarrassment? My lord, may I remind you that within six days you stand to lose your title outright?"

"How did you know about that?"

"An open secret is well known to those who are assumed to not be listening and beneath attention." Meaning every servant in the City probably knows, because they love to gossip about their respective lords and ladies. Granted, they'll never share that information, unless it's assumed you already know. Fae politics don't just stop with the noble class.

"What about my being a mystic? You planning on spreading that around?" I see his jaw set, his eyes narrow. I think he's trembling. "I'm sorry, Sim. That was uncalled for."

After a few seconds, he continues. "Your Excellency, please, this concerns your House. Better it weather some minor humiliation than fall into ruin." I'm about to protest that this isn't all that minor when his face softens. "Please, sir."

Why is that working? Damn it, I'm the noble here, how is he managing to get his way? Still, he is making a bit of sense. I don't have time to whine about this when I have a means of killing the demon without the Azure Blade. Finding it though...

"I don't know what to do, Sim. I mean, I have to be a mystic to do this but what can I do other than set a sword on fire? That'll be great when I'm fighting, but how do I use it to track a demon that's supposed to be dead?"

"It killed Count Kendrick, yes?" He's right, there. "And Father once told me that the same demon killed Count Llewellyn?" Again, correct. "Perhaps it lives in St. Benedict then, my lord?"

It would certainly make sense. Having a demon around tends to drive down the property values. It's why the north side of Allora isn't *anything* like the rest of it, since apparently the demons started moving in. Yet another reason it's all the more puzzling Jen would get paired up with me. A sidhe knight of the Demonbane line would be in high demand in that area, to fight as well as to breed. With her training and lineage, Jen should've had her pick of who she'd marry, or at least *a* pick. Why me?

"I think I would've noticed a demon around, even if it wasn't in my county. They tend to stink up the place."

"Are they not great deceivers, my lord?"

"He's got a point." Deathsinger steps out from behind Sim and appraises him. "Don't worry, he can't see me, and I suggest you not talk to me either, lest he start thinking you've lost your mind."

"Supposing that were true..." I look between both of them. "My family apparently had the grudge, not the demon. It killed Dad when he was trying to avenge Grandfather, and who knows why he was after it other than it being a demon. If it had a problem with my line, why not come after me whenever it felt like it?"

"Sir, please. Perhaps it's in your family's records where your father fell? It is worth checking." I doubt the trail can be any colder starting there, but I don't have any better ideas. I relent, but not because it's Sim's idea, but because, well... Oh, damn it all.

"I'll call Jen, she could look it up, save me a trip back." I take out my cell and dial. The line rings several times, but finally I hear her pick up. My hallucinatory ancestor just watches, inspecting my cell phone, intrigued by its appearance.

"That you, Dick?" She sounds tired, slightly exasperated.

"Yeah, I need a favor. Could you look through the family records and tell me where my father slew that demon?" There's a pause on the line. "I'm serious, could you look it up for me?"

"I won't ask why, probably has to do with the oath, right?" I don't answer, I don't need to. After almost a minute she comes back on the line. "It was at the Lake of the Dead, where the sun weeps blood for the moon's fallen children, wherever the hell that is. Sometimes I wish we weren't so overly poetic."

"If we weren't there'd be no wonder to us, and we'd fade off and die, remember?" I take a second to think it through. "Lake of the Dead... That's a cemetery, a big one. Where the sun weeps blood... Sunset Grove Cemetery, just outside the City."

Her tone is a little incredulous. "Damn, you understood that?"

I smile gently and look to Sim. "I knew someone who taught me to think creatively. How are things with the guards?"

Simaron looks away a moment. Again, mentions of his mother are not appreciated, but eventually I'm going to make him accept her.

Jen comes back on the line, and I turn my attention to the

phone. "Well as can be expected. They're all knights, all with experience. They listen to me though, for now. I should be okay here. Besides, I've got the blade should anything go wrong, right?"

"Might as well. It only likes one of us at present."

"I'll let you head on out then. Have fun storming the castle."

I grin. "You think it'll work? It'll probably take a miracle." Thank the gods Dad had no problem with me watching every sword-swinging movie I could get my little hands on growing up. Jen laughs in return, but I can hear strain in it.

Because there's no guarantee I'm coming home alive.

"Take care of yourself, okay?" She doesn't give me the chance to return the goodbye, the call ending. Probably doesn't want to make it any harder. I put my phone in my pocket and look to my manservant and my hallucination.

"Sunset Grove, as good a place as any to start." I take another long drink from my water, finishing off the bottle, and get into the car after tossing the empty in a nearby bin. Sim joins me soon afterward. Deathsinger leans in the window, inspecting the cabin.

"I don't really think she's right for you."

"I didn't ask your opinion. And I like her. I could've ended up with much worse, you know."

"My lord?" Shit. Sim. He looks at me oddly. "I offer my apologies, Your Excellency, if you believe I did not approve of your marriage to the Countess Stone." He sounds more flustered as the seconds tick by.

"Simaron, it's okay." I'm about to admonish my infamous ancestor when I notice he's vanished. How convenient for him. Asshole. "I'm more talking to myself than anyone else. I suppose

I'm still a bit overwhelmed by the stress of everything happening so close together." See what I did there? If you really look at it, I'm not lying, but I danced around the truth with ease.

"If you say so, my lord." Meaning he knows I'm full of it but he'll leave it alone. This is one of the reasons I like having Sim around. "Will we be proceeding to Sunset Grove then, sir?" I nod in assent. "My lord, please forgive me, and I know I speak drastically above my station, but..."

I start the car. "What is it, Sim? Just say it."

"My mother." He doesn't look at me. "Why do you insist on bringing her up at every opportunity? Why do you constantly remind me of my shame? There are so many times that I find you a kind and generous viscount, sacrificing so much for the good of your lands, but why must you insist on such cruelty with me?"

"You think I mention her to mock you?"

"Why else, Your Excellency? She was a madwoman, her mind torn asunder by her hubris to believe she could hold court with the Fair Folk. I endeavor to carry my burden in silence but you seem to take joy in bringing it to light again and again and..." His face is a mask of pain, rage. I had no idea he was taking it this badly, but...

"I respected Lady Teresa." He stares at me. "I say that with my most solemn oath. I respected your mother. The day she came into my House was a blessing. Her music, it..." I can remember seeing the tears in my parents' eyes at hearing Simaron's mother play. "She brought wonder into our lives. She showed me how to think through my problems, and when I've actually followed her advice it's only turned out well for me. I bring her up because such a magnificent woman shouldn't be forgotten, especially not by her son."

I take a deep breath. "And yes, your mother's madness was a result of living in our world. No human can live within a dream forever." But many of them try, which is often what claims their lives in the end. "She left her mark though, with you. Perhaps you're seen as a mistake by the rest of the Fae, Sim, but not me. I knew your mother, and I've known you all my life, and I refuse, I *refuse* to let her memory fade or die in shame."

A moment passes. Then another. I decide to pull out of the gas station and start the journey out of town to Sunset Grove. I don't turn on the radio, despite the obvious need for something to fill the silence. Maybe this has been building up for a while with him, and he ended up in an argument he hadn't rehearsed for. I don't know how I could've come across as mocking, but then, I've never told him that about his mother before. I thought it was obvious, really. Maybe it looked different from the other side.

"What will my punishment be, Your Excellency?" His voice is small, scared.

"For what?" I glance at him, and his hands are in his lap, fingers gently wringing, fidgeting. "For what you just said? Forget about it, Sim. There's nothing to apologize for."

"Sir, I am your servant, and I admonished you. You are far above my station, and I have not earned the right to question your behavior. Your Excellency, I—"

"Call me Richard."

"My lord, I will do no such thing, to refer to you so informally—"

"Will be an adequate punishment for your transgression, Simaron." I smirk at him and shift gears. He closes his eyes a moment and shakes his head slightly.

"I shall obey then..." He swallows hard. "Richard. I am

curious about one thing though."

"That being?"

"The records mentioned Sunset Grove, I understood that as well." I nod, pleased, and wait for him to continue. "But it is an immense cemetery, it will take some time to search."

"That's why there was the second part, 'the moon's fallen children'." I shift into the next gear. I'm not risking my life just yet, so my Fae luck is still helping through the light traffic. If I'm driving to my death, I might as well make good time while I'm at it.

"That part confuses me, sir—" I look at him, and again he sighs in defeat. "Richard."

"Not that hard, if you've ever hunted them or know people who have."

The moon's children were the weres, obviously, and until a good portion of them learned how to play human well enough to live in the City, they lived on the outskirts, in the wild. The Sunset Grove Cemetery was put near their territory.

Their burial grounds, to be specific.

Chapter Twelve
Thumbing My Way

I've never been a fan of going to cemeteries at night. Lack of light, surrounded by the dead, you're pretty much a horror-movie cliché waiting to happen. Throw in that I was driving a sports car, was not a virgin, and had engaged in more than my share of premarital sex, and I might as well wear a T-shirt reading "First Victim Here". Every terrible story that's been passed around a campfire or college campus about Sunset Grove I assumed was true, and the idea of strolling into not just a burial ground, but a burial ground for werewolves, werecats, werebears, you name it, and looking for a demon…

It makes me rather relieved that I'm going in at eleven in the morning on a cloudless day. Hell, it's practically picnic weather. Considering that the weres don't use grave markers, their grounds look like an adorable series of grassy knolls that overlook the cemetery. Ye gods, there are even daisies growing on some of them. Granted, I'd expect that cuteness evaporates the second the sun goes down and the fog rolls in.

It certainly doesn't look like a place where my father fought a demon, much less where one set up shop, but then again, it is the middle of the day.

Daisies can be intimidating under the right circumstances, right?

"I feel we've gone to the wrong place, Sim." I sit on the grass, taking in the view of rows upon rows of headstones. There are smaller graveyards in the City, but they tend to be for more upscale dead people. Sunset Grove is for the middle to working class, people from Beckettsville and some parts of Grunstadt, the various suburbs and exurbs that spoke out from the City itself, bedroom communities and the like.

"It may very well be where Count Kendrick defeated the demon. There was no guarantee that the creature would be about, especially so openly. An odd place for a battle though. I suppose the demons prefer more urban locales." It's difficult enough for Sim to cut the constant honorifics, but I doubt he'll call me by my name unless I pressure him to. As I said, it's an adequate "punishment". I'm sure he sees it as one.

"So now what..." I look around, not seeing any signs of life as it were, save the pretty flowers. "I hardly like the idea of standing here waiting for something to happen. I don't exactly have the time to be reactive in this situation."

"It surprises me you are not more emotional over this." I give him an inquisitive look, and he appears quite cross. "Count Kendrick gave his life to defeat this abomination, and yet it still apparently lives. This is an opportunity for the son to avenge the father."

"Dad was trying to do the same thing, that's what killed him." I exhale softly. "Possibly getting killed by a demon isn't going to do the county any good, Sim. And if I kill it? There's probably a thousand in hell waiting to take its place. What's to say the next won't come looking for some payback when I'm not ready? Why put my ass on the line and leave the county defenseless?"

"Noblesse oblige."

I shake my head, looking down at the grass. "Simaron, the

only noble responsibility I was born into was a shit ton of property taxes and an eventual arranged marriage." My face is then greeted with a slap, and Simaron's face is red with anger. "What...the *fuck*?"

"You want me to address you as Richard? As an equal? Then I shall treat you as such. You are *sidhe*, a living dream, a noble among the noble race. To humans, you are the epitome of eloquence, beauty, skill, and your grace lies in the dreams of your subjects. Even with your...your *debaucherous* 'films' you still sow the seeds of wonder in the minds and dreams of those who see them, a perfect male to save them, to love them, their ideal. Their vision of perfection is what keeps you alive and you *dare* to suggest you are beholden to nothing more than simple taxes?"

"Sim, I..." Whoa.

"You owe them, Richard Stone! You have a responsibility to them and I will be damned if I will see you mock your birthright one second longer."

Holy shit.

I think that bears repeating. Holy shit.

"Sim? Where did that come from?" He sets his jaw, and I quickly put up my hands. "No! I'm not mocking you, it's just that... How long have you felt this way? Why didn't you ever say anything?"

"If you can speak to me about accepting my mother, my heritage, you should hear the same criticisms. To be perfectly honest, I am surprised that..." He stops, looks away.

"No, keep going, you're on a roll." I can't get him to answer. "Sim, I want you to be honest with me. Hell, I don't think anyone's ever been this honest with me."

"I am surprised..." His voice is softer. "I am surprised it took this long for you to shame yourself."

Ouch.

I slump, rub my face a few seconds, fill the silence as best I can. I can't exactly apologize my way out of this, or say something cute or tell Sim to never speak of this again. I should be angry, considering a mere servant just dressed me down concerning issues that are none of his damned business. Quite a few Fae would agree that humans don't really matter in the long run, either. It's not like you see the other nobles doing much for their communities other than soaking up the wonder and creativity.

To be honest, I feel a bit shitty right now. And I don't like it at all.

"Richard."

"Sim, I don't think I'm quite ready to talk to you yet."

"*Sir.*"

"I just need a couple minutes, okay?" I then feel my head pulled up from staring at one of those daisies to look down the hill, where I see four armored Fae marching up. Literally armored. All are armed. "Ugh." I get to my feet and open up my jacket, letting them see the crest. They stop several feet away, at attention, wearing shining Fae-steel armor, long green cloaks with no heraldry. Odd. Their skin is pale, pointed ears, no helmets. All sidhe knights with bastard swords at their sides. The only real difference between them is their eyes. Blue, green, purple and orange.

One of them steps forward, the orange-eyed one. "Count Stone?"

"That would be me. You boys sent to protect me? I'm pretty sure I'm fine on my own." I gesture to the grassy knolls about me. "Turned out the daisies here weren't as intimidating as expected. Bad lead."

"Sir." Simaron sounds a bit nervous, but his hand is

steady, near the hilt of his saber.

Orange Eyes glares at Sim. “Your servant is forgetting his place, Count Stone.”

“He’s my servant, so it’s little of your concern. What are you doing here?” It is odd. How did they even know I was here?

Orange Eyes doesn’t respond. Green Eyes looks toward Sim, and Purple Eyes places his hand delicately on the hilt of his blade. Blue Eyes steps forward to reply.

“This is a dangerous place for a noble to be, Your Excellency. Especially when armed insufficiently.”

“Is that so?” My hands remain at my sides.

“Indeed, my lord. One might say you could be dispatched by inferior numbers. Even a...” Blue Eyes smirks, “...*Knight of the Realm*, such as yourself.”

Ah. I get it. I’m being set up to be embarrassed. Couldn’t finish the quest without outside help. How humiliating it will be for me, how fortunate that the as-yet-unnamed noble sent them to protect me from my own incompetence.

I tilt my head at Blue Eyes. “Are you questioning my martial prowess?” Sim shoots me a glance, wanting to shake his head quickly. He doesn’t, but I can see the almost-gesture. “We aren’t made Knights of the Realm for passing a correspondence course.” I can tell he doesn’t quite get the reference. I step closer, getting in his face. “I hunted and killed a nest of wererats when I was thirteen using only a long knife and a short bow. What deeds have you done? What stories are told of you in your county, *Knight*?” I can actually feel the weight of my authority, no matter how meager, pressing onto their shoulders. “Now tuck your tails between your legs like good little lapdogs and return to your master. I have no need of your assistance.”

Blue Eyes doesn’t back off. Fuck. “I’m afraid that isn’t possible, Your Excellency.” I hear the sound of swords being drawn. Shit, shit, shit. This just got entirely too serious.

They're here to kill me.

"Should I bother asking my crime, or would it be too much to assume you're literate enough to read my execution order? We nobles can use some awfully big words you know, like 'cat' and 'the'." Hey, if I'm scheduled for execution, I plan to be as snarky as possible. It's not like being nice or begging will change their minds on the matter.

"As thrilling as it would be to test my mettle against yours, Count Stone..." His eyes drift to my right. "You aren't who we're here for." Toward Simaron.

My father taught me how to use a sword, for when the grace of my blood would forsake me. I know how to parry, riposte, swing, thrust, disarm, block, dodge roughly and gracefully, and generally handle most adversaries on a variety of terrains. Three at a time is my personal best, but that was sparring. This is not going to be an easy situation. Hell, I'd be amazed if Sim and I came out of this alive if I relied purely on my sword. The only thing I have going for me is that I could call for proper dueling rules, act as Sim's champion, and take them on one at a time with naught but a practice saber.

I'm also an adult film star, in a *very* bad neighborhood, and my coworkers often take me out for drinks in some pretty shitty dives where bar fights are par for the course. And sometimes you get involved in those fights, no matter how pretty you are, because some drunks have a bit of a problem with you fucking some other guy on film, and see this as a perfectly valid reason to kick your ass. These sorts of people don't give a shit about proper dueling protocols and as a result cause you to learn some rather...creative methods of problem-solving.

For example, should there be some uppity douche bag in front of you who's standing too close for punches, kicks or melee weapons, and his attention is currently elsewhere? You are left with little option but to either retreat and get adequate space to engage him in fisticuffs, move even farther to draw your blade, or rear your head back while he's looking the other way and ensure your forehead makes full and fast contact with the bridge of his elegant, graceful nose.

Fuck, that stings!

I stagger from the impact, my head a little fuzzy as I draw my sword quickly. Blue Eyes is on the ground and holding his face, which is stained blue, the weight of his armor making it rather difficult to get up right away. Now I've got that three-on-one I was aiming for.

Granted, according to my vision I'm fighting nine of them, and they're spinning about. Tricky bastards.

I take a guard position, trying to focus, but there's a growing pounding sound in my head as I put myself between the three of them and Sim, who has his saber drawn.

"Sorry, boys, no one's laying a finger on my manservant." Ye gods, I sound tipsy. Remind me to never headbutt a sidhe again.

"Our apologies, Count Stone. The order comes from above even your station. The Tainted One will come with us, and whether his head is brought back as a trophy is entirely your prerogative." Orange Eyes helps up Blue Eyes, the latter of the two staggering back into formation, rage in his eyes. At least I think it's rage. Could be a concussion, but whether it's mine or his is anyone's guess.

"You'll have to go through me." I hold the sword up at Orange Eyes. "You will have to *kill me* first."

He bows elegantly and takes a guarded stance. "As you wish, Your Excellency."

Simaron steps in front of me. "I would think not. I believe

His Excellency is in no shape to fight, especially not on my behalf."

"Sim, what the hell are you doing?"

"The *Tainted One* will fight for himself." He lowers his saber to his off hand and cuts his palm, smearing his purple blood along his blade. The knights step back in revulsion. "If you wish this to the death, Sir Knight, I advise I will take every action to level the field. Do you believe the stories, Sir Knight? That the Nightmare rides in my veins? That merely a wisp of my blood will devour the life of your dream?" He flicks the blade in the direction of the knights, a few errant drops sailing through the air. They scatter as if before a live grenade.

Simaron takes an aggressive stance and points at the lot of them. "Who shall be first?"

What you're seeing is one of the reasons those like Sim are openly hated by the Fae. It's long been suspected that mixing Fae blood with "base human waste" will taint the perfect living dream of Fae existence. And what's a tainted dream? A Nightmare, to the Fae. Their unnatural blood is simply proof of it.

Granted, most tainted ones are killed while still infants or children, the human parents as well, more often than not. Simaron's the exception simply because my parents were a hell of a lot more open-minded and we're far enough out on the fringe that no one pays much attention. Most who see Sim at first glance assume he's just a human who's been brought into our service, a sign our county's on hard times, yes, but not unusual or wrong.

If you've got purple blood and you make it to Sim's age, chances are that someone knows about you and wants your head as a trophy. The Fae can't openly hunt the "purples" though, hence the lack of heraldry on these knights. No tracking them back to their masters. Still, no noble would willingly allow one of his servants to be executed without fighting for him, that's just common sense.

This still might be an attempt on my life.

Luckily the adrenalin's starting to flow, making the pain a bit more manageable, my vision clear enough to fight as my stance regains its confidence. I still have an ace up my sleeve if I want to get through this without fighting, which I'd vastly prefer. They might be assholes, but killing fellow sidhe is usually a big no-no. It's not like we breed a lot.

So, I take a deep breath while the knights regroup, and I begin to sing. I focus my anger into the notes, filling the empty staff of Simaron's blade with the music of Sigil, the bloodied sword igniting with a blaze of silver flame. Sim stares at his sword, but only for a second, and advances toward the knights, who understandably panic and retreat. They probably never imagined that tainted blood would also burst into what I'm sure will be described as the unholy balefire of the Nightmare.

"I was really expecting a demon when we got here, Sim. What the hell was that about?" I slump back down onto the grass, rubbing my head, my face now feeling tender. "How did they know you were even out here? That I was out here? Is it common knowledge what I'm questing for?"

"Either that, sir, or we were simply followed from the manor. We have not exactly been vigilant." He cleans his blade and sheathes it, and then rips a strip off his shirt to bind his hand. "The fire. That was you, sir?"

I touch my forehead and wince slightly, but manage a nod in reply. "You're supposed to be calling me Richard, Sim." He sags visibly. I have to grin slightly, though. "What about you? The blood of the Nightmare?"

He smiles softly, sitting next to me, before it becomes a full grin for him as well. “I do love taking advantage of the ignorance of fools. Nightmare, indeed! All my mother’s heritage has granted me is the inability to receive blood through transfusion.”

“And lie. You know for a fact your blood won’t do a single thing you threatened. A Fae couldn’t have done what you did.” He shrugs, doing his best to hide another smile.

“You did request I utilize creativity, Richard.”

Chapter Thirteen
Life Wasted

"So this noble quest is becoming a bit of a bust, isn't it?" I try to keep my head still while Sim inspects my bruise. His touch is light, gentle, exactly what I need right now.

"I still cannot believe you struck a knight with your head, Richard." We're in the car, in the cemetery's dirt patch by the entrance that serves as a suggestion of a parking lot. It's early afternoon. I almost wish we had brought a picnic lunch, no matter how morbid the location. Sim finishes his examination. "It should be fine, just tender, but there will be a bit of discoloration."

I shrug, letting my eyes avoid the rearview mirror. "Battle scar, right?" I lean back in my seat, flipping on the radio. "I suppose I've probably given some of the Fae even more cause for a hunt on all half-bloods."

"So is that the sobriquet you prefer?" I look over at Sim, his eyes on me as he continues. "I would have you know my behavior is more the exception than the rule for my kind."

"I would hope so. I'd hate to think you could be easily replaced." I smirk lightly, but apparently this is not the time to crack jokes. I roll my shoulders and grab one of the bottles of water he bought earlier. "Yes, it's the term I use. It's the most literal, without any mocking. You're half-Fae, half-human. Half-blood works. How do you know how other half-bloods act?"

"You often wonder where I manage to procure good wine, fresh fruits?"

I nod, and it sinks in. "Farmers and vintners, huh?"

Sim shakes his head, and I'm a little surprised.

"What then?" I ask. "You'd think they know their way around a wine considering how good that stuff you bring back is."

"They have to. They must be entirely self-sufficient. Humans shun them much as they would a Ra'Keth, and the Fae, well..." He smiles gratefully. "Not all are as fortunate as I was."

Ra'Keth, those are sorcerers, the god-killers. They're human, but humans just know that they're...off, and tend to avoid them. There's only one true Ra'Keth out there now, but I'd have to say he's not anything to worry about. Yes, I'm speaking from personal experience, and yes, it's a story for another time. Probably after many, many rounds.

I take a swig of my water and offer it to him. He looks at me for a moment, and takes it, as if to return it to the bag.

"I was offering you some. Equals, remember?"

"Suffering under a punishment to call you by your given name will hardly make us equals, Richard."

"We survived a battle where we were outnumbered and outgunned. If anything, that makes us brothers-in-arms, and I couldn't call the Firemanes a warrior's line if I didn't say that makes you an equal in my book." I shrug slightly. "Then again, I've never thought of you as beneath me."

"I find that difficult to believe, sir." I give him a hurt look, but he seems undeterred. "Granted, you are not a difficult person to serve, but I am often well aware of my place with you."

Ouch again.

"If I ask you a question," I say. "Will you answer me honestly?"

"Questions like that are only asked when the answer is expected to be a lie. Are you under the impression that I've been anything but honest with you?"

I could easily come back with the fact that that isn't a yes. Another reason that half-bloods aren't liked: it's not that they can lie, it's that they can lie *very* well. The human capacity for falsehood mixed with a Fae's unquestionable sincerity?

Still, he smiles warmly. "But yes, I will answer truthfully, whatever your inquiry."

"Do you like me, Simaron?" He furrows his brow, confused, and I clarify. "I mean, are we friends? Or do you think we could be? Because I get the feeling that..."

"Complete honesty?"

Great. This will not be an answer I'll like. I nod though, because the curiosity will kill me otherwise.

"There are more times than not that I see you as pompous an ass as any other noble of the City. I see you shirk your responsibilities with a flagrancy that is nigh repulsive to one in my place. And I believe you to be as hedonistic as a satyr whenever you find yourself given the slightest opportunity. So I suspect there would be a difficulty in a friendship between us that would make me constantly weigh the effort against the merit."

My heart feels like it's been cored.

He takes a moment. "But..."

I lean back heavily into the seat, exhaling. "Thank the gods there's a but."

"I have seen glimpses, Richard. I have seen the nobility within you, that you show only when certain none are watching or sometimes in spite of yourself. You show great concern for me when such treatment is neither expected nor warranted. I am always under the impression that my well-being is of great importance to you, that to you, my heritage is a negligible trait compared to my other abilities." He looks down for a moment. "It would be good for you to commit the same concern to your county. I am certain it would only benefit from such attention."

"It would seem that you'd make a far better advisor than servant, Sim." I try to smile. "At least I can trust you to be honest with me. How long have you been holding all of this back?"

"Some time. However, it is not malice or belief that there is some pedestal you need to be knocked from that makes me say these things. If we are to be friends, then, as a friend, I feel obligated to tell you the territory that you are treading dangerously close to." He takes a drink from the offered water. "I must confess that I feel a loyalty to you as well."

"I should hope so, considering I've known you since you were born."

He manages a slight grin in reply, his eyes looking away a second. "That would be one reason, yes, Your Excellency." I give him a look, and he chuckles lightly. "Richard."

"So now where do we go?" I take out my cell phone and dial up Jen.

It rings several times before she picks up. "Took you long enough. You leave your phone somewhere?"

"Sorry, I wasn't expecting your call." A second passes before she asks, "You find the demon?"

"Nope. Found a few mercs. Tried to poach our butler."

"Is he okay?"

"He's fine. Just a little scratch. I've got a bitch of a headache, thanks for asking." I take the water bottle back from Sim and have another swig. "There's still some daylight left so I figure we can do some more investigating before we head out to North Allora. I'd prefer not to traipse about demon territory, so do you have any leads from poring over the family's history?"

"Nothing I can think of. There's not much about your father's demon hunting, save a list of names of the ones he killed." Another pause.

"C'mon, you're a Demonbane. Some of the names must be familiar."

"A couple, yes. Any demon would be a valued kill, especially made in service to the Fae. It is impressive that your father was able to kill as many as he did." This is a way of saying that my father probably did decently considering he wasn't properly trained and, obviously, not a Demonbane. It's also a way of saying the kills weren't that impressive at all, but she is talking about her father-in-law. "Your grandfather, Llewellyn, managed some good kills as well before meeting his end. He was more oriented toward the warrior ways than your father?"

I shake my head, even though she can't see it. "Actually, no. Grandfather was a poet. Luck just favored him, at least until the end. Where did he fight the demon?"

"I don't know about this way of generating leads. No guarantee that the demon's going to be there or that you'll find a trace of him." I can hear some papers rustling before she comes back on the line. "I don't suppose you know any scryers? Maybe a human with a little talent?"

"I doubt going to a Ra'Keth would lift any shame on my part, and I wouldn't want to risk going to another mystic." Nor mention to my blushing bride that she's married to one, and she'll be carrying my tainted children. Probably should only have one, go Dad's route. "Hey uh...is anything in there about me? Maybe in my dad's journals? About when I was born, in particular?"

A few seconds pass. "Why are you asking? I mean, I found the usual stuff. You know, the silver bard, the crystal sun, the phoenix tree, standard fare. Why? What should I be looking for?"

I know that's a bit confusing for the uninitiated, so I'll lay it out. On the day a Fae is born, a musician is inspired to compose his or her *magnum opus*, tumultuous weather vanishes as the sun breaks perfectly through the clouds, and the oldest tree in the surrounding area dies and is replaced by a sapling as if by magic. What can I say? We love to make an entrance.

"Forget it. Is the blade safe and secure? How are the guards doing?"

"The sword's fine, and I got rid of the guards for a while, they were getting on my nerves. Kind of liking this new authority. They should be back later, probably out patrolling. That's what I'd do. If you really want to go check it out, your grandfather fought the demon on the Benedict Shores. It's not any more specific than that."

"Got a name?" I look over at Sim and shrug. Should I have to go to a diviner on the down low, having the demon's name would help.

"The demon? Terrach. I think I'm pronouncing it right. Oh yeah, some guy named Will called. I told him you're unavailable for the time being. He sounded pissed."

I sigh softly. "My director, for my work. I'll have to call him later, smooth things over. For now that's our sole source of income and it'll be hard to maintain the manor if the City takes it from us for not paying property taxes." Another couple of silent seconds go by. "I'll call you later. I'm going to head down there, see how it goes. I doubt a demon's been hiding out in my county, but uh..." I look to Sim. "Perhaps I need to be more vigilant, right?"

Jen wishes me luck, and I end the call, leaning back in the seat again. I'm on a damned wild goose chase and I have no clue how to track this demon. I have the name though. That should count for something.

Sim looks a bit concerned. "Richard?" I pull the car out of the dirt patch and onto the road, heading back into the City. I glance over at him to cue him to continue. "I must confess I know little of what your heritage bestows on you..."

"Are you referring to my being a mystic? Don't tiptoe around it, at least not when we're alone. You haven't been about being half-blood."

"Fair enough. Knowing the demon's name, could you perhaps divine the location yourself?"

It's certainly an idea, but currently all I know how to do is set things on fire, and the hallucination of my not-so-illustrious ancestor isn't playing backseat-driver at the moment. I hardly plan to start singing Sigil in the car. I don't want it to catch fire or anything. I'm aiming for discretion in this quest, after all.

"Not a clue. I don't suppose you know anyone who can find lost demons?" I chuckle, because it's ridiculous, of course. "Damn it, Sim, I really want to hear a mocking and derisive denial to that question. I don't think I can handle much more today."

"If you wish that, Richard, I'm sure I can come up with some retort that will be adequately offensive. Shall I include veiled insinuations about your mother and unwashed livestock?

Granted, all of it would be a lie."

I grit my teeth. He looks downward, away from me.

"I apologize if I was not forthcoming. It is simply that you would not be welcome there. Even I am looked upon with some suspicion by my kind."

I turn up the music. Sim reaches over to turn it back down.

"But considering the desperation inherent in our circumstances, I believe the attempt would be warranted. They have made use of a cloaking charm which renders their home all but invisible to the outside observer, but I can lead us there. Pull over, please, as I will need to drive."

I do so, and we switch up. Sim drives well enough, but I can see the tension in his hands. He's betraying his people. There's no guarantee that I won't remember how to get back there once we leave. He's making a leap of trust for me. That's probably why he's scared right now.

As we continue along the highway though, coming back into the Benedict, it starts sinking in why he's nervous. When we finally arrive at a large factory complex that I could swear had been leveled years ago, I see evidence of life and a lived-in quality...

The half-bloods have been living almost all in one place.

In my county.

I am in such deep shit.

Chapter Fourteen
Indifference

Ever been to a club, or a bar, and seen some stranger walk through the door, and the second you see him the only thing that goes through your mind is "my God, what a fucking douche bag" with a deep, almost instinctual conviction? Maybe you lean over to the person next to you to point this guy out, whisper to each other, have a private little laugh? It's okay, you can admit it. Hell, I've felt that plenty of times.

Never been on the receiving end of it, though.

Granted, this isn't really a club. It's apparently an indoor commune for half-bloods set up in a gutted paper mill not six blocks from my house. And the lord of the land is certainly not a welcome sight. There's no fear, no one scurrying away, just scowls and derisive looks. Should be expected, they do outnumber me, so they can probably spend the next hour or so spitting in my face with relative impunity.

"You could have stayed in the car, Richard."

I give a playful shrug. Sure, I could have stayed in the car, but it's not like I can change my mind now. Best to see it through and take in the surroundings without trying to be too obvious.

All of the equipment that was here has either been removed

or broken down and repurposed. There are skylights, surprisingly intact, to let the sun in for the gardens where they've broken through the concrete floors. It's like a little village and park, all enclosed in a red brick factory. I can even see the small vineyards.

"They can't possibly grow enough to support them, can they?"

"We bottle wine here, mostly." A woman dressed in coveralls, her hands dirty, face dusty, her hair and forehead under a do-rag, but I can see two bumps where the edge of her scalp is. Horn stubs. Probably half-troll. "The rest, well, there's this magical place called a supermarket where you can find preserved foods and fresh produce."

I immediately look to Sim. "You've been buying my produce all this time from a fucking grocery store?"

Sim bows his head slightly. "I purchase it from the commune, sir. Which they buy from the fucking grocery store, yes." I blink several times. He then smirks. "They have an excellent selection from what I hear."

"Did you actually just say fuck?"

The woman practically growls at Sim. "Why did you bring him here?" I hold my hand up at her, and she responds with indignation. "Did the blueblood just shush me?"

"Lady, he used a profanity. You have no idea how much I want to savor this moment. It's like watching your child take his first step."

"We're here to see the seer, please." Sim is doing his best to ignore me. "It is of the utmost importance."

The woman motions us over to a secluded area behind a shack made from sheet metal. It's one of several that are inside the factory, built along the walls. Once there she reaches into her coveralls and takes out a knife. Cold iron. I can tell. *Believe me* I can tell.

"You bring the lord of the land into our home? He'll return with a garrison of knights and we'll all decorate the trophy room of this blueblood with our heads." She points the knife in my direction and I hold up my hands. "Unless we take care of him quick."

"Yes, Hope, because I'm certain no one will come looking for him if you do that." I gape at Sim as he speaks to her. Ye gods, what kind of life is he living on the side? "If it weren't for his rule over these lands you wouldn't even have this home you take such pride in."

She doesn't take her eyes off me. "Is that a threat, Simaron?"

Okay, time for me to try damage control. "Whoa, whoa, whoa. Hold up just a second, okay?" The knife gets closer. "Seriously, I'm not here to kick you out, all right? There's no need for your pissing contest. I don't mind you guys staying here as long as you keep it on the down low."

Hope lowers the knife slowly, out of danger, at least. "From what the seer tells us, blueblood, your opinion on our residence won't matter much in a few days." She takes a hard slap across the face, from Sim. Holy shit.

"That is your lord, Hope, and even if the seer is accurate in these matters, until he is deposed, you will address him as Your Excellency." She glares at him. Betrayal. Sim takes a breath, and continues. "Now, this needn't be more complicated than it is fast becoming. May I suggest we set aside our prejudices and resolve this matter so we can address the true problem at hand?" Simaron turns to me. "You will not reveal the location of this commune, yes?"

I nod.

"You will swear an oath to that effect?"

A second passes, and I nod again.

Hope doesn't seem impressed. "If he's deposed that oath will mean little." The knife hasn't been sheathed yet, and I'm trying not to stare at it.

"So it would be in your best interest to ensure he retains his title then, yes?" Sim motions toward the knife. "And I imagine it would best for our people if you would refrain from threatening our one vocal supporter in the Fae court."

She looks me dead in the eye. "I won't bow to you. We will not offer tribute. You will leave us in peace and not return here, do you understand?"

I grit my teeth. Yes, I'm rather lapsed when it comes to the nobility thing, but it's not often that a *serf* orders me around. I could just as easily call them freeloaders and get them the hell off my land. I can't do that though. Otherwise I'd be the asshole they so desperately need me to be.

"No bowing, you refer to me as 'my lord' or 'sir' at most, and I will expect a bottle of your commune's finest wine delivered to my manor once every full moon. If you want me to act as your advocate, you had better accept these terms." Her grip tightens on the hilt of the blade. I don't back down. "It's not difficult to see you're the one in charge here. You have to appear in control for your people, am I correct? It's the same with me. Hell, I could give a rat's ass if you burned me in effigy on a daily basis and sent me bottles of year-old goat piss. But when the big wigs come strolling around, I want to appear like I've got a handle on the situation and not potentially allowing a militia to take root in my county. You see where I'm coming from, right?"

Hope chews her lip for a moment and still shows concern. "You plan to reveal us then?"

I shake my head. "I'll simply admit the truth, there are half-bloods in my county, they're productive subjects who pay tribute, and they are under my protection from poachers. If necessary, I can gain support from the Duchess of Tolon Wood. I am descended from Sunleaves." I take a step toward her. "I won't reveal the location of this commune, I'll swear an oath to that right now, but this can't be all one way, okay?"

"And in return, you only ask to see the seer?"

I shrug slightly. "For now, yes, but I won't make any requests that you don't approve of."

"Is that so?" she asks, an incredulous look on her face. She waves the blade gently at me. "Well, I don't approve of a blueblood seeing the seer." Sim glares at her and her eyes dart to him, narrowing. "I have agreed to nothing yet, Simaron."

He stands his ground. "I would hardly imagine that Count Stone is pleased that our people have taken residence on his lands for so long, without tribute, without his knowledge, when he more than likely would not have objected. It would appear there are parts of this arrangement that both of you will have to live with."

I know I have to take the first step here. I'm on their turf, no matter how much ancestral claim I have to it. With a deep breath, I breathe out the oath in Sigil, yet another chain of Fate wrapping around me that I'll never be free of. Honestly, we Fae are not supposed to swear this many oaths at any given time. In fact, it's expected to be damned near impossible to get us to commit to a promise.

And half-bloods aren't bound by any such oaths. They can all lie. I'm showing a lot of trust here and they can put me over a barrel if need be, and I'm sure they won't be as gentle as Sim was that one time I actually had him put me over a barrel.

"All right then." She puts the knife back inside her coveralls. "We'll try this out for a while, see how it goes." A second passes before she looks at me. "*Sir.*"

"Thank you. When will it be possible to see the seer?"

She sighs softly. Great, problems already.

"Hey, a deal's a deal, right?"

"Tonight, more than likely, after sundown."

My eyes go a little wide. "Your seer, I'm not waiting on a vampyr, am I?"

She laughs, and it's a rough sound, but genuine. Even Sim cracks a smile.

She motions for me to follow her into the shack we've been standing by, presumably so that we can wait out the day. "No, my lord, we do not offer shelter to vampires. The seer is...resting, currently. And once she is awake, it must be made certain that she is in the right mood to receive guests. Her father was a sidhe mystic, and the talents carried over to her, but they can be difficult for her to process."

"So the half-bloods have mystics as well? That's intriguing. I didn't think Ra'Keth blood could still be that strong after all that time." The shack is nicer than I expect on the inside, but still pretty cramped as it's clearly meant for one person. The floor is concrete, a washbasin, a futon, table, all of it looking like it was bought from a thrift store and restored with a fair bit of love. It smells like the vineyards, actually.

After Sim and I sit on the futon, Hope pours some wine. "From what I understand, the god-killers were human, and it would seem that mystic talent cares little for the purity of the blood. It shows itself when it wants to."

I take a sip, and it is the same that I've been drinking for the past few years. "Any reason in particular I can't see her until after sunset? I'm kind of on a tight schedule, you know?"

Hope takes a pull of wine directly from the bottle, doing her best to stifle a laugh. Sim sniggers before regaining control.

I'm beginning to feel that leaving in a huff would be justified. "Is this all some big joke? Seriously, why can't I see the seer right now and just command her to help me out?" Sim places his hand on mine to keep me from leaving.

"My lord, I seriously doubt that Her Royal Majesty herself would find a six-year-old girl responsive to commands when she has been woken prematurely from her afternoon nap."

Chapter Fifteen
Just a Girl

I've never been good around kids.

It's not a hatred thing. Children, at least human children, tend to see the world as it really is. Maybe not in its full-on glory, but enough to have good reason to sleep with a light on and never allow any part of their bodies outside the safety of their covers.

To a human adult, I'm the hottest guy they've ever seen, whether they swing that way or not.

To a human child? I'm the wicked fairy from their bedtime stories looking for any reason to snatch them off and leave a changeling in their place. (Bad PR, mostly. A few bad apples in a very big bunch. We had to come to the New World to escape that shit.)

Imagine how a half-blood child's going to see me. At least she has good reason to be afraid. She's probably been hunted since the day she was born.

"No weapons, no bindings, no anything, and I'll be in dagger's reach the whole time. These are the terms and they're not negotiable. Yes or no?"

I'm standing in front of another shack, this one by a modest flower garden. I'm rather amazed at how well they've used the space in this factory. The skylights above have been pulled open to ventilate the smoke from a few small campfires. I guess a big downside of living off the grid is the lack of electricity. I can only see about a dozen of the shacks along the interior of the factory walls, all of them looking cobbled together from junk. The seer's shack isn't as ramshackle looking, and there are a few small bundles of flowers placed in front of the door. Daisies, mostly.

"Don't really have much choice." I remove my saber from my belt, my belt as well, and hand them to Hope. She takes them and heads inside for about a minute, maybe two, before peeking back out the door.

"She'll see you." Hope then motions down to the bundled daisies. "Bring those in."

I nod and bend over to pick them up, the flowers still somewhat fresh, their colors dim in the fading light. I can hear some small engines being started up. Generators for electricity, I'll bet.

The room inside is hardly extravagant, a small bed to my right, table to my left, a rug making up the floor, probably fished out of a dumpster and cleaned heavily. I can still make out cigarette burns in the light provided by the camping lanterns in the room. Hope is seated at the table, and the kid sitting cross-legged on the floor is probably the seer.

She's dressed in a pair of jeans and a T-shirt that's for a girl a couple of years older than her, her arms thin, face slightly gaunt, skin pale. Her hair is a soft sandy blond, her eyes a bright purple as she looks up at me, the light hitting her shirt and showing characters from a children's show.

"It's an honor to meet you, Seer. I understand you can help me find what I seek?" She nods eagerly.

"Can you do a braid?" The girl shakes out her hair, which

is longer than I first thought, and it's a tangled mess.

I blink, tilting my head at her. "Beg pardon?"

"I like braids but I always get pigtails. Do you like braids? Your hair is long." I look over at Hope in a panic.

"Is she..." I nonchalantly tap the side of my head. "Okay?" No answer, but she's stifling a laugh. Bitch.

The seer stares at the daisies I'm carrying. "Are those for me?" The daisies are snatched from my hands, and she buries her face in them, sniffing deeply before picking one of them out. She proceeds to pluck the petals off one at a time. "He loves you, he loves you not..."

I rub my face, approaching exasperation. "Dare I ask who you're doing that for?" She giggles and tosses the half-plucked daisy to me.

"You can do that one. You don't like daisies though." She grins big. "You like roses, but you don't want people to know what color."

I take a deep breath. "I'm trying to find a demon, I know his name. Can you help me find him?" She looks at me and turns away from me. For a second I think I'm being dismissed, until I'm handed a brush by Hope.

I really have to brush and braid her hair. I start from the bottom, holding her hair from higher up to get through the snarls without hurting her. After a few minutes of silence, I get the impression I won't be receiving a response. I wish that Sim had been allowed in here. He could give me a hint, maybe. I start on the braid though. "Okay, what kind you want? French? Regular? Warrior's braid?"

She looks over her shoulder at me and then at Hope rather crossly. "There's *different kinds*?" The seer folds her arms and pouts while I start on a regular braid. Hope keeps on stifling those laughs, adding on an "if I only had a camera" look to her face.

Okay. Focus. I can get through this. "I'm surprised you're letting me anywhere near you, actually, Seer." Now that her hair is brushed the braid goes pretty easy, just a matter of the motions.

"Why would I be scared? You're a narcissus, not an oleander." Once I finish the braid, she reaches back to feel it and smiles big. "Do you know any games? I like hide and seek but you're already playing that, but you're not playing it well."

Wait, this might be going somewhere.

"Yeah, I get the feeling I'm looking in the wrong places. Think you can give me a hint?"

She nods once and beckons me close. "The best seekers cheat and yell olley olley oxen free so all the hiders can get caught 'cause they think it's safe."

Okay, that was a bit of a goose egg. "You have no idea where the demon is, do you?"

The seer smiles in reply and gets up, taking the half-plucked daisy from me and putting it in my hair. "You only like games you can win. You're scared to lose. That's why you don't like daisies. You don't like picking the wrong petal."

I'm sure you can feel my frustration at this point. Just once I'd like to meet a seer or precognitive who gave direct answers.

So when I get up and leave, I'm rather proud of myself that I don't use any profanities, don't slam the door or otherwise yell at the kid.

A couple of minutes pass before Hope comes out and promptly slaps me in the face.

"What the hell?" My face is going to be sore for a bit.

"She's crying, you *asshole.*" My belt and sword are then literally thrown in my face. Luckily I catch them fast enough to avoid more bruises.

"Oh c'mon, you expected me to deal with all that cryptic bullshit while you had a good laugh about it? I saw you over there."

"She was *happy.* Other than her father, you're the only sidhe she's ever seen, and what do you do? Treat her like some fucking information service. Like a thing. You think she understands what's going on with her?" She shakes her head. "Deal's off, blueblood."

"Whoa, whoa, hold on." She shoves me back a couple of steps away from the seer's house, and I can hear a growing commotion. Great, I'll have my own angry mob. I raise my hands in surrender. "I'm sorry, okay?"

"Yeah, I'll bet you are." She reaches into her coveralls. I know what's coming out of them. "Get the fuck out of here."

"Can I apologize to her, at least?"

A disbelieving smirk in retort. "Yeah, it'll be real sincere."

I narrow my eyes at her. "Unlike some who shall remain nameless, my sincerity can only be genuine." That gets the knife out. "Hey, I'm just giving what I'm getting, lady." I take a breath. "I'm not good around kids, okay? At all. I didn't have any brothers or sisters, no cousins who dropped by. All I had growing up was Sim, and I think he was born an adult, honestly. I don't know how to talk to children, all right? So I screwed it up and apparently made a little girl cry. I *do* feel bad about that. I wasn't expecting it."

"You actually feel bad about it?"

I roll my eyes at her. "Ye gods, lady, I do have a *soul.*" A second passes. "C'mon, could she be that broken up about it? I didn't spit in her face, I walked out on her."

"Just like her father."

Ouch.

Hope shakes her head and motions the crowd to disperse. "You think it's her fault she's like this? You think anyone would ask for that?"

"I sure as hell wouldn't." I probably meant that as part of interior monologue. "Okay, will you give me a chance to apologize or not?" Hope heads back to the door.

"Depends on whether she wants to see you." She cracks the door open and dodges a flying half-naked Barbie doll. She then smirks at me. "The seer will see you now."

Bitch.

When I enter the room I'm not quite as fast and catch a Ken doll to the neck.

"Ow, dammit." I wince. "I mean, I'm sorry, okay?"

"You're mean. You're a narcissus!"

I've been called worse.

"I think you mean narcissist." This time I catch Barbie's niece or cousin or something in the chest. Kid's got an arm. "Hey, quit it." I'm tempted to tell her I'm not her father, but I get the feeling that would really be a dick move on my part. And to think, a couple weeks ago I might've done it. Look at me grow. "You're going to mess up your hair. I didn't get time to tie it up."

She sniffles a bit and reaches around to her now-disheveled braid. More sniffling, her face scrunching up. Oh no, please don't do this.

"C'mon, don't cry. I can fix it." I step over to her cautiously. I don't know whether Hope was full of it before about her crying, but it was pretty apparent she was about to, and it would be my fault. And making a six-year-old girl cry is just... I really would be a douche bag.

She lets me get closer, and I kneel next to her, picking up

the brush from the floor and starting through her hair again. "I'm sorry I walked out."

"You wanted answers. But you didn't want to hear them." She sniffs again and looks over her shoulder at me. "Can I have a French braid this time?"

I nod, smiling gently. "So you like flowers, huh?" She wipes her eyes with the sleeve of her T-shirt, and I tap her shoulder lightly with the brush. "Hold still. Don't want it to be off-center."

"Uh-huh. They're nice and they're pretty, and Mommy told me they have their own language." Considering that Hope hasn't mentioned her mother, and definitely isn't the mother seeing as she's a half-troll and the seer is half-sidhe, I decide to step around that potential landmine.

"My mom told me about the language of flowers too. Every one has its own meaning. I never learned all of them though. Did you?"

She nods, and I stop braiding for a second.

"Head still, okay?"

"Would your mommy like some flowers?" She turns, and I stop braiding, but there's a sweet smile on her face. I close my eyes for a second.

"She's a broken... She's not around anymore. She left so she could be with my father."

The seer sniffs softly. "My mommy did too." My guess is that her mother didn't do some elaborate suicide ritual. But if a human went off to find the Fae father of her child, well, it probably didn't have a fairy-tale ending. (No pun intended.) Not everyone can be like Simaron's father. Hell, even in that case it ended badly. "What's your name, mister?"

"Richard. What's yours?"

She swallows hard and manages a friendly face. "Casey."

My eyes go wide, not because I recognize the name or anything, I still barely know this poor kid, but something else popped up on the revelation radar. I know the name and location of a half-blood mystic. This kind of information could be commanded out of me by people who would see her as nothing more than an information service. Or a trophy. This...is not good for her.

"Casey, will you let me make you a promise?" She looks at me oddly for a moment and then shrugs. I move around in front of her and take her small hands in mine. "You're going to hear me say some strange words, but don't worry, it's only to keep you safe. I'm making an oath that I'll never tell anyone outside this building your name, where you are or what you are. Okay?"

She squeezes my fingers and giggles. "I know what an oath is, Richard. My daddy's a sidhe like you."

With that, I swear the oath. I tie myself to it, more than a chain to wrap around me. No, this is a big one. The Sigil slides out of my mouth, down to my neck, to my chest. I swear I feel the words sinking into my skin.

"And just what do you think you're doing?" Deathsinger is standing behind her, looking her over. "You are aware of the consequences if you break this."

She's only a kid. I don't want to risk anything happening to her should I get captured by demons or get asked some very direct questions by the nobility that I don't want to answer.

"So you'll tie your own life to this? Willingly?" The Ra'Keth chuckles lightly and inspects the braid I put in her hair. "Sure, she's cute and everything, but is she worth dying for?"

Like I could live with myself if I heard some noble brag about having her head mounted in his trophy room. As I said, I do have a soul.

The Sigil wraps around my heart, a gentle reminder pulsing through my mind of my promise.

“Wonder which bloodline she dragged herself out of.” Deathsinger smirks. “Don’t worry, I’m not threatened. She’s not one of mine so I’m a bit curious. She lives to breed a couple generations that mystic blood could produce a Ra’keth for a grandchild.”

I squeeze Casey’s hands. “It’s okay now.” When I look up behind her, the ghost of my ancestor is gone. “And for your information, I like jasmine as far as flowers go.” She giggles again. “What’s so funny?”

“You like roses. But not yet.” Damn seers.

“So, can you help me find the demon? Would it help if I told you his name?” I squeeze her hand again. “Please?”

She shakes her head. “I only see the future. I...I can ask the flowers though.” She runs her free hand over the bunch of flowers I brought for her. “It’ll take time though. They need to listen for the name.”

“Will it get you in trouble? Could they find you?” She gives me an indulgent look.

“Richard, no one ever suspects the dandelions.”

Chapter Sixteen
Last Kiss

"Would you mind telling me why you couldn't be around for any of that?" I'm outside Casey's shack, next to a small campfire where Sim is sitting in a plastic Adirondack chair. I'd tossed a ball of paper into the flames a minute before that bore Terrach's name, because you don't say a demon's name out loud if you can help it. Casey had seen it and would set to chatting up the local flora in the morning.

"Miss Hope asked me to run some errands, courier work, mostly. And to quell any concerns, none of her requests have ever interfered with my duties at the manor, sir."

"And how exactly did you accomplish this courier work so quickly? I was only in there maybe an hour tops."

He tosses something to me, which I catch. My keys.

"You took *my car*?" I am, understandably, a tad perturbed. "That's my car, Sim."

"A car which, I might add..." he actually smiles with a nigh-mischievous edge, "...corners like it's upon rails."

I blink once. "What the hell, Sim? Have you always been like this?"

Sim reaches over to rub my shoulder. "You disapprove?"

"I'm more shocked than anything. None of this is exactly...proper."

He pulls the half-plucked daisy from my hair.

"Hey, give it back. Casey gave me that."

Sim returns it with a slight bow. "I am surprised you have not finished it, sir. And as for my untoward behavior, I believe I can lay it at the feet of your corruptive influence, Your Excellency." Sim leans over to poke at the fire. "I rarely have the opportunity to be this way, Richard, to say what is on my mind. I never imagined I would be able to be completely honest with you. It is new territory for me."

"Same for me." I idly start plucking the petals, keeping track in my head. Loves me, loves me not.

"I hear the seer will be aiding you in finding the demon." Loves me. "I do apologize for taking your vehicle, though, Richard. I know it is important to you, it having been Count Kendrick's, but the urgency of my errands left me little choice." Loves me not.

"I don't suppose I can ask what those errands were?"

He shakes his head in reply. Great.

"I thought not. And yeah, Casey's checking it out for me." One of the nice loopholes in my vow is that I can discuss her, say her name, as long as I'm in the building. And besides, I swore not to reveal her identity, and since Sim brought me to her in the first place, it's not like I'm revealing anything regarding her. "I don't know, something seems weird about this whole thing." Loves me.

"The quest to track down the demon?" We both know his name is Terrach, but c'mon, even when you're pretty sure a demon is dead, you still don't go saying his name out loud.

"Kind of. I was with Dad when he died, and I would think

he'd tell me if he wanted me to avenge him, you know? He ended up dying from the wounds that thing gave him, but he brought back the Azure Blade dripping in ebon blood. If he wasn't sure the demon was dead, why would he come back?" Sim only shrugs in reply. Loves me not.

"Perhaps to not leave his family behind? Given how deep the love was between him and Countess Regina, it would stand to reason that he would not wish to die anywhere other than in her arms." Sim looks thoughtful for a moment. Loves me. "However, Count Kendrick was dedicated to the knightly ways, so it would seem odd for him to flee a battle. Perhaps the demon escaped?" Loves me not.

"Demons don't run. At least not the kind that the Fae hunt. The tempters, they run, yeah, but no way a succubus or an incubus took down a sidhe knight." Loves me. "And by sidhe knight, I mean my grandfather, even if he was never officially knighted. He was twice the warrior Dad was, what with the luck he had, and Dad was no slouch." I chuckle slightly. "And then there's me. Diminishing returns, huh?" Loves me not.

"You act as a patron of the arts, my lord. Woe to the Fae who thinks of that as a wasted endeavor. I am certain your grandfather would have words for such as they." Loves me.

"I act in porno movies, Sim. I'm hardly a muse for the next Fellini. Hell, I'm probably more inspired by this world than I inspire it." Loves me not. "There's just so much here, you know? So much beauty to see, taste, hear, that's why I tend to concentrate on music. You can have it anywhere, no matter what you're doing. I hate to bring her up again, but..." Loves me. "Your mom taught me that." Loves me not.

"My mother was a classical pianist from Destry Bay, Your Excellency, not a mumbling vocalist from the Pacific Northwest, so I would question how you ended up preferring that music to that which she played. I...” Loves me. “I would thank you on her behalf, for acknowledging that she had a positive influence on you.” Loves me not. “I see you’re nearly finished with your flower. Dare I ask who it’s for?”

I chuckle nervously and slide the stem back into my hair. “I’ll check it later.” I know how it’s going to end. I can count and only an idiot couldn’t work it out that far ahead. My cell phone goes off, and I check the ID. It’s home. Jen, probably wondering if I’m alive. I get up to find a secluded corner so she won’t hear the people in the background.

“I’m alive, don’t worry.”

“Where the hell are you?”

I grin in spite of myself. “God, we sound married already. I’m fine, I’ve got a lead but it’s going to take a little time to pan out. How’s everything at home?”

“That’s not an answer, Dick. Where are you?” A bit more authority in her voice this time. Look who learned her noble voice all right quick? Still, it’s not all authority, there’s...worry.

“Jen? Is everything okay? You didn’t exactly answer that either.” I take a breath. “Are the guards in place?”

“They’re all here. Everything’s fine, would you come home? Check your lead tomorrow?” That tension remains. “Where are you, Dick? Seriously, this is the kind of behavior that might cause your bride concern.”

Shit. I can feel the two oaths I’ve sworn coiling a bit tighter around me. There’s only one way to handle this, really, without breaking the vow or pissing off Jen.

“I’ll be home in an hour. Gotta allow for traffic, you know? Want me to stop somewhere, pick up some milk?” I smirk a little.

“Asshole. All right, I’ll see you in an hour. If you’re late, I’m sending out a search party." She's probably serious too. The phone clicks off, and I put my cell back in my pocket before heading over to Sim.

"The little missus wants us home in an hour. So this is how it starts, huh?" I try to smile genially but it's been underlined again that I'm definitely no longer part of the swinging bachelor lifestyle. "I guess checking out the Benedict Shores can wait until morning. Losing track of how many days I've got left. Six, I think, or five and some change. At least we'll be staying somewhere safe tonight, right?"

Sim gets up, stretching. "It will be a relief to change into more comfortable attire, as well. Casual dress has never appealed to me. It's akin to going to war in camouflage instead of armor."

"I'll take your word for it." I knock on my shirt, which has a solid sound considering the crest is affixed. "So let's say our goodbyes and meet at the car in a couple of minutes, yeah?" He nods in agreement, and I head to Casey's shack. Hope is standing guard outside, as expected.

"I'm going to be leaving," I say and stifle a yawn. "But I'll drop by tomorrow afternoon to check in with the seer, see if she's turned up anything. Unless she's got a cell phone and can call me."

"You think we'd allow something that can be easily traced in here? We use couriers, mostly. When the situation calls for a phone it usually involves four trains and a bus." Hope looks toward the door, in thought for a couple of seconds. "I think she likes you. Don't abuse that, okay?"

"Like I said, lady, I do have a soul."

"But you're Fae, my lord. And my people have never meant much to the Fae."

"Well, there's an exception to every rule."

She glances at Casey's door before turning her attention back to me. "I know. I'd like to think you could be different, considering how Simaron is around you." I arch a brow, and she pulls the flower from my hair and plucks a petal. "He loves you." Another. "He loves you not." She hands it back to me. "If it makes it any easier, I'm pretty sure the feeling's mutual."

Fuck.

It appears I have found the right circumstance where a daisy is intimidating.

"What the hell should I do then?"

Hope shrugs in reply.

"I don't think anyone has the answer to that question, sir. You take it day by day, until eventually, everything just feels natural again. Don't worry though. Everyone has to go through this at least once in their lives, everyone with a speck of human in them. I suppose that Fae would have to deal with it as well." She smirks slightly. "No offense."

"None taken. Hard to be a living dream and abhor your dreamer." I extend a hand to her, and she takes it, shaking it firmly. "I'll see you both tomorrow. Tell Casey I'll give her a warrior's braid?"

"Don't mess this up, okay, blueblood?" It's not so much warning this time, there's a pleading in her voice. *Don't be like her father*, that's what she's trying to say. I don't have any plans to, but I have the feeling I've signed on for a bigger commitment than just dropping by and braiding her hair.

Funny. That doesn't seem all that bad.

I leave the factory/commune, heading out to a small garage adjacent to the building where Sim parked the car. There's no evidence in or around the car to indicate where he might have gone on his errands, but I'm trying to not let it get to me. If he actually were doing anything to plot my downfall, I'd have been dead a long time ago.

My guess is that he's delivering messages, trading supplies, part of the movement that keeps the half-bloods going, keeps them hidden. If I weren't the viscount of this area, I would probably have to report him or have him arrested for treason or something. At the very least, I'd have to lead an assault on the commune. But I am His Excellency, and I am allowed to exercise my prerogative and shoulder the burden of responsibility should it all come crashing down. I've already tied my life to so many oaths, it doesn't seem too much to put my life on the line again.

Hell, I'll probably be killed by a demon within the next few days anyway, right?

Simaron emerges from the building a few minutes later, carrying a paper shopping bag that I can tell has fresh grapes and probably a bottle or two of wine as well. He places the bag in the backseat of the car and secures it. "It would appear we are ready to depart, Richard." Simaron steps closer to me. "I would assume my punishment will cease once we return to the manor? It would not be proper to refer to you by your given name before the viscountess."

"Yeah, that'll probably work. Back to the real world." I lean against the car. "We'll need to drive around a bit, kill some time. Don't want to get home too early or she'll be aware that I wasn't really all that far away."

"I understand, sir."

"Richard. For a little while longer. It's nice to be referred to informally."

"My lord, you must accept that you are the viscount of these shores..."

"That's not what I'm talking about, Simaron. I know full well that I'm nobility, okay? It's nice to be referred to as an equal. By you. I've been brought up to consider you beneath my station, but I've known you most of my life, you know? It's good to be on equal footing for a change." I turn toward him, and he's standing there, not expectant. Not anything, really.

"I am at a loss for words, sir. I'm not quite sure what you want to hear."

I take the daisy from my hair, look at its bare face, then pluck the final petal and let the stem drop to the ground. In the next second Sim is in my arms, my lips pressed to his, and he's returning it. Really giving it back. I don't know if I can call what I'm feeling for Simaron at this moment what I think it is. I don't know if that's fear or just uncertainty.

All I know is that I'm standing here with Simaron, in a moment where he and I are together, and equal, and there's no one to tell me it's wrong, no one to chide him for stepping beyond his station. There is only him, there is only me, standing inside a moment that I will keep inside my heart until I draw my final breath.

Chapter Seventeen
Gone

The ride home is understandably quiet.

I mean, I shouldn't feel bad about this. That's what I keep telling myself, though the exact reason continues to elude me. My father did plenty with Sim's father and Dad was deeply in love with Mom. So I shouldn't beat myself up for a simple kiss with someone who isn't the bride that I'm only seeking friendship with.

But then, Sim isn't just someone, is he?

The stereo's on, one of the band's acoustic sets providing more atmosphere than entertainment or distraction. I'm grateful I told Jen it'd be an hour. I've had plenty of time to drive the streets of the Benedict without speaking, trying to come up with words to say. Sim's been silent since we both agreed to get in the car and go home. His expression is relaxed, and I wonder how he can be so calm and accepting about this when it's causing me all sorts of stress that even Eddie Vedder can't soothe.

I want to pull the car over again, to have a few more minutes to figure this out, even though I don't know what exactly I'm figuring out or stalling for. The manor is drawing near, though.

"I suppose I should proclaim that your punishment is officially lifted, so that you can go back to all the honorifics." I glance at Sim, who nods curtly in reply. "But, you know, if no one else is around, and you want to call me Richard, it's okay."

"It would be best if I did not do that, Your Excellency. For both of us. It would not bode well for either of our multitude of obligations if you were to be shamed in such a fashion. We should operate within the dictates of Fae society." He reaches over and squeezes my hand. "I offer apologies if I have complicated matters for you, my lord. Upon reflection, perhaps my actions were not in either of our best interests, especially not where the fate of the county is concerned."

Gods, I can't do this anymore.

I want to say screw it all. I want to give up because I'm tired of this, of the responsibility that I never wanted, that I have to prove myself to ancestors I could care less about, that I have to shoulder the burden of being a mystic, that being a mystic could be the reason my parents never had any more kids, that so much depends on me, all the time, when all I want is to just leave it behind and be with...

"Simaron?"

"Your Excellency?"

I swallow hard, proceeding through the gate to the not-so-long drive to the garage. "Sim, I..."

"Your Excellency."

"Sim, I really need to get this out."

"My lord, there's something amiss."

"I know, Sim, but I feel once I get this off my chest—"

"*Richard.*" He points out the window, where there are four knights standing in front of the garage, all in armor, practically identical, no heraldry, no way to tell the difference between them save the color of their—

"Oh *fuck*!"

I understandably slam on the brakes even though we're only doing eight miles an hour. It's just what you do.

"Simaron, stay in the car. If things get rough, you take the car and you go. That is a *decree*." Sim glares in response, because a decree is not to be disobeyed. At all.

I get out of the car as Sim slides over into the driver's seat and hands me my sword from the back. I draw it quickly and point it directly at Blue Eyes.

"Leave my lands, *now*." Okay, maybe I was angsting earlier, about wanting to give it all up and run off, but it doesn't mean I'm about to let four assholes who tried to kill me and Sim walk onto *my* lands, and stand in front of *my* house. "You are trespassing on noble lands without my leave, and I am perfectly within my rights in both Fae *and* human society to show you a glimpse of the Nightmare that a sidhe knight can be."

I'm so pissed off even I believe that.

And where the hell is Jen? She didn't notice four knights-errant in the damned driveway waiting for me to get home?

"I would choose kinder words, Count Stone. But as these are your lands, and protocol is protocol, you will have the right to exercise your noble prerogative."

The garage door opens behind him, to reveal Jen bound in iron chain, and held by a fifth knight with long black hair and dark blue armor. He has a blade to her throat. Jen is limp from the touch of the iron, her face pained.

This is not good. Iron is bad enough for Fae, but for sidhe it's especially bad thanks to all those centuries of a limited breeding pool. To think we sidhe will take pride in this weakness, like it makes us more Fae than anyone else. I'm sure

Jen would disagree right now.

Blue Eyes continues. “Either we will take your wife…”

“And all of the Fae will be on you when you do. You’ll be taking a noble, and any number of Houses will be after your blood.”

The black-haired one speaks up. “I would doubt that, Count Stone. Arrangements have been made. We would discuss the terms, but we are under oath. If you like, we can leave your wife and instead take the tainted dream. He is wanted for…” the black-haired knight smirks, “…*questioning* in several matters, among other things.”

Fuck that.

I whisper as softly as I can. “Rem, Ra’Keth, please, I need you.”

The apparition appears at my side, overlooking the situation. Everyone is oblivious to his presence. “So now my services are required? You Fae do nothing halfway, do you?”

“Help me, ancestor. Grant me the power to sing their deaths.”

“You don’t get it, do you? I’m not some demon or tempter, Richard. And now the honorifics come? When you want something? When you believe I can snap my fingers and solve your problems? I can help you understand your power, but not in the time you will have to resolve this crisis. It lies at your feet, scion. Not mine.” And he vanishes. Fuck, fuck, fuck!

Okay. I can figure a way around this. I point the blade at the black-haired knight.

“And if I decide to fight?”

“That would be your third choice: We kill you here. I am well aware that you are forbidden from drawing the Azure Blade, Count Stone.” He holds up the scabbard of my family sword. "It is a good thing that I suffer from no such limitation."

He shoves Jen to the ground, where she falls in a heap. The four knights part to allow their superior through and then secure my wife. The knight-captain draws the Azure Blade. My father's blade. My family's blade.

And it ignites in a brilliant cerulean blaze.

My knees threaten to buckle. "No..."

"Would that it were so easy to take it from you, Count Stone, but protocol is protocol." He drops it to the concrete below, where it clatters loudly. I can feel tears welling in my eyes. The knight-captain looks over at me and smiles. "I would suppose that the Firemanes are not as privileged as they would make us believe. Custodians of the Azure Blade, are you? A common pooka could wield this trash." He kicks it away.

"Fuck you." The words are soft, hurt, my authority bleeding out of me. I still hold the blade steady as he turns his back on me, another insult.

"Kill him. Make it quick. Let him die a noble's death." The knights advance toward me, and I draw in breath, preparing to sing.

"Stop." Sim is out of the car. No, no, *no*. "I will not permit you to harm him."

The knights laugh in return.

"Sim, get in the damned car and go."

"No, Your Excellency." He steps forward, toward the knight-captain. "I will go with you."

"*No!*" I launch myself forward but find four knights holding me back, pushing me away from the scene. "Sim, you can't do this. I won't allow it!"

"Leave him alive and unharmed, as well as the Countess Stone, and I will go with you freely." Sim kneels before the knight-captain. “I want your vow on this.”

“I see no reason to honor the request of a tainted dream.” The black-haired knight raises his sword, and I fight harder against the four knights restraining me, my throat raw from my shouting, my tongue unable to find the words in Sigil to sing.

Sim stands quickly, his hand vanishing for a moment inside his coat before I see a familiar blade in his grip. Hope’s knife.

Hope’s cold-iron knife.

Which Sim presses eagerly against the sidhe’s neck. “Then perhaps you would honor this?” The knight lowers his blade, but the four holding me don’t let up. “It is a simple enough arrangement, well in line with the one you originally offered the Count Stone, only I am making the choice, not him. I go with you willingly, you leave Count and Countess Stone unharmed, and you are allowed the exquisite privilege of continuing to breathe. These are the terms, and they are not negotiable. What say you, Sir Knight?”

My panicked cries and shouts and commands are falling on deaf ears.

The knight-captain grits his teeth. “I am left with little choice. Agreed. You have my vow that no harm will come to Count Stone or Countess Stone tonight. They will be left here, provided you come with us of your own will, surrender that blade and face the charges that will await you. Assaulting a Knight of the Realm is a grave offense.”

“Punishable by death. I am aware. Agreed.” He pulls the blade from the knight-captain’s neck and drops it, away from the two of them. Before the knife hits the concrete below, Simaron is reeling from a gauntleted fist backhanding him across the face. He doesn’t make a sound. I yell, tell the knight I’ll kill him, that his suffering will be of legend, even in the

Nightmare itself. Again, it falls on deaf ears as a vehicle comes up the driveway, a nondescript van, goblins behind the wheel.

Goblins...working with sidhe knights? What the fuck is going on?

The knights holding me shove me back hard enough that I tumble onto the concrete, next to the Azure Blade that I still can't wield. The knight-captain glares at me as Sim is led to the van. "Breach my agreement, Count Stone, and I'll kill all three of you."

I want to reply, make all sorts of vows for the vengeance I will rain down on him, but I catch Sim's eye, and he shakes his head quickly. *Don't do it. Please.* I can't sit here and watch this. I should sing, ignite my pitiful practice saber with silver fire and show them who they're dealing with, but again, I see Sim shake his head. He's putting on a brave face, trying to comfort me.

The black-haired knight motions to Jen. "I would attend to your wife, Count Stone. You know as well as anyone that prolonged exposure to iron would not be healthy for a Fae, especially not for a sidhe."

The door to the van slams shut a few seconds later, and the van speeds out in reverse as I rush to remove the chains from Jen, the iron stinging like a cutting wind against my bare skin. I'm exhausted by the time I get the chains off her and drag her across the garage floor away from them. Her breathing is weak, but there. She'll live, that's for certain.

I wish I could say the same for Simaron.

Chapter Eighteen
In Hiding

This is probably the first time I've ever seen a naked woman outside work. If I were more of an asshole, I'd probably comment that the current view would reaffirm that I'll stick with guys, but not like this.

Not like this.

Jen is in the tub, my hand supporting her head. Her skin is covered in bruises, burns, cuts. Her skin is paler than usual, her breathing still labored. Iron can do that to us. I've added more hot water, to keep her warm. I don't know what else to do, really. My own strength is laughable at this point, but at least I didn't have to wear the iron chains, so it falls to me to take care of her. Still breathing, just passed out. I had to carry her up the stairs. Well, drag, actually.

When this is over, I'll have a bathroom put in on the first floor. Maybe with a Jacuzzi.

That's right, make some jokes, have a good time. Don't think about how I just let Simaron go off with people who are going to torture him until he's begging for death. Don't think about Jen being wrapped in death-chains because I left her alone. Don't think about how it's my fault. All my fault. Fuck.

Fuck.

"*Fuck!*" I punctuate the word with an elbow into the wall and slump to the floor, my other arm getting sore from keeping Jen's head out of drowning depth. I hit the wall again and get a stinging pain for my effort. The wall isn't all that impressed.

"Keep it down..." It's a mumble more than anything, but I lean over the tub to see her face scrunched up in pain, like waking up with a nasty hangover. "Where am I?"

"In the tub. The bleeders have closed up, so mostly you're in there because I'm too weak to pull you out."

"Dick?" She actually sounds disappointed.

"Yeah. Hell of a honeymoon, huh? Bet you're regretting whatever got you stuck with me." I move my hand to gently stroke her head. "How're you feeling?"

"Like I charged into a warrior demon and came out the business end. And then drank a case of rum and went to a concert, where I banged my head against the speakers. And probably threw up on them."

"Nah, that was your shirt." I swallow hard. "Tell me what happened? Where were the guards?"

A few seconds pass. "Those *were* the guards."

"Those are the guards who were sent to protect us? They had no heraldry. You didn't think that was suspicious?"

Jen gives me a somewhat annoyed look, as best she can manage, probably. "They had signed orders from the duchy, all right? Looked authentic enough."

"They drove off with a van full of goblins at that." She doesn't react. I felt that was a bit of a shocker when I saw it, considering that sidhe and goblins *do not get along*, but I guess either the years of knightly training or just the multitude of bruises was masking her concern. "Jen, they took Sim."

"They told me they were going to make you choose. I'm

sorry, I know that must've been hard for you, to pick me over him. For what it's worth, I'm grateful."

"I didn't pick you." That gets a reaction. If she had her strength back she probably would sit bolt upright and backhand me across the face. Instead she cranes her neck forward and furrows her brow.

"Run that by me again?"

"I was ready to die, Jen. I would've fought them for you and Sim. I wasn't going to choose. Sim stopped me though. He went with them on the condition you and I be left alone."

A silence falls over the room for a few seconds. I hear her slip gently back deeper into the water, dipping her head completely beneath the surface for the space of a breath before emerging, weakly bringing her hands to her face to rub it slowly.

"This is getting too complicated."

"Damned right it is." I rest my head against the wall. "I've got to figure out how to handle this. I need to find Sim and rescue him before he's killed. Fuck the stupid demon, this is more important." I try to get up, but fail. "Damn it."

"Cold iron, Dick. Neither of us are going anywhere." She strains to adjust her position. "He gave himself up? Just like that?"

"You're the viscountess, Jen. The lady of the House. What, you think he'd let anything happen to you?" I chuckle softly. "I'm really going to have to rescue him now, so you can get to know him." I give her battered body a once-over and wince. There's marginal improvement, and it'll heal quick, but I still expect her to look better than she does every time I check. "You stay put, I'm going to climb to the sink and get you some aspirin or something."

"Don't bother. It won't help."

"Let me do something, okay? We were sent guards who bound you in iron chain, tried to kill me and hauled off Sim to be tortured, all right, Jen?"

"Fuck, this is getting too complicated."

"Jen, it's just aspirin."

"Richard, stop calling me Jen, okay? I fucking hate being called Jen. My name is Jennifer, call me by that." I blink twice.

"You're telling me this *now*?" Okay. Out of left field. "Why didn't you say something, oh, the night we met?"

"Because I didn't want to marry you and I wanted a reason to think you were a dick no matter how nice you acted. Hell, why do you think I've been calling you Dick?" She struggles to lean over the side of the tub and generally succeeds.

"Firstly, they call me Dick at work, I've gotten used to it. Secondly, I wasn't keen on marrying you either, but that's the bitch of being a noble. I could've done a lot worse. Also, Sim is *gone*, okay? He gave quite possibly his *life* for you, so maybe a little more concern for him? And I swear if you mention him being a—"

"Whoa, whoa. I don't want to see anything happen to him, but look at us. What can we do? Even if we're well enough to search for him, protocol will keep one of us here unless one of us dies." She makes a passable attempt at shrugging. "Unless there's a formal event, like the tournament."

"I know how it works. It has to be me. I want to kill every last one of them."

"He means a lot to you," she says, her gaze softer. "Doesn't he?"

I nod.

She averts her eyes. "You'd charge off for him, not caring what you had to do so you two could be together, right?" She manages a weak smile. "Richard, it's okay. I think it's obvious you and I aren't going to have that kind of marriage. Neither of us wanted that anyway. Gods know I didn't. Still, it would seem that I owe him my life. That's a debt I can't ignore."

"I can't get over the feeling that I'm missing something. Why did they come here? Why take Sim? I mean, his heritage has been common knowledge all of his life. My standing in the community took a hit for keeping him on, but I didn't care. Why take him now?"

"They weren't here specifically for him, remember? They made you choose."

I nod, and the confusion clears up slightly.

They wouldn't have offered me a choice if they didn't have all of my choices covered.

"And those options were either they take you, they take Sim or they kill me." I run through those options in my head again. Not much else I can do, really. "Let's assume it's a win-win-win situation for them no matter which way I lean."

"Not much of a stretch."

"So what's the motive in this? I mean, those same guys tried to take Sim earlier today and—"

"The guards were the mercs you mentioned then." She spends a couple seconds thinking, as if trying to find the words. "Well, I'd hate to feed your ego, but you are the viscount."

"Well, yeah. You sure you don't need that aspirin? You're stating the obvious."

"Ugh, Dick, think about it, would you?" Kind of curious why she's not just spelling it out, must be trying to make me a little more self-sufficient or something.

"If it's about me, then why not kill me and be done with it? Of course, the line would go to you, but they could kill you then and that's it for the House of Stone. And how does Sim factor into this? His dad was a commoner, it's not like he can stake a claim on any title." Hell, the only reason I could see for someone taking Sim wasn't possible for anyone to know—I would do anything to get him back.

Holy shit.

I would do anything to get him back.

"They need me to do something for them that only I can do." It starts to click together, if only one piece. "They take Sim, they can coerce me to do what they want. They take you, they can coerce me to do what they want. They kill me, well, they can probably get you to do whatever they want. They had you wrapped in iron chain, that's convincing no matter what kind of Fae you are." I rub my head.

Jen inches herself up, straining from the effort. "So why wouldn't they kill you and make me do whatever?" She shrugs with a tad more confidence. "Just saying. Might as well cover all the options. It's not like I'm unbreakable."

"For starters? If I die, you're not instantly in charge of the line. There has to be a ritual, my funeral, you have to be cleared of any suspicion, it takes time. You would be head of the line in the interim, but you wouldn't be able to do anything major. You'd have to be accepted by the House as its new master, the Benedict Shores would have to accept you, you'd have to be made the new custodian of the..." No.

It couldn't be that simple.

"The Azure Blade." I know I'm onto something here. "I'm the custodian of the Azure Blade." The knight-captain had made a big deal out of that, even after the sword ignited for him. *Would that it were so easy to take it from you, Count Stone.* "Ye gods, this is about the damned sword." I elbow the wall again. "Damn it, this is all about a stupid sword!"

"Does anyone else know about your problem with the sword?" Nice way of putting it.

Sim knows about it, of course, and I'm sure someone could point a finger at him, considering he willingly went off with the enemy. I'm not about to sully his sacrifice though. To hell with that. Jen knows, but I doubt there's a Fae alive who would allow themselves to be bound in cold iron to allay suspicion. The only person left after that was...

The person who promised to send guards. Guards who came with signed orders from the duchy.

The Duchess of Tolon Park.

Aunt Cadwyn.

Chapter Nineteen
Once

I am riding the Nightmare.

This will require clarification, I'm sure. I've mentioned on numerous occasions that we Fae are living dreams. The living dreams of humans, to be accurate. Most of the time, we're just that to them—something out of a fantasy. We're perfect, beautiful, ethereal, noble, everything that the best of humanity wishes it could attain. That's not ego, that's the way you want us, and we're happy to play our part.

Then there are the other times.

The downside to having that speck of human blood is that we can be as subject to the turbulent swells of emotions that normal people are. Add in the fact that that speck is *sorcerer's* blood and you get a whole 'nother thing. We go from exalted radiance to terrible beauty, the most refined, distilled, perfect expressions of your negativity, and if we're not careful, it'll consume and destroy us. We call it the Nightmare.

And I am deep in it.

I'm in the car tearing through Beckettsville doing about sixty. This is not recommended. I should be pulled over and given a ticket. Or arrested. I know for a fact that what I'm doing is dangerous, so my Fae grace is not in effect. There is no luck, no little guardian angel flying wingman. No, there's something else entirely.

Right now I am the living personification of road rage. I am cutting people off. I am blowing through four-way stop signs. I am running red lights. I am blasting loud and violent music. Right now, I do not care if I hit something. Maybe not even someone.

Somewhere deep in the back of my brain, I am screaming and scared shitless of what I'm doing, what I'm allowing myself to be, but I'm not seeing many options here. My own flesh and blood sold me out and kidnapped Sim for a *sword*.

Said sword is in the backseat, in its case. Jen is at home, holding down the fort. I want her to recover, and this is my fight anyway. As far as her protection was concerned, I called her mother and asked her to send some of her House's guard. It's not much, but I have to figure Jen wouldn't be screwed over by her own family. I get the irony in that statement considering where I'm going right now.

"I have to admit, you do mindless rage perfectly. Mercia was quite good at that, you know?" I'm aware of someone in my passenger seat, but I don't care. I accelerate, turn up the stereo. "Not a one of you does anything halfway, do you?"

"Fuck you, you fucked off to fuck knows where when I fucking needed you."

"Eloquent as always. I do love my Fae." I hear a soft chuckle. "And I don't know if you can actually use that word that many times in a sentence." I swerve into oncoming traffic to shave some more time off. I'm going to cause a major accident any second, I know it. "You do realize, Richard, that I'm not really flesh or blood, so if you manage to kill yourself I won't be spited at all."

I push the speedometer past eighty and slide back into the

right lanes. I think I just blew by a cop.

"Are you going to think this through at all?" He glances out the window. "Oh look, that store is having a sale." Rem turns back to me. "Well, think about this a little past the point you're at now, that is?"

"Shut up. Go away."

"What's your plan? Charge in there, break a few oaths and possibly kill yourself in the process? And to do what? Accuse the highest ranking noble in the area of trying to kill you? Kidnapping? What if she's innocent? Imagine how red your face will be." A second passes. "Tell me what you have to support this, besides circumstance." I cross into Allora. Rem sighs audibly, which I hear even through the music. "Oh come now, it's not like you can get rid of me. Might as well answer the question. What makes you so certain it's her? You're flying off half-cocked, if that's the right use of the phrase, and why?"

"They took Sim."

"Sim went on his own. For your sake. It's admirable that you want to get him back, but charging in will likely get you killed." He waits on my answer but I don't give him one. "Why do you want him back? He's a butler, isn't he?"

I can feel my grip on the reins loosening, figuratively.

"More than that, eh? Special fuck buddy? That's the term, right? I can understand. I had plenty besides Mercia who fulfilled some special needs for me. To be honest, Mercia wasn't my wife. Just one of the mothers."

I break one hundred. *Shut up, Rem.*

"So what exactly is it that he does for you that you're willing to accuse your own kin of plotting your death? Must be a hurricane in the sack. That's the expression, right?"

"Fuck you."

"The stock reply." He leans over to check the gauges. "You're ruining what I'd assume is a classic automobile, or at least you will when you hit something." Rem settles back in his seat. "I'm going to need more than that, though. Even if he does windows, as well as doing you, I don't see the point in—"

"I love him, okay!" I look at Rem, shouting, the Nightmare fueling my voice into a roar. "I fucking love him and I'll kill the son of a bitch who took him away. Is that fucking good enough for you?"

"Relieved you finally admitted it. Richard?" His face is expressionless.

"What?"

He points out the windshield. "Truck."

The rage gives way to fear. The Nightmare slips its reins and leaves me.

I hear a chorus of screeching metal as the car collides, flips up over the truck, tumbles again and again through an intersection. The cacophony fills my ears, sounding like the world is being torn in half by a very angry person. I hear shattering glass, feel pain all over my body, see flashes of light as I clench my eyes shut. The seat belt strains to keep me still as the rolling subsides, my body wracked with echoes of force.

There's warmth, then heat. My skin feels sheared in places, pain mixing with a weird numb tingling in my left leg and right arm, my forehead knocked by something hard as the rocking and spinning finally seems to settle exclusively to my head. I think I smell smoke.

"Get out of the car, Richard." Rem's voice is just as expressionless. "You want to get out, trust me."

I can't move my arm.

"Use your left arm and unbuckle yourself." I try to, my

hand seeming to float slowly as I become aware I'm inverted. After a few seconds I find the buckle, but the button won't depress. "Okay, you'll need to cut it then. You need to sing, okay, Richard? Burn the belt off. Drag your finger over it and sing."

I can barely think, let alone speak, let alone sing. In the future, I'm never going anywhere without my crest on my shirt. If I have a future, that is.

"Do you want to die?"

I don't know.

"Do you want to die without letting Sim know how you feel?" Cheap shot, but okay. I'd already wrecked my dad's car from confessing my love for Sim.

Holy shit, I really do love him.

"Richard, please, time is of the essence here."

I sing his name. I search my mind for the syllables and sing Simaron's name in Sigil. A silver flame dances along my fingertip and severs cleanly through the belt near the buckle, my body suddenly slumping downward as I do my best to crawl and worm my way through the open window, across the broken glass that litters the street of the intersection. There are cars all around me that are stopped, plenty of fender benders, but the pillar of black smoke that's coming from the Trans-Am draws the most attention and gives any onlookers reason to vacate the scene.

My Fae grace didn't spare me any pain from the accident, but at least I haven't killed anyone.

Sirens wail in the background as I slowly crawl from the car. After a few seconds I become aware of someone picking me up, supporting me, dragging me from the wreck. I feel more pain, yeah, but right now I'm glad to be away from the potential explosion.

"Stay with me, buddy, okay? Ambulance is on the way." I have no idea who's talking to me. I think it's a guy.

Nice thing about Allora. Accidents get taken care of right quick. Tax dollars at work. If this happened in the Benedict, I'd probably be dead. Granted, in the Benedict there wouldn't have been a truck to hit.

"C'mon, buddy. Stay with me. Talk to me, what's your name?"

"Richard." That kind of sounded like me, if I was wheezing it through a plastic bag stuffed down my throat.

"Richard, you are not going to die today, all right? Just hold on." I don't really have any plans on dying, honestly, but it's always nice to hear someone agree.

I can't make out who's talking, but seeing as Rem never called me buddy, I assume it's a good Samaritan. The pain isn't as bad as I thought considering all the parts of me that don't seem to be working right. But that's probably shock.

"Hold on, Richard. You're not going anywhere." In any other circumstance, that would probably be a bit ominous, but there's no malice in that voice, which I still can't put a face to as my vision's blurry. All I want to do is just close my eyes and sleep for a while. The sirens are getting louder or my hearing's getting screwy too. I'm not in a state of mind to discern one way or the other.

A few seconds later, I hear loud and excited talking, several voices of varying genders, all talking about me. We sidhe do love to be the center of attention. I feel my wallet being pulled from my pocket, and for a couple seconds I'm rather pissed that someone would have the nerve to mug me after I wrecked my beautiful car, until I hear my vital statistics being recited off my driver's license, along with a couple people remarking that I don't look thirty-four, and then a bit of cursing as my "rare blood type" is noticed.

Fae can't get blood transfusions from humans, just not done. Normally, I'd get wrapped up in herbs and given extracts and stuffed full of Fae cuisine, and maybe a mystic would be grudgingly brought in if things were dire. But that's the Fae method. I've been picked up by humans.

As I'm loaded into the ambulance to be taken to the nearest ER, it occurs to me they'll be calling my listed emergency contact to give me a transfusion.

The one I was going to see. The one who sent the guards. The one who very well might have taken Sim.

The Duchess of Tolon Wood.

My Aunt Cadwyn.

Chapter Twenty
Alive

I wake up to the smell of flowers, which scares me slightly considering that I associate flowers with funerals. I'm breathing though, always a good sign. I can hear steady beeping somewhere off to my right, and when I open my eyes I can see a metal stand holding a large bag of clear liquid inside, a tube running down into my arm.

So this is what being in the hospital is like.

I look down at myself and my leg is elevated, as well as my arm, both in a cast. My chest feels odd and tight and sore and violated in a way. There are stitches when I lift my cheap gown enough to peek at my chest. Shit.

My surroundings are a bit more encouraging. I'm in a room, the walls in muted colors, windows with a nice view of the bay, a TV in full view, no other occupants. A private recovery suite. Whatever those humans did to me, it apparently went well.

To my left is a small table with a bouquet of flowers in a dirty-looking vase, the blooms all white. I strain a bit to check them when a woman enters the room, dressed in faded jeans, a T-shirt and a fleece jacket. Considering that neither of us are holding court, there's no need to dress formally.

She holds a small suitcase, sets it next to the table and sniffs the flowers for a moment, furrowing her brow then smiling. “Narcissus and white heather. Seems like someone's looking out for you despite having met you before.” The smile is pretty forced though, and it only lasts another few seconds before the woman leans over my bed and squeezes me tightly in her arms.

“I was so scared, Ricky.” Aunt Cadwyn pulls back, her face stern, but that, too, is forced. “How could you be so irresponsible? You could've been killed! Thank the gods you were able to hold on long enough for me to get down here and give you a transfusion. These humans can't just let us handle things. They thought I was crazy and...and you almost... And if you did, what would I say to your...” Tears are streaming down her face. This is the person who was my prime suspect.

I am such an asshole.

“I'm sorry, Aunt Cadwyn.” Ugh, is that me? I sound like I've been gargling razor blades and broken glass. “How long have I been here?”

“A couple of days, you've been working on your third.”

I do the math in my head and figure I have about three days until the solstice. All that time lost to the Nightmare. How could I have been so stupid?

“Your wife is worried sick,” Cadwyn says. “I'm working on getting her a dispensation so she can see you here. It seems foolish in situations such as these, but protocol is protocol.” She doesn't sound all that impressed with the rules right now. “Tell me what happened?”

“I wrecked the car.” I remember all of the other cars around me. “Was anyone else hurt?”

She shakes her head. “Apparently your grace had its work cut out with everyone else. You were lucky. The physician told me you shouldn't have made it to the hospital, much less long enough to get a transfusion. 'Rare and incompatible blood type' was the term he used. Even when shown proof we're not human, they find ways to convince themselves we are. A saving grace, I would suppose." She wipes her eyes. "I would count yourself lucky your father is with your mother, otherwise I'm certain he'd have ridden the Nightmare until you were all but trampled."

Her face then grows severe. "I swear I will punish that half-blood, though."

My eyes go wide. No. Please, no. "Why?"

"For letting you drive so recklessly, of course!" Exasperated, she clenches her fists tightly. "It's his duty to look after you, attend to your needs. Once I'm certain you're well, I am going to your manor personally to drag him before my court to explain his negligence. If you were not in any state to get behind the wheel, he should have offered to chauffeur. I see that he couldn't even be bothered to stop by, the—"

"You don't know." How could she be behind it? How could she have arranged it all and admonish Simaron like that? Fae can't lie. She couldn't announce that she was going to retrieve Sim from the manor if she knew for a fact that he wasn't there. She couldn't accuse him of negligence if she was going to have him brought up on charges of assault.

There is no way it could be her.

"Know what?"

But there were signed orders from the duchy and...

"Did you send guards to protect the manor, Aunt Cadwyn?" She arches a brow and pulls over a chair to sit at my side. I look at her more intently. "The four guards and the knight-captain."

"I was going to send Sir Gaius." My aunt's personal

bodyguard. A Knight of the Realm from the Icehand line. He's older, looks to be in his sixties to humans, well over a hundred, actually. He guarded Aunt Cadwyn's mother first, but he is still one of the most feared and respected knights in the City, if not the kingdom. "But Duke Tremaine was kind enough to offer a contingent of his own knights. The amount of effort he put into making the offer, it was impossible to refuse without weeks of protocol, and I didn't want to risk your safety. I allowed him to send the guards for three sunsets, and then afterward I would send Sir Gaius."

She looks at me matter-of-factly. "You of course will have no issue with him watching over your lands while you recover from your injuries and your wife holds vigil at your side?" She smiles softly and takes my hand. "Now, you interrupted me, a rude action, I might add, while I was dressing down your absent manservant. I can only imagine that you had a good reason, so no apologies are needed for the slight. We'll simply account it to the medications these humans have churning through your veins."

I'm still reeling from the revelation about who signed those orders.

"Duke Tremaine sent the guards?" She nods once. I can't be sure though. The knights could have been acting on their own. "He knew them? Trusted them?"

"Ricky, what's wrong?" Concern in her voice, obviously. But this is now a matter that is becoming so very, very delicate. I can't just announce that a duke kidnapped my manservant and will probably kill him if I don't give him the Azure Blade. For starters, it's merely speculation. More than that, even *I* don't know if that's true. It's a guess that holds a little water, but it's still a guess. And sidhe nobles do *not* guess in matters such as this.

But I've still been out for three days. And Simaron...

Oh gods, Simaron might be...

Aunt Cadwyn is looking more concerned as she sees the panic rising in my eyes. I have to throw her off the trail.

"Is my sword okay?"

She sighs. "Ricky, try to focus. One thing at a time. Let's start with how you managed to get in an accident." Might as well start with that.

"I was riding the Nightmare." Her face turns deadly serious, but I do have to tell the truth. "I was angry. Very angry. We were attacked by four knights twice on the day of the accident. No heraldry, so I don't know if they were errant or just concealing their master. They bound Jen in iron chain." A gasp from her, to be expected. Using iron is a very big deal, especially for sidhe, as I mentioned. Strange though, that Jen didn't tell Aunt Cadwyn any of this. Then again, Aunt Cadwyn was the primary suspect until I rolled the Trans-Am through downtown Allora. "And they took Simaron."

"I can understand then, considering what was done, that you would seek vengeance, but to lose yourself to the Nightmare, Ricky..."

I look at her for a moment, shamed. I don't want to say it, but she can see.

"The guards. I said I would send guards and you... And the accident was in Allora and..." The tears are brimming again. I expect rage, not this. Oh gods, Aunt Cadwyn, please don't... "You thought me responsible?"

"I didn't know what to think. I couldn't rule it out. They had signed orders from the duchy assigning them there. The seed of doubt was planted, and it grew and twisted, and I was so messed up over them taking Sim and..."

"And the Nightmare took you." She closes her eyes a moment. "I must admit that I have fallen thrall to it myself. The rage, it seems to clarify everything, condense all confusion down into a simple point, onto an easy target. I have only felt it once, but I must live with the consequences." I nod in shamed agreement, and Aunt Cadwyn looks away. "You say Simaron was taken?"

I explain the events of the evening just before the accident. The choice, the sword betraying me again to shine with cerulean fire in the hands of that bastard, and Simaron offering himself. I leave out the part where I'm a mystic. I doubt she could handle that.

"He offered himself to protect the two of you..." She covers her mouth a few seconds. "I regret ever thinking him capable of negligence. He assaulted the knight-captain, though?" She taps her finger against her chin. "I don't know whether he could be held accountable. What sort of blade was it?" She smiles nervously. "As long as it wasn't cold iron, I'm certain he wouldn't receive more than censure considering the extenuating circumstances."

Oh shit. She reads my face well enough.

"I see. I'm curious where he would obtain such a blade. But I will make inquiries, find out if he is being brought up on charges. If so..." She doesn't need to finish that sentence. This is all we can really do. Sure, I could march to the duke's estate and kick down the door and accuse him, but I'd probably be killed by his guards for spouting madness and be accused of being lost to the Nightmare. I would need proof.

"What you say about the sword, Ricky, is alarming. Has it...*always* been like that, I wonder?" I shrug, well, half shrug, as my right arm's in a cast.

"This situation is growing quite cloudy," she says. "I've half a mind to seek out a mys—" She looks away a second. For some reason, Aunt Cadwyn has always had a problem with mystics. See why I'm not forthcoming?

"So." She inspects the various beeping machines and then my battered body. "I would suspect you should be recovered by tomorrow evening."

I know this sounds insane, considering I was in a major accident and my arm and leg are in a cast. But try to remember I'm not human. And considering I'm no longer riding the Nightmare, my grace will be back in full swing. A car accident isn't like hunting down a demon, after all, so with some Fae cuisine replacing my hospital food, I should probably mend up well enough to at least be on my feet and sawing out of these casts within twenty-four hours.

Which reminds me, I need to check in with Casey. I would guess that the flowers were left or sent by her. It's not too much of a stretch to figure a seer would know I had been in an accident, and that narcissus was used in the bouquet pretty much seals it. Can't ask Aunt Cadwyn to read me the card though without her asking me some pretty direct questions I won't be able to duck around. Best to wait until she leaves.

"Ricky?" Right, I forgot to answer her.

"Yeah, as long as I get some home-cooking, I would guess so."

She kisses my forehead gently. "I will do what I can to find Simaron. I only ask you tell me one thing. Rather, I would like for you to confirm something for me. A suspicion I have held about him for some time now. I have always suspected from his behavior that he has been hiding something, something that, well..." Please don't ask me about the half-bloods, Aunt Cadwyn. "And as you are most familiar with him, I can suppose that you might shed light on this matter, perhaps clear up some confusion." She looks away a moment, not meeting my eyes. "I suspect he has committed or at least will commit severe breaches in protocol. Breaches that will have dire consequences for him."

Oh shit, she knows. She knows about his courier work. She might even know about the commune. Oh shit, shit, shit!

"Just ask me, please, Aunt Cadwyn."

She takes a deep breath. "Should we be able to recover him, Count Stone..." She referred to me by title. Not good. Not good.

A moment passes by until I can't stand the tension any longer. "What?"

"It is suspected that he seeks to step far outside and above his station. The other day, before your wedding, he visited my library to gather research materials for the ceremony. He told me that it was to help tutor you in proper vows, so you would not mispronounce and potentially embarrass yourself. At first, I thought it was odd. You are a Fae noble, such vows should come easily to you, but he assured me somewhat sheepishly that you had been neglecting your studies." She sighs. "This was not at all unbelievable."

Okay. Fair point. But I don't remember Simaron coaching me on my marriage vows.

"I am used to commoner sidhe as servants now, and Simaron is very well-behaved, so well-trained for his profession that for a moment I forgot his heritage and..." She closes her eyes for the space of a breath. "Forgot his ability to spin falsehoods. I believe that your manservant lied directly to me. This alone is a severe breach." Yes. Yes it is. Why would he take books on those vows? It's not like they're closely guarded secrets of the Fae. You can't twist them into anything sinister. They're binding vows of loyalty and devotion, that's all.

"What do you mean about him stepping above his station?"

She takes a moment, using her duchess voice now. "His sacrifice for your safety, the taking of materials on loyalty and devotion vows of the sidhe court, his behavior for the last several years that is visible to the vigilant eye... It is a suspicion, but as a duchess of this kingdom, I cannot allow suspicion time to grow and bloom. So, I apologize for the intrusion, but I must ask and, Count Stone, for this next question I require your complete and absolute honesty." I can already feel the weight of her authority. No way around this. No clever wordplay will save my ass or pull me from the fire. Direct honest question, direct honest answer. "What is the nature of the relationship between you, Count Stone, and your manservant, Simaron?"

Chapter Twenty-One
Release

"I don't see how this question relates to my duties as Viscount of the Benedict Shores." That's right, I'm stalling. She asked me as a duchess asking a viscount, so I am permitted to give that answer until she can provide good reason that my relationship to Sim, whatever type it may be, is in some way hampering my responsibilities.

And she sees right through it.

"As a Fae of noble birth, it is your responsibility to continue your bloodline and remain a member of good standing of your House. We have suspicion that your relationship to your servant has changed in a way that has shamed you in the eyes of your forebears. If this is not true, you need merely tell us the nature of your bond to the half-blood Simaron, and we will assume your shame comes from other sources." She's brought out the "royal we". It's not just a status thing with the Fae, it's authority, a reminder that she is well above me in station and her patience is wearing thin.

"I have done nothing wrong, Your Grace. Of this I am certain."

"But your servant has. He has spun lies to a duchess and used his position to obtain knowledge of Fae rituals without so much as a 'by your leave'. And in the wake of his actions, his master has been shamed. We are finding difficulty in thinking him completely innocent." I look at her pleadingly. *Please, Aunt Cadwyn, please don't do this.* "Answer the question, Count Stone. No more queries, no more refusals, no more stalling." Her voice becomes hushed. "Ricky, don't make me command you."

Even in a hospital bed, my arm and leg in a cast, my voice still sounding more than a little scratchy, she won't show mercy. And I know why: she promised my mother she would look after me. There's no spite here, she's well aware of what she calls my self-destructive patterns. This is yet another example of her needing to save me again, clean up my mess before I ruin myself and my House.

"I haven't done anything wrong."

Her face grows more severe, putting back on her mask of authority. The command of a duchess will be coming soon.

"No, Aunt Cadwyn. I'm telling you, nothing of what I'm doing with Simaron is wrong."

She sighs. "I'm aware that you and Simaron do many things together...in private, that we won't speak of." Still a quiver of arrows, even outside the court. "And they are to be expected, as you were not yet wed, but I fear that perhaps Simaron has begun to see things where they simply aren't." Meaning to her, this is an obsession that needs to be dealt with now that it's causing real problems.

"You think he's in love with me." A few seconds pass in silence, the words on the tip of my tongue. Gods, just say it, get it out there. Granted, when I admitted it before I ended up in my current condition, but I had to doubt my bed could collide with a truck.

"That is the suspicion, Count Stone, yes. And if he swore

any kind of oath of devotion to you, it might have affected your standing with your House."

I shake my head quickly.

"Ricky, you can't know for sure. I must admit he's performed admirably, but if he is truly in love with you..."

It probably won't end well for either of us. I'll be humiliated, of course, as it'll be assumed I'm being unfaithful to my new bride, and doing so with a half-blood (though the more offensive terms will be used). It's a nice little slap in the face to my romantic aspirations; no matter what I feel for Sim, he and I can probably never be together.

You know what? Fuck that.

"I think he is, Aunt Cadwyn. But more importantly, I love him back." She stands, speechless. I summon what strength I can. "And I'm not doing anything wrong. So I love him, so he's a half-blood, I don't care. It's thanks to him that I want to actually be noble, not just be a noble. It's because of him that I even give a damn about Fae society, about what we're supposed to do for our duchies and counties and baronies and fiefdoms and kingdoms. I might actually end up a better man because of him, and I love him for that. And if the House falls because of it, I'll just build a new one."

"Nothing will change your mind?" She holds up her hand to me. "Don't answer, it was foolish to ask, perhaps." She takes a step away, her back to me. "Please understand that this is unprecedented, and especially considering your recent marriage and..."

"Aunt Cadwyn..."

She turns to face me. "Right now, Her Grace, Cadwyn, Duchess of Tolon Wood, is speaking to you, Count Stone." She straightens her posture. "Do you realize the difficult position you put us in? You have betrayed a marriage vow within days of making it. You have disgraced yourself to your bloodline. Count Stone, you have not only embarrassed yourself as a Firemane…" Her face grows more stern. "But as a Sunleaf as well."

Oh shit. I've potentially embarrassed the royal family. Not good. Not good at all.

"How many others know of this infidelity, Count Stone?"

"Only you and me. Simaron doesn't know how I feel yet."

I can see emotions warring in her eyes, but relief wins out as she delivers her judgment. "Then you will keep this matter between only the currently involved parties. Do you understand?"

I nod once. "I'm sorry, Duchess Cadwyn."

She leans down and kisses my forehead. "I never asked for an apology, Ricky." She sits. "Perhaps it is the wisp of humanity that causes us to do these things, to make our hearts so fickle, untamed, to choose who they will. Regardless, we cannot help who we love, I suppose." Her hand is on mine now, and she squeezes it. "Since you have shared a secret with me, I feel I should relieve the debt." She takes a deep breath. "It is about Regina."

My mother.

"What about her?"

"As I mentioned, I have ridden the Nightmare once. It was shortly after Regina announced to me that she would be undergoing the Ritual of the Broken Mirror." She seems ashamed. "I terrified even Sir Gaius in my rage. I thought her such a coward for leaving you behind, that she was spitting in Kendrick's face by joining him rather than raising his son." She bows her head slightly at me. "I apologize for thinking so badly of her, Ricky."

"That's it? You were pissed at Mom for killing herself? Why feel guilty about that?"

"I'm not finished." She squeezes my hand again. "Ricky, there is something I have wanted to tell you for so long, but I swore an oath before Kendrick's death that I would not say anything." Her eyes meet mine. "But as his son, you can release me from it if you choose. I must warn you, though, this will be very difficult to hear."

I take a second, but curiosity doesn't let me delay long. "I release you then." I take a breath, realizing this has to be done formally, and I manage to croak out the same words in Sigil with some difficulty.

"Are you aware of the Tomb of Keres?" I am, of course, but my own oath to Catrin prevents me from saying anything more, prompting Aunt Cadwyn to continue. "It was not always so, as you know. A Ra'Keth lived there, until his death, and while he was well hidden, it was possible to find him if one were patient enough. Kendrick, Regina and I once visited the Ra'Keth's sanctum." I blink. Holy shit, my family trafficked with a sorcerer?

"Ye gods, Aunt Cadwyn, what did you do?"

"Regina and Kendrick loved each other deeply and wanted to conceive an heir, but there were difficulties. So, they went to the sorcerer for aid, that Regina might bear a child. After a long negotiation, the sorcerer agreed to a working. You were the result of that working." My jaw understandably drops, and she pats my hand. "Worry not, there is no more sorcerer blood in you than any other Fae. Your father is Kendrick Stone, no one else." She looks away.

"Are you saying this is why I have no brothers and sisters? Because Mom and Dad needed magical assistance to conceive me?" Suddenly the question of why *I'm* a mystic is a lot closer to being solved.

"That is why you have no siblings, yes." Cadwyn swallows softly, closing her eyes a moment. "And why I bore no children of my own."

"Aunt Cadwyn, why haven't you ever told me this before? I would've released you from that oath ages ago if I'd known this."

She shakes her head. "You had nothing to tell me that would carry the same worth. You have confessed a secret love for a half-blood within a week of your arranged marriage, Ricky. It's a secret that's worth this one."

"You gave up your ability to have children? That was the deal?" I grit my teeth. This is why I hate sorcerers, they deal like demons.

"It turned out that the sorcerer had little in the way of expertise in matters outside conjuring and scrying. It took much to convince him to attempt the working. We had to absolve him of any unintended effects..."

"Covered his own ass, pretty much."

She nods once.

"Well, okay," I continue, "I was some weird magical version of a test-tube baby. Doesn't seem all that major, really. Maybe a little embarrassing for Mom and Dad, but they're beyond any point of caring. And you, what's embarrassing about making that kind of noble sacrifice for your sister? I mean, you gave up your ability to make life so she could have one child, and then she commits suicide and you feel guilty over being mad at her about it? Why have you been beating yourself up over this?"

"I was afraid you'd be angry with me."

"Why? Aunt Cadwyn, Mom left me without a family when I was twelve, and even before that, Mom and I weren't that close. She was so devoted to Dad. I was closer to Simaron's mother, to be perfectly honest. And look at you, you're a *duchess* and you were still making time for me. You're pretty much the only family I have. Any time I have a serious problem, I know I can talk to you, that's why..." I exhale. "That's why I was riding the Nightmare. I suspected you were involved with what happened to Simaron. I feel so stupid now for considering it."

"You thought I was capable of doing such a thing to my own flesh and blood?" She sets her jaw, fighting off the tremble that often accompanies tears. "Ricky, I could never do something like that to you. Ever."

I nod. "I know, I'm sorry. Like I said, I feel like a prick."

She shakes her head. "That's not why."

"What, you swore an oath to never screw me over?"

She shakes her head again. "No, I would never need to swear such a thing."

"Then what?"

"Your father was quite charming."

I arch a brow. "Okay..."

"Mother had grand plans for us, to marry into strong Houses since, as you know, we are not of the primary Sunleaf line. Unfortunately for Mother, Regina and I were both quite enamored of a young Knight of the Realm who watched over the Benedict Shores."

I blink. "You and Dad?"

She shook her head quickly. "No, no, nothing of the sort. He chose Regina and that was that. Then I had my little coup and established the Sunleaves as the proper rulers of Tolon Wood. I carried feelings for Kendrick, in secret, until the end of his life. I was still longing for him when he and Regina came to me wanting to see the sorcerer. That they would ask what they did of me, to give up my fertility so my sister could flaunt another victory, that she had now borne the child of the man I ached for, and that that child was nothing more than an heir to her... I was distraught and angry. So..." She starts wringing her hands together as she speaks. "I made my own arrangement with the Ra'Keth." She attempts a smile, but it's weak, strained. "Your magical test-tube analogy was not all that far off."

I can't speak. My heart can't settle on an emotion.

Her voice starts to break as she pushes through it. "In a way, I thought it would be a solution where all would be satisfied. Your father would have an heir, your mother would bear his child, and I..." She closes her eyes again, a tear slipping down her cheek. "I'm sorry, Ricky. I've wanted to tell you for far too long."

I need a minute to work through the sheer nonsense of this. This can't be true, right? I mean, Fae can't lie, but all those times I called her *Aunt* Cadwyn and she never corrected me? Why she's never referred to me as her nephew, always as her family, her flesh and blood? All the times I poured my heart out to her, *especially* when Mom died, and she couldn't just let me know that it was okay, because my mom hadn't really abandoned me, because...

"Are you trying to tell me you're...my mother?"

Chapter Twenty-Two
Rearviewmirror

It can't be true.

But Fae can't lie.

Granted we can omit the truth, stand mute, say we're under oath and can't reveal secrets. There are countless ways to mislead someone while remaining completely "honest" in a technical sense.

"I need you to leave, now."

"Ricky, please."

I stare at her. "You cannot drop something like this on me and expect me to accept it and move on. If you really are..." Gods, I can't say it. "Well, then you should know that. So you need to leave me alone and let me deal with this on my own. Please." Stay strong, stay strong.

A few seconds pass in silence, and her face betrays that she wants to say something, summon some last effort to make this end with a tearful hug instead of me ordering her away. It should be a happy occasion, after all, finding out that I'm not an orphan. I shouldn't feel lied to because she had all the bases covered, had the best reasons and of course "the best of all intentions" for what she did.

If this is what the Fae do to the people they love, I can

understand a little more why any human who dares to love us in return eventually loses their mind.

"Just go. Please." A nod is all I receive in return, and she steps outside. When the door opens, I see an older man in full armor outside, armed with a bastard sword. Sir Gaius. When she vanishes out of sight, he remains. A guard. Her best guard.

The door closes and with that the tears come.

"Have to admit I'm surprised at all this." Rem is now seated by the bed. "I hope you don't mind that I stayed out of that scene. I figured the last thing you needed were questions regarding your sanity."

"You're surprised that she's supposed to be my mother?"

"More at the little rules you set up for yourselves, the oaths you bind yourselves with. It's hard to believe you were meant to be our living dreams."

I shake my head slightly. "I'm sure you'd love a philosophical debate, but I'd really like a few minutes to be overemotional. Please, leave me alone, let me cry and scream and throw things until the moment's passed and I can think rationally. I'm tired of acting proper, okay? Just let me act—"

"Human?"

I stare coldly at him.

Rem only smiles. "Why do you think you're a mystic, Richard? Because somehow there's more of my blood in you than anyone else in your line? That doesn't make any sense. I'm part of your *human* ancestry, and you're allowing yourself to act human. You're being more than a dream."

"What the hell are you talking about?"

"Do you think a proper sidhe would want to throw some violent tantrum if he learned what you did? Have you considered the political gain for your House from this revelation? The information you now hold over your mother? The advantages that are firmly within your grasp? No, you wish to cry, be angry, confused, and try to make sense of it all. You feel betrayed. All understandable reactions...for a human."

"What are you saying, I'm turning human? That's why the line rejected me?" He laughs, and even though I know he's not there, I throw the TV remote at him, which passes through him and hits the wall.

The sound immediately alerts Sir Gaius, who comes into the room with his hand on the hilt of his sword. He scans the room quickly, checking behind the door before turning his eyes to me.

"Sorry, Sir Gaius. It's just not my day. It's all right, I'm fine as I can be." He nods once.

"I'll be right outside, Your Excellency." It stings to be called that, because it reminds me that Sim is imprisoned somewhere and there's nothing I can do to save him in my current condition. Gaius returns to his post and closes the door behind him.

I look back to Rem, who's still chuckling. "What the hell is so funny?"

"How do you know what lines you're descended from?"

"We have records." Extensive genealogical records. We Fae take our bloodlines very seriously.

"And how do you know which House?"

"For the most part it's patrilineal. There are a couple of houses that follow the mother's line, but mostly the father's."

"And the bloodlines are split rather evenly between male lines and female lines? You can trace your lines back to specific Fae. What about the Houses? What are their roots?"

"Father said they were the Houses founded by the

originators of the bloodlines."

Rem nods. "Did you know that Ra'Keth don't just pop out of the womb slinging spells and what not? Most of us were completely unaware of the power we commanded until it awakened within us. I, for example, had a rather simple existence. I was a peasant, common as dirt. How embarrassing for you, eh?"

"What an inspiring story. Go away."

"Do you know what line of work my family practiced? What art my father passed down to me, that his father had taught him and so forth?"

"Well, you were called *Deathsinger.* My guess is that you were a bard."

He shakes his head. "I'm afraid my singing voice was not that refined. It was simply how I did my work. To answer the question, we were stonecutters." He smirks slightly. "A house of stonecutters, if you will."

"Your point being?"

Rem rolls his eyes. A house of stonecutters... And the Houses were founded by the bloodline's originator.

"You're the progenitor of the House of Stone?" I rub my face. "Ye gods."

"The people may have called me Deathsinger, particularly *your* people after I was dead and burned and scattered to the winds, but I served a purpose. Unlike many of my sorcerous brethren, I tried to keep the world from being ended again and again. We still believed that the world itself was a tree back then. Before it had been other things, a flat stone, an island in a sea of celestial blood, a cloud of breath, a waking dream, a giant turtle's back..."

I blink. "The world was seriously all of those things?"

"This question coming from a Fae, a race that professes itself as the living embodiment of dreams." He nods once. "Yes, the world was all of these things and more. There were already things in the dark that we had created, and some of us believed the best way to deal with the ones that had gone awry was simply to end the world and make a new one where our problems simply didn't exist. It would be, as it was explained to me in 'small words a peasant would understand' like chipping away parts of a stone that detracted from the natural beauty of the sculpture that lay within."

"I kind of follow so far." I think on it a second. "But if you keep chipping away, there won't be any stone left after a while, right?"

Rem's eyes go wide. "You cannot know how relieved I am to hear another being say that."

"Again, are you trying to convince me that you were the lone and righteous wolf amidst a crowd of evildoers? You were Ra'Keth, and Mercia killed you for a reason."

He nods. "I made mistakes, of course. I was only human. But I was against any attempt to end the world as we knew it for frivolous reasons. I figured that if the world was a grand tree, then I would be the mountain that kept it out of reach." The crest. A mountain's peak holding up the roots of a tree that enveloped the whole summit.

"It is your House." I slump in the bed, my body sagging.

"All this means, Richard, is an emphasis on what you as Fae already know. You're descended from the sorcerer-kings of old."

I stare at him. "It means that the Houses we seek to uphold, the banners we carry out onto the battlefield, the glory we earn for our families, it's all to honor *you*. The ancestors we don't speak of, that we *despise*. It makes us so...hypocritical.

Why are you telling me all this? This doesn't help me with anything, not with what Aunt Cadwyn told me, not with Sim..."

"You're calmer now, yes? Able to think rationally?"

I sigh. "Maybe a little."

"So let us examine your problems. First of all, Cadwyn. If she is your mother as she claims and has little reason to mislead you about, what changes for you?"

"It means she's been keeping things from me."

"And if you had known all your life, what would have changed?"

"Well...Dad would've been humiliated. I would've been sent to live with Cadwyn or live among the commoner sidhe, as our House would've been disgraced. Simaron's father would've been dismissed or reassigned to a new House..." And Sim never would've been part of my life.

"And if she had told you after your mother became a broken mirror, as you put it?"

"I wouldn't have believed her. And I would've resisted her, hated her." And my family would have been humiliated, and I probably would've taken it out on Sim. Chances are the feelings he developed for me never would've taken root.

"And now that she has told you, what changes?"

"I'm going to be mad at her for a while, but if I can get Sim back, I'll have him and Jen to lean on. Sim will probably convince me to patch things up with her, simply because of how much I've tried to get him to reconcile with the memory of..." I look down.

"His mother, yes."

"Yeah." So this probably was the best way it could've turned out, considering the circumstances. I hate not being right.

“And concerning Simaron.” He gestures at me to get my attention back on him. “Do you truly believe, in your heart, that he is dead?”

I shake my head quickly. “No, of course not.”

“And you have eliminated your mother as a suspect.”

“Yes, thank the gods. I still feel like an ass for believing that.”

“Who then, I ask, is left?”

An excellent question, I have to admit.

“Well, there are duchies outside the City, and the higher-ups live out there too. The Queen lives upstate, near the capital. And of course, there’s Duke Tremaine, but that wouldn’t make any sense.” Because it wouldn’t. He already has the only other magical sword currently possessed by Fae in the kingdom. Embarrassing a viscount doesn’t really do anything for him one way or the other either. Even the half-bloods wouldn’t matter much. He’d just storm in and kill them and that would be that.

“Think, Richard. What has changed?”

“Since when?”

“Since this all began. What have you learned that has always been true?”

I arch a brow at him, confusedly. “Well, I’ve learned that I love Sim.” He gestures that I keep going, so I try to follow the logic. “And that the sword will burn in any Fae’s hands but mine, it seems.”

“Yes, keep going. You’re nearly there.”

“This just affects me, though. What the hell does it matter to a duke? All he cares about is showing up Aunt Cad—” And the puzzle piece clicks into place. “I’m her son. I’m her son by someone other than her husband. I’m her *only* heir. If everything happening with me comes out then…”

“The humiliation will be hers to share as well. There is a grand gathering of your people fast approaching, yes?” The Summer Solstice. Even the Queen Herself will be attending. My aunt...my mother would be disgraced before Her Royal Majesty.

Leaving His Grace, Duke Tremaine, to offer to perhaps “watch over” Cadwyn’s duchy while she recovered from the embarrassment, a stewardship that would likely not have an end until the two duchies were simply combined.

“The tournament would be the perfect place to reveal everything. The only question would be how he’d know all of this. Cadwyn’s sworn an oath, there’s no way she could’ve told anyone but me. So unless Tremaine can read minds...”

That’s ridiculous, though. Duke Tremaine doesn’t need to have any oracular powers to know all of my family’s dirty secrets. He doesn’t need to be a mystic.

Not when he’s already married to one.

Chapter Twenty-Three
Go

“I really appreciate this, Sir Gaius.”

I’m currently in the passenger seat of the duchy’s “carriage”, namely a fully loaded Mercedes Benz. Gaius is driving, obviously, because it’s difficult to drive with a broken arm and leg. I have a set of crutches in the backseat. I refused the wheelchair because I probably won’t need it in a few hours.

“It is no trouble, Your Excellency.” He’s curious why we’re driving to Destry Bay to see His Grace, Duke Tremaine. He’s more curious why we stopped at an electronics store, but he doesn’t say a word. Not his place to question the actions of nobles greater than he, after all. “While you were fetching your devices, I received word that your blade has been recovered and is being sent to your manor at Her Excellency’s request.” Good, at least the sword made it, and better that Jen has it than an enemy. He looks down at the smartphone docked in the center console. “Humans and their technology. Eventually they may even surpass their Ra’keth ancestors.”

“They’ll always need sorcerers, Sir Gaius.” I’ve been carving into the thick clamshell plastic that encases my prize, my ace in the hole. “And I think in some ways it’s necessary for us to follow them, lest their dreams of us be anachronistic.”

"As long as we do not follow them too far, Your Excellency."

Despite his acclimation to the current times, Gaius would be most happy were every day like the Victorian era, when manners and etiquette still meant something, at least in his eyes, a noble title still carried weight, it was gauche to admit that a *table* had legs, and most importantly, when service such as his was respected instead of ignored, or worse, pitied.

The drive continues on in relative silence. To be honest, it's nice to not have to talk to anyone.

I really don't know how to explain what I'm doing. If I confirm what I suspect, I don't know what I can do with that information. Let's just say for argument's sake that Duchess Catrin used her powers as a mystic to glean plenty of embarrassing secrets from Duchess Cadwyn. (I'm still not comfortable calling her my mother yet.) Why not make a play herself?

Well, she'd have to tell how she found out for starters, and the only way to do that is to imply she'd been trafficking with demons, sorcerers or mystics, or confess that she's a mystic herself. If she does that, well, whatever information she gives up had better be a lot more impressive than the scandal that will erupt from how she got that information. And the wife of a duke being revealed as a mystic? Duchess Cadwyn will find a way to spin her dirty little secret eventually. Duchess Catrin cannot.

And it wouldn't make any sense for Catrin to burn herself as well as Cadwyn. Granted, if she knew that *I* was a mystic, that would probably tip the scales in her favor, but it seems that no one knows that so far, save myself and Simaron.

Duke Tremaine can't exactly use his wife's information either. He'd be in pretty much the same boat, wouldn't he? So he has to keep it quiet.

At least publicly.

The duke will always have that information, he can always hold the *threat* of it over whoever is involved. In particular, Cadwyn. But I only just found out about my parentage, so I can assume that Tremaine thinks me ignorant. If Cadwyn's "crimes" are revealed, I can play dumb and suffer minimal repercussions.

I rub my temples. The duke is a sidhe, he'd have worked this out so that no matter what happens, he wins. So let's run through the scenarios.

He reveals Cadwyn: Damage to his own reputation, but he can shunt it off on his wife and have her dealt with as a mystic. Since she does her best to keep it secret, he can play dumb and survive the ordeal with his own duchy intact and the Duchy of Tolon Wood without a ruler. Either he becomes a steward of the duchy or it goes to the heir, which would be me. Assuming Tremaine has Simaron, the duke trades my oath of fealty to him in exchange for Simaron's life and the Azure Blade. The duke wins.

He keeps it quiet: Over the following years, he gets minor concessions here and there from blackmailing Cadwyn which over time add up. Sidhe can be patient, he can wait decades to get what he wants. In the meantime he uses Sim to secure fealty and the Azure Blade. Eventually Cadwyn dies (probably from an "accident" when there's nothing more he can take from her), I'm revealed as the heir, and the duke rules both duchies. The duke wins.

I go after the duke: I challenge him. He invokes the right to a proper duel during the tournament. I'm forced to use the Azure Blade, and my shame is revealed in public (should I not find the demon first, which is starting to look highly likely considering I haven't heard from Casey yet). Duke Tremaine either disgraces me or outright kills me in the duel, or uses Sim to make me throw the fight, and the Duchy of Tolon Wood is left without an heir. Cadwyn eventually suffers "an unfortunate incident", he becomes steward. The duke wins.

And of course, Cadwyn can't exactly come forward and just confess all the secrets to escape Tremaine's hold on her. It would not only shame her out of her title, it would bring shame to the House of Stone, as it would reveal my family trafficked with sorcerers. I'd end up a pariah even if I weren't a mystic, simply because I was conceived through sorcerous means.

The only x-factor in all of this is my being a mystic, which I still have no idea how to utilize. I can hardly use it in the tournament, as the sword is supposed to burn blue, not silver. I'm sure I could *eventually* learn to do more than just sing fire into my blade, but if what Rem told me is anything to go by, I can't accomplish it in a few days.

I need to question my ancestor more at some point.

Sir Gaius breaks through my reverie. "We are nearly arrived, Your Excellency."

Well, after I take care of matters here, that is.

The duke's manor is, obviously, far nicer than mine. Destry Bay is a rather upper-class suburb of the City, though most of its residents would probably argue it's *the* upper-class suburb of the City. You can't take the train in, nearly all transit is by eco-friendly buses or walking. As a result it's very quiet and clean, and the property values are astronomical. The duke's neighborhood is a "walk-able" area, where you can't even park a car or take a bus. The roads are narrow, made of cobblestone. It's like stepping a century or two back in time, save the modern storefronts.

Gaius parks about five blocks away from the manor, about as close as he can get, and escorts me to the front gate, looking every bit the kindly grandfather aiding his grandson in visiting some well-off relative, when he could probably cleave three people in twain should he perceive them as a credible threat, and then pass judgment on their parentage and education, more than likely.

There's a guardhouse built of brick much like the wall that encloses the estate, and a tall sidhe, wearing functional armor and armed with a longsword, exits the house when we approach. Well, he looks like that to us, at least. He probably looks like a heavily armed guard in SWAT gear to the regular people.

"State your business."

Gaius steps forward, his voice rumbling with authority. "His Excellency, Count Richard Stone, seeks an audience with Her Grace, Duchess Catrin. It is of the utmost importance that he speak with her in due haste." Gaius gives me a look, to let me know he's putting himself on the line and I had damned well better not be exaggerating about the urgency of my request.

The guard, seeing my relatively broken body, appears concerned. "Do you require aid, Your Excellency? And does your visit pertain to your injuries?" His hand brushes the hilt of his sword.

Gaius steps in front of me, his hand on his blade as well. "His Excellency was quite recently injured, but we are not bringing accusations, no. Conversation is all His Excellency requires of your lady, nothing more or less." I lean on my crutches, trying to look as pathetic and nonthreatening as I can.

A few seconds pass, the guard and Gaius exchanging intense looks until the guard finally breaks.

"Wait here." The guard motions over another Fae, shorter, I would guess a brownie (though brownies nowadays tend to be taller than they were overseas). The brownie then dashes off to the manor proper to deliver the request, and in the meantime, we wait. After a few moments, the servant returns, slightly out of breath.

"Her Grace will see him, but she requests he be alone. The knight must wait here at the guardhouse." I nod in assent to the terms before Gaius can protest.

"I'll be fine, Sir Gaius. As I said, I'm simply here to talk. Besides, these are our friends, yes?" I wink at him, and he sighs in defeat. He knows for damned sure these are *not* our friends, as Duke Tremaine and Duchess Cadwyn have been feuding ever since she ascended to the title. But on the surface, all the Fae call each other brother.

It takes a few minutes, thanks to my slowed pace, but I eventually enter the manor, and the House of Storms apparently doesn't put much stock in modern technology. The lighting is by gaslight and candles, even in the late afternoon. There are commoner Fae, mostly brownies and a few sidhe, among the house staff. Trolls and common sidhe make up the guard that is posted here and there, but none look familiar, and I don't see anyone who looks like a goblin.

Then again I doubt goblins would be allowed to just stand around in plain sight if they knew anyone from outside the household was coming.

"Excuse me, but before I see Her Grace, could you direct me to the restroom?" The servant gives me an odd look, and I lean in conspiratorially. "It is something I'd rather not discuss, if you get my drift."

I give him a knowing look, and after a second, he nods once and leads me to a short hallway and opens the door to a lavish bathroom. Everything's marble, gilded fixtures, the lighting given by candles. Ye gods, did he have to be period about everything? Still, the lighting's adequate to do what I need to. I adjust my sling for comfort's sake and take the device Gaius mentioned out of my pocket and slip it into the palm of my broken arm. It's small enough to be concealable, thankfully.

I wait a few seconds, both to make sure I'm ready for this and to better sell the misconception that the servant probably has. Hey, I said I needed to see the restroom for a reason I'd rather not discuss. I don't want to discuss what I'm bringing. If he thinks I came in here for some baser reason, that's his mistake.

And shame on him for thinking me so coarse.

I wiggle my fingers, only wincing slightly, thankful that my bones are knitting themselves back together. Big upside of the blue blood, both literally and figuratively. I should be walking without the crutches by tomorrow evening, and back to fighting form by the following morning. If only I could say the same about Sim.

I exit the bathroom and allow the servant to lead me to a special chair that's been fetched. A few commoners gather around it to carry me so I don't have to embarrass myself by hopping up many flights of stairs. After sitting and nodding to them, the chair is lifted and up we go. Ugh, I feel like some cartoon royalty. The only thing that's missing is being fanned with palm leaves and fed grapes. I keep my fingers clenched tightly around the device, concealing it from sight, my hand still tucked inside my sling.

It takes a few minutes and I'm carried down halls and up stairs lined with oil-painted portraits, the previous Dukes of Destry Bay. The good duke is from the line of Bran the Duskstar, who led the great insurrection against the Ra'Keth known only as the Emperor, which is practically the only thing that line has ever done. Yet they're just barely behind the Sunleaves in terms of claim to the throne.

"You're taking me to see Her Grace, Duchess Catrin?" I've

never been farther into Tremaine's manor than the ballroom for a formal function, so I need to confirm that I'm not being carried off to some torture chamber.

"Yes, Your Excellency, of course. That is what you requested, yes?"

I nod in reply. It makes me thankful we can't lie. The duke could always hold me captive under some pretense and apply all the pressure he wanted, if he knew the truth about my relationship to Cadwyn. And I have willingly walked into his house in a condition that would make escape a laughable prospect.

After being carried up another flight of stairs, I'm taken into a rather barren-looking room probably meant for storage. The chair is set down, and as soon as I get up, the servants practically scurry out. Shit, shit, shit.

"Shut the door, please, Count Stone." The duchess steps out of a darkened corner. She's wearing a simple gown, white, albeit slightly dirty. Her hair hangs about her face, which looks a bit thin, almost gaunt. I obey her request and advance toward her.

"Your Grace?" The closer I get, the farther she backs away. And then I see the reason for her skittishness.

There's a fading bruise on her cheek, and given how quickly Fae heal, it means that something has struck her in the last few hours. No, given from her shying away from me, it was some*one*. And there is only one person I could imagine who has the power to do such a thing.

His Grace, her husband, Duke Tremaine.

Chapter Twenty-Four
Better Man

There's only silence for the first few seconds. She can see that I see the bruise, that I know what it means and who gave it to her. If a servant had done it, he'd be dead, no question. If a goblin or some creature had done it, she wouldn't be hiding in a storage room, staying in darkened corners. She's here because she feels ashamed, afraid. I try to find the right words to say and especially how to say them.

"Did your husband do that to you, Catrin?" Simply asking, so directly, especially by her *name*, would normally be considered such a breach of protocol I could easily be censured for it. I personally don't care if they drag me naked over hot coals, because if she answers in the affirmative I'm going to kill that son of a bitch.

"I cannot answer." Her voice is soft, lacking the strength it had at the Tomb of Keres. Of course she can't answer. It's a safe bet to assume he swore her to an oath to never discuss it. Can't exactly have her revealing what he's done to her. We are the dreams of the humans, after all, and there are plenty of nightmares to learn from in the human psyche. "Please, do not press further. Why have you come?"

I shake my head. "I can't do that, Your Grace. I can't allow you to be treated in such a fashion. It's *wrong*." I take a deep breath. "You are sworn to secrecy, aren't you?" She doesn't answer, but if she weren't being made to stay quiet, she'd admonish me for even suggesting it. "Then I'll offer a secret of my own in trade."

"Count Stone, please. The matter is being handled. Why have you come?"

"You have a bruise on your face, Catrin, and gods know what else that's healed up in the last few hours!" Maybe I'm overreacting. Maybe this isn't any of my business. There is still Sim and my myriad problems that all have a clock ticking away at them. But something needs to be said, right? "I will give you a secret I have revealed to only one. A secret that could easily result in the downfall of my House. You need only tell me the truth."

She looks away, keeping her bruised cheek out of my sightline. "The Fates have told me much. I am aware of your parentage, Richard. And the manner in which you were conceived. And of your relationship with the half-blood. Nothing you can tell me is worth this, nothing that I do not already know."

I take a step forward. "I am a descendent of the Ra'Keth Rem of the Northern Plains—"

"Your House's birthright is known to all the Fae."

I step closer. "And his blood sings in my veins." A more eloquent way of confessing that I am mystic, like her. She turns her face back toward mine, disbelief there, but she gently nods. The secret is enough. She speaks no words, but her face is wet now, her chest quivering to hold back sobs.

I don't know what to say to her. I don't even know what I'd want to hear were our roles reversed. The words that tumble past my lips feel weak, contrived, obvious.

"It's not your fault."

I can't believe I just said that. Of *course* she knows it's not her fault, right? That what he's doing is wrong? That's obvious. She knows that, doesn't she?

The sobbing sounds are louder now, and she sinks to her knees. I follow her down, kneeling very awkwardly before her, fumbling with my non-broken arm to find a handkerchief or something she can use to dab her tears. I don't really know what to do. Do I hug her? Tell her it'll all be okay? I mean, I wanted to say something, and I did and now...

"I will never tell a soul, Richard." She looks at me. "What he would do, if he knew Cadwyn's son was mystic..."

"She'd be humiliated, I know. I think the more pressing concern right now is you, Catrin."

She shakes her head slowly. "He'd call for her abdication. And your head. He hates our kind, Richard. We're...tainted to him, to many of the Fae. They see us as too human." She closes her eyes a moment. "I myself was unaware that the sorcerer-blood sang the song of Fate in my soul, not until some time after Tremaine and I were wed. Suddenly I could see things, I knew secrets no one could know. I thought Tremaine could use the information to improve his standing..."

"But he could never truly explain how he came by it."

"He was furious, so much power, so much information he could never make use of. And then there was my curse. It would be passed down to his heirs, he feared, and we were already wed. All of his grand plans suddenly had difficulties arising, and I..."

I take her hand, and she doesn't shy away. "And he blamed you for it? It's not your fault you were born mystic."

"My abilities did not manifest until recently. Within the last year, in fact." She pulls her hand away now, slowly. "But nothing can be done. He is my husband, we are bound together, and I am bound to never speak of this to anyone. I doubt everyone would be so free with their secrets as you, Richard. There is so much I wish I could tell you, but..."

"Forget about me, what about you? Is there anything I can do to help?" I want to ask about Sim, but it doesn't seem right, does it? At least not this second. "What if I offered you refuge in my county? You could get away from him. Make an appeal to the Queen to have your marriage dissolved. She could easily release you from the oath keeping you from making his treatment of you public."

"From what I know, Richard, your lands are far from safe, and the duchy would suffer without me. This is not something I can simply run away from. Please understand."

I cast my eyes down at the floor. "There must be something I can do for you."

"I do appreciate what you've done. The trust you've shown in me. You cannot imagine how it feels to confess what has been done to me, to be reassured that the blame is not mine, or at least not mine alone. You have given me words to draw strength from." She then looks at me. "The device you've been hiding, do you intend to use it?"

I blink and check my sling, where it's hidden still, and sigh softly. I can't really play dumb. "That was before...well, all this." I take out the device, a digital voice recorder, and show it to her. "I figured if I repeated everything I learned from you at the Tomb of Keres, I could use it if I recorded it on this. You know, play it back for other people and not break my oath, since I wouldn't be repeating it."

She smiles weakly. "A clever gambit, using the tools of humans, but you would still be breaking your oath, Richard. You would know, in your heart. For all our vaunted honesty and sincerity of speech, we are excellent at lying to ourselves, aren't we?" Catrin rises and helps me up to my feet, which is a bit awkward considering my leg's still in a cast. "Your wife does not even know you are here, does she?"

I shake my head. Jen's probably worried sick. She was expecting to visit me in the hospital and here I am in the lion's den.

"Your Grace." I still need to know. It feels wrong to ask, but she might have the answers. I need to know Simaron's all right. "I came here originally seeking my servant, who was taken from me three nights ago. I know I risk much simply by suggesting he is here, but—"

"But there is little you wouldn't do for him, I sense." She already revealed that she knows. It's apparently an open secret among the aristocracy how I feel about Sim. I wonder how many other people knew before I did?

"Where is he, Catrin?" I know she probably can't tell me. He'd make anyone involved swear an oath to keep it secret. No announcements have been made of Simaron's "crime", so I have to guess he'll use that information to better leverage the sword out of me, or whatever it is that he wants.

"I cannot tell you."

I nod knowingly. "I figured as much."

"But I would suggest you take the matter up with Tremaine. He might be able to advise you on where to seek your servant." Clever woman.

"Thank you, Your Grace." I get my crutches from where the servants set them by the door. "I would suppose His Grace is already coming up to see me, as my visit was to be expected eventually."

The duchess nods once in reply, and I start toward the door. "Count Stone."

I turn to face her. "Worry not, Your Grace, I have not forgotten what transpired here. If you ever have need of my aid, you need merely call." I bow. I can't exactly tell her that if she ever wants to leave the son of a bitch, I'll be here with a U-Haul. No real proper protocol for that other than what I just said.

"It's not that, though I am grateful for your courtesy." She looks toward the door, some fear there, but she steels herself. "My husband is a negotiator, in his own eyes, at least. If you were to enter into a conflict with him, he will have many ways to solve it with words, and more often than not to his own great benefit. I would suggest you remember your birthright, whether words are your weapon of choice..." Her eyes meet mine. "Or not."

I bow again, with some difficulty, knowing that'll probably make perfect sense in the time it takes me to find His Grace, Duke Tremaine, Lord of the House of Storms.

As I hobble down the hallway, I'm joined by another servant, a sidhe this time, who feels the need to escort me. To think, I could be in a semi-uncomfortable studio right now filming *Ass Commando 8*. Ye gods, what world was I living in?

"I'd like to see His Grace, if it's at all possible." The servant doesn't blink or break his slow stride.

"The duke is expecting you, Count Stone, if you'll just follow me." Wonderful.

We stay on the same floor, which is a bit odd since the duke's receiving rooms are supposed to be on the first floor. More than likely a little surprise, and me without a sword.

My arm is starting to itch, the "broken" one. Aunt Cadwyn left me plenty of food before I departed from the hospital, so I obviously snarfed down as much of it as I could. I mentioned that I heal quick, even quicker once the food and wine of the Fae are involved. Easy to fix a broken dream when there's plenty of good dreamstuff to chow down on.

Those dreams you have of endless feasts of the most succulent foods you've ever seen or tasted, what do you think happens to that food when you wake up?

That's where the whole thing about never eating Fae food comes from, after all. It'll never sustain you, because it's just a dream, but it's better than anything you'll ever have, so everything else will taste flat and lifeless. We don't make the food, you do. That's why you forget how the food in the dream tasted. If you could remember you'd probably starve to death.

The Fae, well, dreams sustain dreams with ease.

"Could you fetch me a blade, Fae-steel?" Before he can refuse, I cut him off and tap my cast. "I need to remove this, I promise that the blade will be used for nothing more than that." Besides, I'm hardly going to physically threaten the duke in his own house. I may be pissed at him but I'm not going to be reckless about it.

The servant sighs for a moment, nods once, and motions over another servant who's standing watch by a simple-looking door. The new servant, a rather burly-looking troll, I would guess a guard in servant's clothing, is asked to escort me to the duke while the sidhe fetches a suitable knife, which will probably be a penknife. It won't matter. Fae-steel can cut through most things with relative ease. In case you're curious, Fae-steel is simply steel made without iron. How do we do that? Sorry, we don't share that with humans. Regardless, the cast will be like slicing open a cloth bandage as opposed to a near-block of plaster.

Despite the fact that my arm's feeling better, my leg isn't quite at full strength yet (trying to kneel on it didn't help), so I'll save that cast for later. Just as we reach the door, the servant returns with the blade I requested, a letter opener. A Fae-steel letter opener. Nice to see what kind of respect I command around here. I take it and slide the blade cleanly through the plaster, cutting through it like I'm cutting through air. Takes a little bit of work, but I can already move my arm. Just a matter of wriggling it out now. It'll give me something to do while the duke is talking, I guess.

When the door is opened for me, I'm treated to the sight of a rather plain sitting room, the furniture all done in wood, a bench by the wall, a couple of chairs in the middle of an area rug that takes up most of the floor. There are a couple of paintings on the wall of the duke's ancestors. The most prominent is of Bran the Duskstar standing over the bloodied corpse of the Emperor, his foot planted on the dead sorcerer's chest, holding the Ra'Keth's head in one hand and a sword in the other. That sword would be the Adamant Heart, a hand-and-a-half blade that the Emperor according to legend used in executions.

"Please wait here." The servant's voice is dark, gruff, and if the guy didn't look like a bearish troll, I'd swear he was a goblin. I'm left alone in the room to look around, perhaps take a seat or place myself into a more respectful position considering the duke is on his way. I decide to work on wriggling my arm out of the cast and put the digital recorder into my pocket.

After about a minute, I hear loud steps outside the door, the duke's escort more than likely, and then the door opens, revealing a servant, sidhe, dressed in finery, who steps in and clears his throat.

"His Grace, Duke Bran Owain Gavin Tremaine Duskstar, Lord of the House of Storms, Knight of the Realm..." No more a knight than I am. "Slayer of the Dagger's Line..." I heard some vampyr were responsible for the majority of that. "Guardian of the Dying Wood..." He threw a pittance into a local campaign to stop the cutting of trees in Destry Bay to keep property values up. I also heard a local goddess was primarily responsible for the measure and its success. "Duke of Destry Bay, and Wielder of the Adamant Heart." Which means he mostly hit the genetic lotto, just like I did.

The duke enters, dressed in his finest, like he stepped out of a well-funded film set in the Romantic era, the Adamant Heart sheathed in its jewel-encrusted scabbard at his side. He stands proud and looks expectantly at me. I'm supposed to be kneeling right now. I glance down at my leg cast to imply that it'd be painful to go to that degree of formality. Yeah, I took the pain for his wife, but I think I've made it clear what my opinion of her husband is.

The duke nods to one of his attending guard, and my good leg is quickly swept out from under me, putting me flat on my ass. Ow.

"My apologies, Count Stone. I'm afraid my staff can take protocol rather seriously." He doesn't ask anyone to help me up. "Would you care for some wine? I've recently received an excellent vintage. You'll drink with me, of course?"

I look up at the armored guard, who's probably waiting for a reason to smack me again, and I nod in assent to the duke.

"Very good." He claps his hands once, and from behind him, a bruised and beaten man steps into sight. Ye gods, no... "Simaron, please fetch us some wine. It appears Count Stone and I have much to discuss regarding your welfare."

Chapter Twenty-Five
Save You

So this is it, this is where the House of Stone could very well come to an end. The duke has me cold. I think everyone in the room is well aware of this. I wasn't lying when I said I would do anything to get Simaron back. I would probably swear fealty, give him the sword, whatever was necessary to ensure that no more harm came to Sim. It's all over now but for the talking, working out the deal.

Usually when someone's going to get screwed as deep and hard as I'm about to, the cheesy low-grade techno starts playing in the background and everyone starts speaking in erotic puns and single-entendre.

Simaron hasn't moved yet. He's simply staring at me, seeing my leg in a cast, my arm still wrapped in plaster. I probably don't look like I'm in all that great shape, but I'll heal quickly. Sim's a half-blood. He won't.

Tremaine looks slightly to his right, in Sim's direction. "Do I need to repeat myself, Simaron?"

I speak up before Tremaine decides Sim needs motivation.

"I would suppose he's a bit surprised at my condition. I was in an accident. But worry not, I'll be fine, and the cause of it is nothing that I bring to your doorstep, Your Grace." The duke's eyes are back on me, and I keep my attention on him, letting Sim be in the peripheral. I'm all right, Sim. I'm right here. "You say you wished to discuss his welfare? I will admit I'm curious how he came to be here, and in the condition he's in. I trust there's an explanation for my manservant's current state, Your Grace?"

We both know damned well how this happened, but I have to act like I'm giving him the benefit of the doubt. Duchess Catrin intimated that the key to this lies in protocol, but not his protocol. It still isn't making all that much sense yet, but I'm good at thinking on the fly when I really need to.

"It would appear that your manservant assaulted a Knight of the Realm, Count Stone, with cold iron at that. I would wonder how such a weapon came into his possession. Might you have some light to shed on this mystery?" It's common knowledge that a servant's actions can be pinned on their masters, especially when cold iron is involved. Just because we're forbidden for the most part from killing each other doesn't mean that some of us aren't devising ways around it.

"To my knowledge, no cold-iron weapons have ever been the property of my House, Your Grace. But if what you say is true, about him assaulting a knight, that is a grave matter indeed. Why have the Royal Inquisitors not been brought in to sort out the truth in this?"

There's a damned good reason the Royal Inquisitors haven't been brought in. It'll ruin far too many people involved once everyone starts getting asked questions delivered with the Queen's granted authority. I take a breath. Imagine a fencing match, full of feints and ripostes and thrusts and parries. On one side you have a junior-college champion, and on the other you have a three-time gold-medal winner. "I would suppose you wish to negotiate a compromise where neither of us suffers any undue embarrassment, Your Grace?"

Guess which one I'm not?

Simaron looks down at his feet. This isn't what he wants, I know it.

The duke seems to relish this. "Giving up already, Count Stone?" I can hear the smugness in his voice, but I'm sparing myself an hour of verbal sparring where I'd more than likely slip up far too many times and give him more leverage. Best to do this quick and dirty, and as far away from the duke's comfort zone as possible. "I wouldn't even know what you would be expecting in an arrangement."

"I want Simaron returned, immediately, and any charges you or yours might have against him dropped and never spoken of again."

He laughs, the bastard actually laughs.

"These are very serious charges, Count Stone! Such things cannot be simply waived off, not without great compensation."

"Fine, what do you want?" Tremaine has a look of expectation, and I grit my teeth. Right, I have to be formal with him. "What manner of compensation would be suitable for repaying this debt I will owe you, Your Grace?"

"Such disrespect, but I suppose it's to be expected from the fringe counties. This is quite a request on your part. It is so unexpected I am afraid I cannot imagine suitable recompense." Another smug smile. "Perhaps you could suggest a means of payment, Count Stone?"

I keep my eyes on Tremaine, but I see Sim shake his head softly. I'm sorry, Sim.

"Perhaps the Azure Blade…"

The duke shakes his head as well, smiling.

"He used cold iron, Count Stone."

"For openers. I could also offer tribute for a decade."

"Three. And please, continue."

I nod. "I could also allow my first-born son to squire under you." I have to swallow the bile rising in my throat just from suggesting that. My own son learning to be a knight from *him.* He can tell this troubles me.

"And your first-born daughter, she will handmaiden for my wife?" Yeah, I'm sure that's all my daughter would be doing for you. Maybe she'll help you in the bedroom too? I wouldn't be surprised if you finally have children after that, you sick son of a bitch. Still, this is Simaron.

"That could be arranged." He hasn't accepted yet. There's only one thing I have left to offer. "And I could swear fealty to the grand and noble Duchy of Destry Bay." I swallow hard. "And fealty to you, Your Grace."

"Fealty? Truly? Though I am afraid that tribute and fealty from a fringe county is hardly impressive, and a squire and handmaiden that are yet to be conceived?" He takes a step forward and motions for Simaron to follow. Sim doesn't get a chance, he's roughly shoved by the guard behind him. "And the Azure Blade? The House of Stone has long contended that only a true scion of Mercia could wield it. That would imply that the sword would have little use but as a trophy for my wall." He smiles. "I have more than enough trophies, Count Stone."

He wants me to reveal it myself. The truth about the sword.

"If you are speaking of the azure flame, the sword will ignite for any of the noble race, Your Grace. The Firemanes act as the sword's custodians, we have never intimated anything more." Which we haven't, but we didn't exactly correct people who assumed the sword only worked for us, apparently. I suppose after a few generations, we began to believe it ourselves. Sure came as a shock to me. "If you drew it, Your Grace, it would burn with your noble fire." The look on his face is priceless. It's of victory. He's probably imagining the portrait of him wielding the Azure Blade and the Adamant Heart already.

Sim is pained, fighting tears. I'm giving away everything, for him. Gods, I don't envy the weight he's probably piling on his heart right now.

I slowly get to my feet. "Would that be acceptable compensation for my requested terms, Your Grace?" The burly guards make no move to stop me. I'm not armed after all, and I've lost. It would be kicking me when I'm down, which the duke more than likely has first dibs on.

"They would, Count Stone." He glances to the guard on his right. "Pick the tainted one up, take him to the viscount's vehicle, keep it quiet."

Simaron is then unceremoniously dragged from the room. "No, Richard, don't do this!"

I take care not to meet his eyes. I can't give Tremaine any more ammunition. I tell myself that I'll see Sim in a few minutes, if I play this right.

The door is closed afterward, and it's just the duke, me and his guards.

And I have to play this right.

"Shall we settle the matter then, Count Stone?" He steps closer, so I can properly kneel, and he can place his hand on my forehead while I swear fealty.

Instead, I stare him dead in the eyes.

"Yes, let's." I then swing my plaster-clad fist, the back of my hand colliding with his face. The impact jars my arm enough that I can slip out of the plaster gauntlet and throw it at his feet. "I challenge you to a duel. You have insulted my honor, my county, my family and my birthright, and I demand the opportunity for retribution. We shall meet again on the Summer

Solstice where we shall engage in single combat, by sword, to first blood. Simaron will be my second, so there will be no detaining him as that will interfere with the duel being carried out. If I win, I receive everything I asked of you, with no recompense paid. If you win, well, let's just say I'll go down fighting before I ever swear fealty to you." I lean in close. "Of course, you could always refuse the challenge, acknowledge me as the greater warrior. But seeing as I'm only the viscount of a *fringe county,* and you're the Duke of *Destry Bay,* well, that would make you a little *bitch,* wouldn't it?"

Holy shit, does my arm hurt.

The room is dead quiet. I'd drop a pin but I'm standing on a rug. That and I don't have a pin. That and I could very well be in the final seconds of my life, considering I just struck a noble and there are no other witnesses save his guards. He could kill me anyway if he wanted to and probably get away with it.

But I've challenged him.

And protocol is protocol.

"If I win, your title, your land, your wealth, your heirlooms, and any noble claim you could make will all belong to me. We will meet at the tournament, before the assembled aristocracy, and the Azure Blade will face the Adamant Heart. My second will be of my choosing, and I am not required to have your permission or clearance no matter who it may be as long as they are under my jurisdiction. As the one challenged, these are the terms I set. Do you agree?"

He's right, and I don't see anything wrong with those terms. I nod once.

I'm then knocked to the floor by a backfisted strike that collides with my face, pain blossoming fresh. Something wet collides with my cheek. Spit.

"Then I accept." I look up to see him turn to the assembled

guard. "Remove this county trash from my home, if you would?"

The burly guards quite roughly pick me up, and I'm essentially dragged out despite my weak struggling. I'd put up more of a fight but my bell just got rung pretty well, and I accomplished what I was trying to do.

Granted, it was a bit of a stupid concession, promising everything if he won. There was a time when I wouldn't care, because I'd be dead, but it's more complicated now. Simaron, the commune, all of them would be subjects to Tremaine, and that wouldn't go well. I have a responsibility to the half-bloods. (Not to mention the idea of Tremaine finding Casey makes my blood run cold. I don't want to imagine the things he'd do to her.) They agreed to be my subjects, so it's my job to keep them safe. I'm their viscount. I mean, it's just a simple matter of...of...

Noblesse oblige.

Holy shit, Sim is having an influence on me.

I'm practically thrown out the front door, but it turns out to be more like a rough shove. I end up face first in the dirt and gravel that comprises the duke's driveway. With a bit of effort, I manage to roll onto my back and catch my breath.

"You can be such a fool, sir." I blink several times and see a hand held in front of me. I take it, and I'm helped up to my feet. "Must my sacrifice mean nothing?"

I smile weakly at Simaron, keeping restraint as we're still standing in front of the duke's manor with guards watching us. "It's not your job to sacrifice, Sim. The county functions much better with you there." I wrap my arm around his shoulder and use him for support as we both start hobbling me back to the front gate where I don't doubt we'll find a very aggravated Sir Gaius. That he left the hospital with me in relatively stable condition and will be returning me home worse for wear will not reflect well on his ability to protect me.

I turn my attention back to Sim. "Besides, you're apparently in a bit of trouble concerning some tomes you borrowed regarding loyalty and devotion vows." I give him a look. "Lying directly to a duchess can be a serious offense, Sim."

"I will do my best to make amends for my transgression to Her Grace, Your Excellency. Would you care to explain your condition, my lord?"

"I wrecked the Trans-Am." I'm amazed how blasé I sound.

"Count Kendrick's... By the gods, sir, what happened?" I look ahead. We're out of earshot of the gate guard and Gaius just beyond it. Why not tell him? If I've learned anything today, it's that you never know what's coming next.

"In a nutshell? I realized that I have loved you for some time now, Simaron, and I more than likely will until my dying breath. The shock of this realization caused my attention to be distracted, I lost control of the car and ended up in the condition you see here." I'm even more amazed I made a declaration of love sound like I was describing what was in a house salad. But I want to know how he'll react, and I can't exactly get down on one knee and confess my love. For starters, I'm too banged up to kneel anymore without delivering my adoration through a mask of agony, and second, I said we're out of earshot, I never said they couldn't see us.

Sim, understandably, has stopped dead in his tracks and is staring at me. "Sir, I..."

I lean a bit closer to him. "Worry not, Sim. I plan to do this again properly once we are both home and have our privacy."

He looks down. "I understand, sir. Declarations of that nature should not be announced publicly."

I smirk slightly before we continue our journey back to the

car.

"I suppose it could be taken that way. I personally would rather we were alone when we made love, as such an act need only be for the two of us."

"Your Excellency, you are hardly in any condition to—" I place my finger on his mouth.

"I could very well be dead in seventy-two hours, my love, I plan to let nothing prevent me from making the most of the time I still have."

Simaron smiles in return. "I can understand that, sir. I was merely suggesting that given your weakened condition, it would be best if I were to take the lead." And he winks. He actually winks.

Gods, I do love this man.

Chapter Twenty-Six
Even Flow

"You are an *idiot*!"

This is about the reaction I expected from my blushing bride upon revealing how everything turned out at the duke's manor. I obviously leave out the details about the Duchess Catrin. I won't gossip no matter how much I might want to tell Jen.

I don't see how she can make me feel much worse, honestly. I already received quite a verbal thrashing from Sir Gaius. Well, as harsh a thrashing as I could receive considering I'm of higher rank than him.

"I've got it handled, Jen, okay? The important thing is that I'm alive, I'll recover, and Sim's back here and safe. It's just one duel, okay?" In front of the assembled Fae Court. In public. Where the Queen Herself might very well be in attendance. And I'll be fighting someone who supposedly is twice the swordsman I am. To the death.

Let's not forget I've still got a demon to track down and kill in the next three days, or instead of a blade burning with righteous azure fire, I'll be drawing a glorified conversation piece in front of those same sneering nobles who probably will love to see me fail.

Apparently I need to work on my bitterness issues as well.

"You put everything on the line for him?" She's in my face now. Yeah, I figured she'd be pissed about that. "Do you realize how bad we are fucked when you lose?"

"*When?*"

I lean against my father's desk. We're in the study, it seems a good place to handle this. Sir Gaius is watching the front door, dressed in full armor. We won't let anyone get the drop on us again.

"Oh come on, Dick, I could kick your ass and I'm but a squire in his eyes. The only edge you had was that sword and it's worthless to you!" She turns away from me. Simaron is standing off to the side. I know he's got more than a few things he wants to say, but his lady is currently speaking, so he has to remain quiet. "Did you think about this? At all? You walked right into what he wanted."

"He wants a public duel with a pissant like me? That he has to devote precious time he could be using kissing the Queen's ass to attend to some skirmish on the tournament field? If I win he loses any influence he has over me. He won't get me, he won't get the sword, he won't get Sim, and he won't get you. The bastard wants my fealty and our children, do you know that? What was I supposed to do, Jen? Negotiate? Grovel? He *insulted* me and you and our House and *no one* does that with impunity." I turn her to face me again, my eyes boring into hers. "I will not let him taint my honor, or yours."

Her face softens slightly. "So you're doing this for me too?"

A few seconds pass as I realize that, yes, I am doing this for her as well. My mind buzzes with that realization, which oddly reminds me of the sound of someone switching a vibrator on and off. Kind of funny that my brain links emotional epiphany to sex toys. I wonder why I thought of that? Gods, I need to find a new day job. Jen's looking a little concerned though, her hands in her pockets. Better not let the pause get too pregnant.

She starts walking toward the door out of the study. "Jen, where are you going?"

Jen exhales before looking at me over her shoulder and then opens the door. "This is...just getting too complicated. I need some time to think, okay? Alone. And no, I don't want to talk about it." The door closes softly behind her.

"That could've gone better." Simaron finally speaks and takes a seat in one of the high-back chairs.

"Don't see how it could've gone much worse. I knew she'd be hurt by this, but it seems like she gets angry with me whenever I do anything for her, you know? Keeps telling me how complicated it's getting."

I sit on my father's desk and take a bite out of an apple plucked from the dream of a seminary student who walked in the Garden of Eden, if only for one night. I'm not going to live forever and I already know right from wrong, but hey, it's still a good apple, and with any luck I'll be out of the leg cast by morning. "Seriously, what's so complicated about it? I'm working on it, trying to do the right thing. Why's she so pissed off?"

"That's not anger, sir. She's in pain. I would wager that Her Excellency felt similarly to you about her arranged marriage. Despite the rapport that the two of you have developed, I do not believe that either of you were expecting to care for each other, even in a platonic fashion, considering the manner of your meeting and the limited time you have known each other." He looks down. "Sir, was it only for me that you went to the duke?"

"I can't lie, remember? You were a big reason, but I meant every word I told Jen. There's other stuff too, but..." I can feel the weight of the chains around my neck. "Oaths, you know?" I shrug slightly. "How long until you feel you'll be recovered? We still have a demon to hunt, and hopefully our mutual source has gathered some intelligence on the matter." I smirk slightly. "That and I owe her a warrior's braid."

"While I do not heal as quickly as my father, his blood is still in my veins, Your Excellency. I should be well enough for service with the dawn."

I get up and cross the room to him. "Even knowing how I feel, you won't call me Richard, will you? Not here, anyway."

"Sir, I would love nothing more, but protocol is protocol." I can see in his eyes that he has about the same opinion of protocol as I do right now. "And I feel I should explain myself, in regards to the tomes I borrowed from Her Grace with no small amount of subterfuge." Simaron looks away a moment. "I have been teaching proper conduct to the others of my kind at the commune."

"What?" So much for him swearing oaths of loyalty to me. "You're going to have to explain that to me, Sim. That's..." I don't really know what that is, but there are plenty of Fae who will want to see it as a treasonous act.

"Despite your recent allowance to the others of my kind, to let them remain in your lands, I felt the need to prepare for the contingency that they could eventually be evicted and forced to find a new home." His eyes meet mine, apology in them. He didn't trust me, nor believe that I would understand. "Should that have happened, I wanted to ensure that they would know proper protocols and procedures for dealing with Fae society. I'm sure you are aware of how proper etiquette can spell the difference between life and death." He's got me there, honestly. "I must do what I can for my people, my lord. I offer my apologies that my loyalties have been divided and driven me to such acts. I will understand if—"

"Sim, just shut up, okay?" I rub my face for a second. "For starters, Cadwyn is the one you should be apologizing to, not me. And believe me, she will devise a punishment for you that will be fitting. She can't appear soft-hearted, not with Tremaine gunning for her. You took advantage of her trust, Sim. That's just..." I sit in the high-back chair now. Let's skip over the embarrassing part where I thought Sim was taking those books of loyalty vows for my sake. "She might've understood. It's not exactly a terrible thing that you're doing. I don't see why anyone would have a problem with half-bloods learning Fae etiquette, unless it's for more ease in manipulation, that is. I'd hate to think that we've been used."

"I could make remarks in the same regard, Your Excellency. My kind have been used by your kind, and I can think of many who would consider returning the favor a just act." He shakes his head once. "An argument of this manner will get neither of us anywhere, I would suspect. I feel there are those who would see me simply exerting influence over you to pursue an agenda that would be beneficial for my kind. I would fear that you yourself would sometimes question my devotion, my feelings for you..." He kneels before me. "Which is also why I took the books. I wanted you to know that my feelings for you are true, that nothing will interfere with my loyalty to you." Sim takes a deep breath, lifts my hand to his forehead. "I wish to swear complete fealty to you, Count Stone, and to no other. Will you accept my vow?"

I remove my hand from his forehead. "No. I will not." Sim looks up at me in shock, but I press gently on his shoulder, keeping him in place. "But remain where you are. You are correct that at some point I could suspect an ulterior motive regarding your feelings for me." I go to the wall and take a live saber from its mounting. "I could someday suspect you of treachery, question your every action."

I move back in front of him. "But I won't, Sim. Because I have offered you my heart, and my love, and as viscount of these shores, I am permitted my prerogative in certain matters. You would offer your fealty, to be a simple servant. I refuse. I would not trust my heart or my life to a butler." I tap his left shoulder, then his right, then his forehead with the flat of the blade. "I ask you, Simaron of the Twin Bloods, what is your heart?" Only once before had I ever heard the term twin-bloods used to refer to one of Sim's kind. It was about as close to an honorific as a Fae could get, as it was more insulting to Fae, personally, considering it implies that human blood and Fae blood can be viewed as equals. Fat chance in this kingdom. But in this county? I've met humans that I've been able to connect to, Fae that are dear to me, and those trapped in-between that I swore to protect. In this county twin-blood will never be seen as derogatory. And I plan to make an example of it now. "Simaron, what is your heart?"

Simaron stares at me, his lip trembling. He knows exactly what I'm doing. If anyone's going to commit an act that's going to be seen as treasonous, then damn it, it's going to be me.

"My...my heart is the mountain, my lord."

"And your blood?"

Simaron bows his head in reverence. "My blood is the land, sir."

"And what of your mind?"

"My mind is the wind, Your Excellency." I can feel the blade trembling in my hand.

I look up, and for a moment see Rem, who appraises Simaron and then nods once to me before disappearing again. I don't know how I know to do this, but the idea is there in my mind. It feels right.

I sing a few bars from my family's requiem, and the sword

ignites with silver flame, the fire not harming Simaron even as it gently licks his forehead.

"And my body," Sim says solemnly. "My body is a house of stone."

The sword flares, a character of Sigil burning brightly into his skin before fading away. The character for "stone". The House...accepted him. I do my best to hold back a grin.

"Then rise, Sir Simaron, Knight of the House of Stone."

Simaron stands slowly, his eyes moist with tears. He's not alone in that regard. I then present him with the saber, and he bows deeply before accepting it. "I will not fail you, Count Stone." He smiles gently, and bows again. "I will protect you, sir, until my final day, until my dying breath." I know the words in his eyes, what he wants to say, but even now, he can't. Despite being elevated to a knightly position, he still can't openly declare his love for his liege, especially not his married one. All that remains is expressing it through other means, other vows.

If Simaron was forced to leave my service, I would always be his liege, as he said, until his dying day. If we had done this before my marriage to Jen, he would continue protecting me, loving me, in ways either direct or subtle. It is whispered in some circles that Sir Gaius has loved Duchess Cadwyn from the moment he laid eyes on her, and though she never returned those feelings, nothing ever wavered his loyalty to her.

It is almost tragic, considering that Cadwyn herself loved my father so, ignoring her own husband and the advances of her knight. Imagine how that must've been for Gaius, but still he remains. That's just the nature of knightly love I guess, utter devotion from near or afar, no matter how...

No matter how complicated it may become.

I stop dead.

This is all getting too complicated...

Complicated.

"Take a scabbard for that blade, Sim, and come with me." Sim quickly does so, looking a bit confused.

"Is there a problem, sir?"

"Nothing that a little chat with the missus won't solve."

Chapter Twenty-Seven
Whipping

Ever been in a situation where, after a while, you realize that nothing adds up quite right? You start to notice the little details, the inconsistencies that, when viewed on their own, don't matter and can easily slide, nothing that you'd give a second thought to, really. But when you consider all of the minor incidents, you get the feeling that it points toward something you've missed.

This is the feeling that I'm getting about my blushing bride.

I knock politely on her door at first, considering that I don't want to tip her off that she's about to be interrogated. After about half a minute, I knock a bit louder, just below that rude banging style of knocking that can only be described as parental. After a few more seconds, the door finally clicks unlocked, and I'm greeted by Jen dressed in a white terrycloth robe that most would think was swiped from a hotel, but the crest of the House is on the right breast of it. Her hair is wet and tied back severely, her face set in a look of annoyance.

"What?"

"Where were you just now?"

She rolls her eyes and motions to the robe. "Where do you think?"

"Were you taking a bath or a shower when you heard me knocking?" I am going somewhere with this. Because how she answers will determine a lot.

"Why do you need to know?" A question answered with a question, that's all I needed to hear.

"Because you just stuck your head under the sink faucet, didn't you? To make me believe you had been in the bath or whatever." She backs into the room, and I follow her. "Because you were doing something else, weren't you?" I grab the bathrobe and pull it open, revealing that she's still wearing clothes underneath. "You didn't have enough time to fully sell it, did you? I want to know what you've been doing, Jen. Now."

She turns away from me and walks toward the bed, and then sits on the mattress. "I can't tell you anything."

"I can figure some of it out. Let's start with the guards, shall we?"

"What about them?"

"How did they find us at Sunset Grove? Sim suggested they might have followed us, but c'mon, no one comes out to the Benedict, much less out to that cemetery. And how would they even know where to look? You knew, though. Because you sent me there. They wouldn't have needed to follow us if you just told them where to go. And those guards were sent by Duke Tremaine. You squired under him up until we were married. You seriously didn't recognize them?" I cross to her, glaring down. "And you swore fealty, didn't you?"

She doesn't answer. One of the downsides to being Fae and not being able to lie, is that you can't produce an enraged denial. If someone's got you cold, you can only stand mute or try to change the subject. That's all.

"This is why you let me call you Jen, isn't it? You told me you hated that name and still you let me go on calling you that.

This is why you wanted to think I was a dick, to make it easier for you to screw me over. But it didn't get easier. It just kept getting more…" I push her chin up to aim her face at mine. "Complicated." I let go of her and look away a second. "You betrayed me, Jen. But you can't tell me a damned thing because you're under oaths, aren't you?"

"Like you aren't, Dick." Jen rises from the bed. "What the hell are you even doing all of this for, huh? Maybe I am looking to screw you, but at least I'm doing it for *something.* What do you stand for? The continuation of the sex industry in your county? The safety of your half-blood servant? Do you have any idea how much of a laughingstock you and your county are? The only thing that makes your House worth marrying into—"

"Is the sword. I know. I'm well aware." I shake my head slowly. "Is that why you were paired up with me? Because if I die the sword goes to you and you can run it back to your master Tremaine like a good lapdog?" I'm rocked to the right, hard, by an open hand.

"Don't you *ever* imply I would call that bastard my master." Her face is pained, the weight of an oath pressing into her lungs, shaping her words. "I despise him, with every mote of my soul."

"But you still have to do as he asks. You swore fealty."

"No. I didn't." Her eyes are wild as she fights through the pain, resisting her oath. "Not to him."

And that…is a direct denial. She can't lie. But she put on that qualifier at the end. She's implying that she swore fealty to *someone,* just not… "You haven't sworn fealty to the duke."

She shakes her head.

"Then…why did you help him? Help his guards? Gods, why did you let them wrap you in iron chain?"

"You wouldn't understand." She looks past me, and her

face softens. “Or...maybe you would.”

I follow her eyes. Simaron is standing in the doorway, the saber now in a proper sheath and attached to his belt. He’s changed his clothes, his finery a little less houseservant and a little more gentleman duelist.

“Your Excellencies, is there anything the matter?” His hands are at his sides, not touching the hilt of the blade. No matter my own suspicions, until Jen outright admits wrongdoing against the House, Sim can’t really take sides.

“Jen, c’mon. Tell me what’s going on. I can’t imagine why anyone would put themselves through what you did for someone you didn’t even swear fealty to.” Jen doesn’t answer. Right, the oaths. I could suggest scenarios all day and she’s not really required to confirm or deny. “Can you tell me why you hate Tremaine so much? We can at least start from a point of common agreement there, right?”

She nods once and walks over to one of the windows near her bed, gazing out at my none-too-impressive county. Dusk passed a few minutes ago, the sky’s varied colors giving way to black. “Why do you hate him, Dick?”

“Because of what he’s done to people I care about. Because it’s a stupid game, really, that we all have to play, and he wants to win at any cost. He’ll hurt anyone who stands in his way, anyone who reminds him of his limitations...”

Jen turns and stares dead at me. There aren’t any words, but I can read her face cold.

You know.

I know what Tremaine’s done to his wife, the abuse he’s heaped upon Duchess Catrin.

It makes sense that Jen would be sore about it, of course, for a *lot* of reasons. High on the list is probably that Duchess Catrin was her lady if she squired under Tremaine. But then, she isn't a squire anymore, she's a Knight of the Realm, much like Simaron is now. I'd assumed that Duke Tremaine had knighted her so she would be elevated high enough for me to marry honorably, but...

"Jen? Who knighted you?"

She doesn't answer.

"It wasn't Tremaine, was it?"

Again, no answer.

"Ye gods, this is starting to make sense." I pull in the little things, make them fit. "You sent me to the mystic. Meaning you had to know beforehand who it was. It's pretty safe to say that mystics don't reveal themselves to just anyone, only people they trust above all others to keep their secret."

Only silence as she turns back to the window. I keep following the evidence.

"When I asked if you'd be moving your handmaiden or squire in, you said you didn't have one. Because the woman you're involved with isn't a handmaiden. Or a squire. And she can hardly pack up and move out to the Benedict, can she?"

"Sir, are you suggesting that Countess Stone is..." Simaron steps deeper into the room.

"I believe her fealty is to the Duchy of Destry Bay." I step closer to her. "Because all she wants to do is protect her lady until her dying breath." Another step. "And she hates Tremaine because it's understandable to despise the person who's abusing the one you love above all others."

Jen turns quickly, her face trembling, her oaths keeping her words in her throat. Her eyes are brimming with tears.

"He's making you do all of this, isn't he? You set me up, or send me off to my death, you become ruler of the county, and you can hand it right over to him, along with everything, and in return he lets you have her, am I right? He stops hurting her?"

Jen nods, just one simple gesture, and her face is immediately cut several times by invisible blades, deep blue blood flowing down her cheek, the cuts forming a terrible Sigil: Oathbreaker.

Simaron immediately produces a handkerchief and presses it to Jen's face as she slumps on the floor, choking off sobs.

"We will all serve that devil his due, Your Excellency, make no mistake of that." He wraps her in his arms, and her face is in his shoulder, streaking his coat with her blood. "We will help your lady find her strength." Simaron looks up at me, almost expectantly, and I slowly kneel, my legs still sore, but thankfully healing quickly. I gently kiss her forehead, it's not much of a gesture, I know, but Sim's kind of got the protective embrace covered for the moment.

"Why do you think I challenged him to a duel, Jen?" I try to smile. "I mean, wouldn't you love to see him cut up and humiliated before the Queen Herself?" I swallow hard. "Maybe it'll give Catrin the confidence she needs to go to the Queen about her husband's abuse, get her to dissolve the marriage. Then she can come here, you two can take care of each other, and if that bastard comes anywhere near the county line, he'll find an army wielding cold iron waiting for him." I gently nudge her shoulder. "Sound good?"

Jen turns slowly to me and shakes her head. "You're insane."

"That would be a solid argument, but no. I'm seeing things a lot more clearly."

She chuckles softly. "You do realize that's what crazy people always say?" She disengages from Sim and stands, still dabbing the cut of her broken oath. "He'll kill you, Dick. He's an asshole, but he's a swordsman. I've never read any of your exploits, and your sword is..." She looks to Sim.

"I am aware of the viscount's current difficulty, Your Excellency." He rises as well to stand near my side. "I will be with him during the duel as his second. I am certain you are well aware that seconds more often than not will become involved in the fighting."

Jen's face goes white. "You can't be his second, Sim."

I step forward. "Jen, at this point, I don't really much care anymore what people think of my opinion of half-bloods. In fact, I plan to show it proudly. It's a stupid attitude and we should set an example." I look to Sim and smile slightly. "Besides, as a newly minted Knight of the Realm he—"

"Just...stop. Before you go any further, Dick." Jen faces me, her arms folded tightly, eyes cast down and to the side, shifting her weight from foot to foot. "Beyond the fact that you made a half-blood a knight..." I can see years of browbeaten prejudice in her eyes railing against the almost casualness of her tone. "Please tell me that you didn't tell Tremaine that Simaron is your second. Tell me you didn't make it official."

I fight to roll my eyes. So what if my reputation takes a hit? Simaron, amazingly, doesn't look insulted at all. In fact, he appears more than a little worried. What, is he worried about his reputation? I seriously doubt that the responsibility and culpability for the situation would fall beyond my own shoulders.

"Why is this an issue, Jen?"

Simaron chooses to answer. "Because she swore fealty to the Duchy of Destry Bay, Your Excellency. No matter who she personally swore it to, her fealty as a Knight of the Realm lies completely with it." Jen nods in assent. I still don't really get it, actually. Sim continues. "Countess Stone was quite eager to conceal what she had been doing before we arrived. Yet she has made no effort to conceal anything in her room. My guess would be a communication with the duchy. Orders, perhaps..." It starts to sink in.

"He called you, that's why you had to leave the room. Your oath demanded that you keep it secret." I remember back to thinking there had been a vibrator in the room. Her cell phone. Gods, I feel stupid. "Tremaine called you with orders..."

I'm staring right at it, I know I am.

She swore fealty to the duchy, and she froze up when she discovered that Simaron would be my second. Sim mentioned that seconds often become involved in duels. But, seconds are only limited to dueling each other and...

"Or he called you with a decree." I stare at Jen. "He decreed that you would be his second for the duel, didn't he?"

"Yes." The cut on her face starts bleeding fresh again, and she lifts the damp kerchief to staunch the wound. She can break oaths now, freely. No one will ever trust her. She could tell Tremaine to eat shit and die if she wanted, but she won't. Her loyalty isn't to him, it's to Catrin, and as long as she's under his thumb, Jen won't risk anything that'll cause her pain. "I'm sorry, Simaron."

The moment the duel begins, I suspect, Tremaine will goad Simaron into making a move, he'll find a way. Hell, just being half-blood will be all the reason Tremaine needs to send Jen after him to avenge his ever-so-slighted honor. And I can make it all go away if I simply back out, acknowledge him as the superior opponent, severely humiliate myself in front of the Queen, and give him everything he wants. If I don't?

My wife and the man I love will be forced to duel to the death.

Chapter Twenty-Eight
Daughter

"Couldn't you just, like, refuse to fight if he tells you to go after Sim?" I look between Jen and Sim, trying to not envision the possible outcomes of a swordfight between them. "I mean, this could work to our advantage, right?"

Jen quickly shakes her head, and braces herself, pressing a clean kerchief to her face. "He has Catrin. If he finds out I'm taking actions against him he'll set his goblins on her and—"

"Speaking of goblins." I look at her. "Sorry to interrupt, I know Catrin's important, but about the goblins. Particularly the ones who attacked us on our wedding night?"

She sighs.

"They knew we were coming, huh?" What better way to get me to trust her, right? Make a good first impression? "So why did they bail and think I was an impostor?"

"They thought *I* was an impostor. Goblins aren't good with our faces, unless they get real familiar. They were there to sell it, yeah, but..." She winces, dabbing the brand on her face again as it bleeds fresh. "But when you burst out of the carriage with your sword *not* blazing... Well, I was supposed to be escorting you, the Custodian of the Azure Blade, remember? And if you're supposedly an impostor, then it followed in their soft heads that I must've been as well. So they bailed and reported back to Tremaine. As a result, he trusted me even less. I stood mute when he questioned me about the sword, later. I figured you didn't want anyone to know."

Holy shit. She actually went to bat for me. Still, and I don't know why I'm asking this, but I have to know.

"Why?"

"Why?"

"Yeah, why did you cover for me? I mean, the whole deal is to screw me over and get the sword for Tremaine, right? Why not tell him that the sword doesn't favor me anymore? He'd have a damned field day with that." I take a seat. "Do you like me or something? I mean that in purely a platonic sense."

"You weren't what I was expecting, okay? That's how this all got so messed up. I thought you'd be some lecher with no self-control and no regard for protocol and generally a dick." She shrugs. "That's what my mother went on and on about when the marriage was announced, at least." Always nice to know the opinion of me out on the Emerald Shores.

"But we got to know each other and realized it wasn't as bad as we were expecting. And it all went to hell."

"Pretty much." She flips the kerchief over to dab it against her cheek again.

"And he's aware that you're wavering."

"That's why I can't try to pull anything with him at the tournament, Richard. If I refuse to act, he'll signal his man in the crowd, who will give the kill order, and then she'll..." She swallows hard, closing her eyes for a moment, her face a conflict of emotions, rage and tears. "He'll blame the murder on the goblins, feign innocence, and round up a blood hunt on all goblins in the City to avenge his dear wife..." She looks away. "And he'll probably take me as his wife afterward, since you'll more than likely be dead by the end of it. And of course, since all your lands and possessions will belong to me…" Jen shakes her head ruefully. "You get the idea."

"Well…I doubt he'd take you as his wife, considering…" I tap my cheek, the same where her brand is, and she bites her lip in reply. "Listen, you fucked up, I fucked up."

She looks at me incredulously. "*I* fucked up? I'm not the one who challenged a master swordsman to a duel to the death!"

"First of all, it's to first blood." Jen rolls her eyes in reply, and I get in her face. "Second of all, I guess I can see your concern. I mean, I *did* put your life in serious danger by making a deal with a treacherous abusive bastard just so I could have a shot at saving someone important to me. Maybe you could give me some pointers on how to live with the guilt?"

Okay, low blow, I know. But she can't play innocent in this. I'm not going to throw her to the wolves or anything, but I'm not happy.

"Jen, our problem is not each other right now, it's Tremaine. I see a lot of outcomes and all of them are bad, except for one. If Tremaine goes down, we all get out of this alive and okay." I shrug playfully, trying to decrease the tension. "So I guess we've got to win."

"As it appears right now, you and I will be cut to ribbons, Your Excellency." Sim steps toward me to further dampen the mood. "I have no doubt of His Grace's swordsmanship, and Her Excellency's reputation with a blade does precede her, somewhat. Armed with a saber, I would stand little chance against her." He sighs roughly. "And there is still the matter of the demon. Of all the times for your blade to abandon you, sir, this is…"

Right. It sucks. I'm ready to move past it, and finding the

demon, finally, seems to be the best method for doing that. I need to drop in on Casey, but be quiet-like about it. I hate to think this about my wife, considering she became that way on *my* account, but she is an Oathbreaker. Nothing to keep her from trading the commune for Catrin. From my side, it's abhorrent, yes. From her side? Well, I have to consider all of the things I'd be willing to do for Sim and his safety. It appears that true love is a dream that can quickly turn as vicious as the Nightmare.

I take a moment to stretch, my muscles and bones groaning in protest, but I'm still in much better shape than I was. "We can sit here and talk all day about how we're going to lose everything and how it'll all turn into a death scene of Shakespearean proportions, or we can get moving and do what we can to find an outcome that's a tad more acceptable to all of us."

"How exactly do you plan to do that, Dick?" There's no negativity in her voice. I'd almost say there's a bit of hope in there.

"I'll figure it out. I'm the viscount of these shores, and I'm not going down without a fight." Jen stifles a chuckle, and I glare at her for interrupting my attempt at a noble moment. "What?"

Oh. Right. Going down without a fight.

"Yes, yes, get in your little porn digs while you can." I roll my eyes, but throw in a grin. "At least I got a laugh out of you, right? And to show your gratitude for that..." Jen arches a brow as she looks at me, probably expecting something lewd. "I need to borrow your bike."

"What are you, some kind of idiot?"

Hope is, as I suspected, none too pleased with how things are going.

Simaron gives her an aggravated clearing of his throat, and she sets her jaw in annoyance.

“Fine, I apologize. I meant to ask if my lord possibly went to school on the short bus?” She holds up her hands in mock surrender. “No, wait, even those kids would look down on you. You challenged him to a duel and put all our asses on the line?”

I shrug slightly. “Did I stutter?”

Hope dragged us to a dark and quiet spot the moment I started spouting off the terms of the duel, probably to prevent panic, or possibly an assassination attempt. I’m still getting dirty looks from people, honestly.

“Hope, His Excellency knows what he is doing.” Simaron is dressed as he was back at the manor. Luckily I was calm enough to just let my Fae grace handle the driving, because I have practically no idea how to ride a Harley. Simaron steps closer to her, his eyes sincere. “There is a chance to settle things once and for all here, to give our people a real home, to stop running.”

Actually, I’m pretty sure there isn’t, that’s just wishful thinking, but there’s an upside of being half-blood—being able to lie, tell people what they need and want to hear. Granted, should I somehow manage to survive all of this, I’ll have to do what I can to make that supposition into truth.

“I’m here to see Casey, though. Would she be okay with a visit from me?” I reach into my coat and take out a candy bar I stopped to pick up on the way. Something with nuts and nougat. (Whatever the hell that is, does anyone really know?) Probably not the best thing to give to a kid, but hey, I’m not her parent. I’m allowed to spoil her. Hope, however, responds to the sight of the candy bar with an exasperated groan, not appreciating the situation in which I'll be putting her.

"She's been asking after you for days." A pause of several seconds. "You doing all right? The accident, I mean?" Wow, actual concern for my well-being?

"I'll be fine. I'm pretty good right now. Just sore." I motion toward Casey's shack. "So...it's okay?" I receive a nod in return.

Simaron claps my shoulder as if to send me off. "I can wait here, Richard." It's new and nice to have him treat me like a regular guy, though I'm certain this will end the moment we're back out in the real world.

As I walk toward the shack, the hushed conversation begins behind me. Even though I'm not looking, I imagine Hope has grabbed Sim by the ear with a look on her face that would threaten an end to television and phone privileges until the end of the school year.

"Simaron Arthur Gray, you had *damned* well better explain why you're wearing a knight's blade..."

"You like roses now, don't you?" Casey is smiling warmly, sitting cross-legged in front of a camping lantern, a few of her dolls strewn about around her, experiments in braiding evident in their hair. "You're still a narcissus, but you want to share your garden."

"Anyone ever tell you you've got the cryptic thing down pat, kid?" I produce the candy bar, which she practically snatches from my hand with a high-pitched squeal of glee. She sets to attacking the confection with tiny ferret-like gnaws, only stopping every few seconds to make mmm-ing sounds with more than a little exaggeration. I just let her eat, watch her. I can't remember ever enjoying something as much as she is right now.

After finishing, she motions to her dolls proudly, all of them having almost-comical attempts at a French braid. Still, not bad for a first-timer. "I want the other one you told me about."

"The warrior's braid?"

She nods excitedly. "That one. That one!"

"Well, there are various kinds. It depends, actually. Different warriors braid in different ways, if they chose to keep their hair long at all." I reach over and muss up her hair a bit. "For one of them, I'd actually have to tie several braids and use oils and some sticky stuff to make them all stand on end."

"You're making that up!" She's grinning though, sitting calmly, eyes fully on me.

"Nope, in fact, one of the Houses outside the City practices that. Their women are among the best archers among the Fae, and they believe braiding their hair that way makes their shots never miss." I nod once before she protests. "It's true. I'm inclined to believe it as well. Only the Sunleaves have more skill, but that's always under dispute."

"What about your family?"

"My father tied charms in his hair. My mother…" I stop for a moment. How do I explain it? Do I tell her how my mother braided her hair? Do I tell her of the elaborate three-foot braid, decorated with Sigil medallions that clinked together softly? I can only imagine it now. I never saw the ritual, but I see it in my dreams. The way she cut through it with a cold-iron dagger, and the heavy thump of the braid hitting the floor a few seconds before her body did. I always wake up angry. "My mother…"

But she wasn't my mother, was she?

"She ties it very simply, when she wears one at all. My mother has had to fight for her honor but once. She has a champion. A noble knight."

She grins big. "Like Prince Charming?"

I shake my head slowly. "No, but he protects her all the same. He cares for her very much, that's why he keeps her safe." I really should be asking about the demon, I know, but... "Kind of like how Hope protects you, because she cares about you very much."

"Would you?"

"Yes. Yes I would." Why did I say that? I barely know this kid. Felt good to say though. And the smile that's on her face...

"No matter what?" She sounds almost worried, her hands fidgeting. "Even if you didn't want to?"

"Casey, what's wrong?" Oh shit, is the commune compromised? Has she been coerced into something?

"I can't find the demon."

"Shit." I wince immediately, forgetting my language. The magnitude of my misstep is only amplified as Casey makes small sputters of breath, her head down, shoulders hunched, starting to sniffle. "Casey, sweetie, it's all right if you couldn't find him. It's a really big city. Obviously you're not going to find one creature in a crowd of several million. There might not even be flowers where it is."

I'm completely screwed and I'm doing everything I can to remain calm and console her. I'm right though, it's not her fault, and it *was* a lot to ask of her and...

Damn, look at me grow.

Maybe Catrin could give me a hint if the Fates are willing, because if I don't find and kill that thing before the solstice...

"No." Casey sniffles softly. "I can't find it because it's already dead. The calla lilies heard it from the white chrysanthemums, and they never lie."

I still have no idea what that means, but...

"You're certain? It's the demon I told you, the same one?"

"The demon Terrach was slain just before the vernal dawn, by the hand of the daffodil queen." I give her a dubious look, and she looks at me quite crossly. "That's what the chrysanthemum said, they never lie."

I am so screwed.

For the moment, I'm going to accept the edited version of what she's told me: the demon is dead and has been for almost three months (as I can only guess that the "vernal dawn" was the Spring Equinox). My entire redeem-myself-to-the-sword plan was dependent on slaying the demon that killed my father. If the demon's dead, then either I need to do something else or I'm proper fucked. Would've been nice if Catrin had filled me in on this and I wouldn't have wasted the last few days. Granted, she didn't tell me directly that I had to kill the demon. She asked me leading questions and let me assume the answers were prophetic.

I'd be plenty pissed at her if I didn't know that Tremaine was pulling the strings and making her do things under threat of violence. That guy really needs to die.

"I'm sorry." Casey's sniffling again, more fervently. "I didn't want to make you mad." I can see the tears slipping down her face in the lantern light. I take a deep breath and pull her to me, my arms keeping her in a warm embrace.

"It's okay, Casey, don't cry." I stroke her hair slowly, knowing that it absolutely is not okay, but I have to be strong for her, not let her believe that it's her fault. I know in my heart she did everything she could. "It'll be all right. I'll figure something out. It's better that you told me. You did good."

I reach into my coat pocket and take out a fresh kerchief, dab her eyes dry. I force a smile, and turn her around slowly, let my fingers work through her hair. "Now let's get you that warrior's braid, okay?"

After a minute the sniffling sounds slow, then stop while I weave the braid in her hair. This could very well be the last braid I ever give her, seeing as I could be dead not too long from now. Best I do it right, after all. It won't solve anything, it won't bring me any closer to proving myself to Mercia or her sword. Hell, that I'm spending so much time with half-bloods probably pisses her off tenfold, but Simaron was right. I do have a responsibility here. I owe it to them, all of them. I am their viscount, their protector, whether it's to defend the county from demons, or the commune from discovery, or even a little girl from having to grow up too fast.

Noblesse oblige.

I'm sorry, Dad. I never got it until now.

Chapter Twenty-Nine
Immortality

In the end I gave her a simple braid, for a Fae noble, at least. Similar to the braid my father would have before he went out to hunt, during his wild days when he kept his hair long, before I was born. Tight, keeping the hair from the eyes in an almost severe fashion, adorned with simple charms for good luck and a safe journey. He gave me the same braid when I was young. I used pennies for the charms in Casey's braid, scratching Sigils in the copper. Maybe they'll work, since I'm a mystic, but I couldn't make any promises.

She's asleep, and since I don't know where to go, I haven't left the shack yet. Might as well stand guard over her while I try to figure things out. I actually sang her to sleep, just a couple of the slower songs from the Pearl Jam catalog, but she went to her dreams regardless. I could feel it, you know, the magic in my voice, flowing out of me, carried on my breath and seeking only to calm her, the silver fire that had been so fierce when it emerged before just a calming light, warm and comforting.

Suddenly the idea of having a child doesn't seem so alien. Not producing an heir, having a child.

"It would be an interesting family, to say the least." It appears my illustrious ancestor has deigned to grace me with his presence again.

"What do you want, Rem?"

"Same thing as before, nothing's changed." When I look up he's dressed similarly to me. "Granted, I'm not the one who needed to change."

I grumble softly under my breath. "How am I supposed to protect them, Rem? I lost the sword's power, I'm an embarrassment to my family and I'll probably be stripped of my title at best after that duel with Tremaine."

"Save the first part of your statement, that sounded like a rote recitation. Do you care at all about your title, your family?" He's kneeling next to her now, looking her over.

I glare at him, because yelling would wake Casey up. "You know I do. I need all of that or I can't help them." I roll my shoulders. "But the nobles of the City will see that I'm shamed the second I draw the Azure Blade and it doesn't burn. It won't matter if I win, not that I could. The blade's a paperweight in my hands and there's no way it could stand up to the Adamant Heart. I don't know if it could if I wasn't shamed." When I look at Rem, he's smiling, almost smugly. "What?"

"The Azure Blade. Quite a pretty name for it, considering..."

"Considering...what?"

"Well, I certainly didn't call it that. It was, if you remember, my sword, until Mercia decided she deserved it more." He stays where he is, waiting almost patiently.

"Ye gods, get on with the story, okay?" No answer, but Casey stirs softly, so I hush my voice. "Fine, what did you call the sword?"

Rem leans in close and whispers in Sigil. "*Rain Cutter.*" I give him a look, and he smiles proudly. "I wanted a blade sharp enough to cleave a raindrop in twain without splattering it. And I succeeded in forging it." I roll my eyes at him, which earns a finger wag before he continues. "You would be amazed how many conflicts and needless bloodshed you can avoid if your opponent is made aware how overmatched he is."

"Bullshit. The blade has never been that sharp."

"Of course it hasn't, not for you. You've been calling it by the wrong name for millennia now." Rem practically snickers. "You've all been pronouncing yourselves as unworthy of it every time you draw it." I blink.

I know that's important, what he said. I need to ask the right question. The sword has a different name, that needs to be invoked in Sigil, and that every time a Fae draws the blade, it shows the bearer as unworthy...

"Rem? How does the blade show its disapproval?"

He smiles. "Did you know that for the longest time, it was believed that witches and demons and other creatures of evil could be identified purely by how fires burned in their presence? It's a belief that's resurfaced several times over the course of the varied histories of this world, even in my time. Do you know what silver magic means, descendant?"

I shake my head, of course. Magic's magic, in my opinion, and it's generally bad and best left to Ra'Keth. "It's bad for weres?"

"It means the magic was freely given and received, without bloodshed or dishonor. Simply put, it was earned, usually in a virtuous fashion, also possibly through hereditary means. Azure magic, well...it identifies the sorcerer as a soul-thief, a murderer." He smiles again. "And when my lovely Fae concubine decided she didn't need me anymore, I didn't have the highest opinion of her, or her descendents."

Another puzzle piece. "So the Azure Blade burns with blue fire because..."

"It's proclaiming you to the world as a murderer, yes. All of the Fae are in some way related to me now, thanks to your centuries of inbreeding. Granted, I only consider those who are directly descended from me to be part of my House, those such as you. The sword cares little for such distinctions, though, so it will burn a treacherous blue for all."

"All but me." I stare at the ghost. "All but *me*. It doesn't do anything for me. Why?"

Rem leans in closely. "Whose approval do you truly believe you require to wield that blade, Richard? While it was indeed tragic that your father died fighting a demon, do you really believe I care one way or the other if he killed it? He accomplished his purpose, at least in my eyes."

"He had children, to continue your line." I stare at him. "That's what I am to you? A means to continuing your bloodline?"

Rem laughs softly. "Richard, that is the purpose of all life, you'll soon find out, to survive as long as possible. I have no real agenda, because my enemies are long dead and forgotten, and I have no issue with their descendents, save my own."

"But...the sword stopped burning after I was with Simaron. That doesn't make any sense, how can I continue the line if I'm with a guy?"

He motions to Casey, and I instinctively put myself between him and her, even though he's a phantasm of my mind. Rem nods once. "You see? Right there. *That* is the reason you are breaking free." I keep my position.

"I don't get it."

"Caring for this child, putting her needs before your own, and suddenly the idea of being a father yourself wasn't so repulsive, was it? Before this, before you forged your connection with Simaron, your children would have simply been heirs, yes? Someone to continue on the line, be a good Fae noble and play the grand game and hopefully marry up to a nicer title?"

I want to eventually have a child, not produce an heir. Actually have a son or daughter and raise them not to be a proper Fae noble or play the game right, but to impart the lessons I've so recently learned, to make them aware of the responsibilities they will carry, to not wall themselves off or hide from their obligations, to know when doing what was right was more important than protocol. Simaron was a part of that, as was Jen, and Catrin, and my mother, and Sim's mother, and Casey, and...

"This is why you approve of me? Because I finally started having paternal instincts? Because I want to protect the people I care about?" I look down at Casey and wonder if I'd have a daughter, imagine the paths her life would take her. Or a son, and if he would turn out like me or take after my father. "I still don't understand."

"What are you willing to give for them, Richard?" He gestures to the world beyond the door of the shack. "Not just her, nor Simaron, but all who live in your county. What of your wife and her lover? What would you give to keep them safe? To spare them pain? A few days ago, I assure you, you would have let them suffer, as it was their own problem to solve. You would've been content to continue as you were, maintaining your own status quo."

"Are you telling me that if I knew what was being done to Catrin, I wouldn't have taken action?" Since I can't reply the way I want to, I just show him a famous hand gesture instead.

"A few days ago you wouldn't have bothered to find out. This has obviously been going on for a while, and had you been vigilant, you might've noticed. I'm sure many have, but say nothing for fear of getting involved in something they feel is not their affair. You, and your wife, did choose to get involved." Rem paces slowly around the small room. "The difference between you and your wife is that you are willing to sacrifice yourself to save the duchess, whereas in the beginning your wife was content to let you suffer. Granted, it can be argued that she was only doing it to protect her lover, and her outlook has changed, as you've discovered."

"That why the sword lit for her?"

"She was aiding in a plot to end my line. Of course I wanted all to see her for what she was. Unfortunately Mercia and her descendents did too well a job of spinning their shame into a badge of honor. Thus, my approval of you will be seen as a humiliation."

I look at him. "So I never had to kill the demon."

"As you've learned, it's already dead. I'm certain Mercia would ask you to find another to slay, but as I've stated, her opinion matters little."

"And it didn't occur to you to tell me this?" I grit my teeth. "I mean, that's just..." I look down at Casey again and flip off my forebear once more.

"Much as with your discovery of your true parentage, do you truly believe you would have accepted that? That it was my approval you needed? Remember, I was your hated and despicable soul-drinking ancestor, Deathsinger of the Northern Wastes, just a few days ago. I believe when it was suggested that you prove yourself to me you were ready to let the House fall before considering such a thing. You jested that I would have you murder gods and lay countrysides to waste to win my favor. How quickly things change in the midst of interesting times, wouldn't you say?"

"All right, maybe you have a little point there." Asshole. "So what, I'm an okay guy in your book now? Doesn't exactly help me, seeing as you're not the one who decides the duel. When I draw that sword, it'll ruin me and your House, and then your line is done."

"Truly? Your people merely need to see it lit ablaze, do they not? You are well aware how to make this happen without any aid from me."

Right. Because I'm a mystic. I can sing a few lines of "Spin the Black Circle" in Sigil and have the sword light up the arena with an argent conflagration. Only one problem with that.

"I'd kind of reveal myself as a mystic, you know. They could very well strip my title for that, or at least find a reason to. Plus it'd all be moot anyway, considering they're expecting an azure flame, not a silver one."

Rem smiles, showing some teeth. "One of your titles is Custodian of the Azure Blade, yes? A responsibility that only your line can carry? What better way to show your House's singular ability to wield it than by showing a talent no others possess?"

"Well..." Shit, he's kind of got me there. I mean, I can do this because of my bloodline, though not the one everyone's thinking of. I might not even be suspected of being a mystic, as long as I'm not too forthcoming with explanations. "Okay, maybe I could do that."

"It appears you have the matter well in hand, then, Richard." Rem starts toward the door, as if to signify our time together is over.

"Wait. Before you go. What's the real reason?"

He turns to face me. "Beg pardon?"

"Why is it so important to you that your line goes on? Is it just for a form of immortality? Because that doesn't hold up on its own. There's got to be something else, right?" For a moment I see his features soften, and his image shimmers, and he's dressed in casual attire no more, rather in simple robes of deep gray and slashes of blue. His hair is longer, tied back loosely with a bit of leather cord, his face marked with Sigil that glows with a silver light. In his hands he holds a sword, my family's sword, Rain Cutter as he named it, the blade stained red, dripping blood that vanishes before it hits the dirt floor.

"You know the tales of my kind, of course. You must have heard the stories of me, of the things I've done. While I can claim that many of the atrocities attributed to my name are false, or gross exaggeration, enough of them are true to weigh on my soul, even over millennia. There are times I wonder where I am, descendant. Am I languishing in Tartarus, awaiting judgment? Flagellating myself in the deeper circles of hell for my crimes until I feel I have suffered enough? Lingering in some limbo or lost in some world long since cut off from the loom of Fate? What I do know is that while the sins of the father do not always become those of the son and grandson, and so forth, the possibility exists to make amends, to return something to the world from which I have taken. If your actions can redeem the House of Stone even to a modest degree, to make this grand world a bit worthier of saving, then perhaps my existence, in the end, was indeed for the greater good."

Holy shit.

"What did you do, Rem?"

His eyes close for a moment, and he looks away from me. "Do you know why your race often takes it upon itself to hunt demons, Richard? Has it ever been explained to you, outside a rote answer that they are evil and must be destroyed? What I have done to you, to my Fae, my living dreams..." He almost trembles, his image shimmering again.

I feel a dread slipping over me, icy and slick. Somewhere deep inside me, I know exactly what he's speaking of, but I refuse to let myself see it.

"The gods were still young then. And we, the Ra'Keth, were still confident of victory over them. Some created weres, others made the walking dead you call the vampyr, and some of us..." His face loses its strength. "You have to understand, I never thought it would go that far."

"Rem." I don't want to know. But I have to. I need to. "Please, tell me what you did."

"The Nightmare. I taught you all how to find it, to ride it, to make its strength your own. But some of you, you became lost to it. You fought so well, even the gods themselves, even other Ra'Keth feared you, and I thought if I let it happen once I could fix it later and make it up to you all but it was a war and you need to understand that..."

"You're rambling, Rem. Cut to the end. What did you do?"

"The demons. They were Fae."

The world stops.

"You made us into demons?" I don't know if I can move. "Demons? You made us into *demons*?" I would give anything to strike him right now, to... "That's why Mercia killed you."

"It was one of the reasons. The reason she gave, at least, but she rode the Nightmare all the same when she struck me down with my own blade. I took my living dreams and turned them into... My anger, my violence, I made you all understand it, use it, make it your own. That's why I need to keep the line going, Richard, to make amends to you all for this. Purge the Nightmare forever from you, from the world, return you to the beautiful dreams you once were. I know you don't want to help me."

I put my hands over Casey's ears. "You're goddamned right I don't want to fucking help you, asshole. But I'm not doing any of this for your guilty conscience. My county and family are threatened. I'll do what I can to protect them. The demons are a danger to our kingdom and the world at large, so I will fight against them. That is my responsibility and I will be honored to do it, but *never* believe that it will be for you."

I take a moment to breathe, pushing down the tendrils of rage that are creeping up through me, the Nightmare beckoning from the back of my mind, seeming even more repulsive than before. "Just go. Okay? I'm going to do this with or without your approval. It's good you want to redeem yourself, but I can't make up for what you've done. All I can do is try to clean up your mess."

I take my hands from Casey's ears, and she stirs again, nearly waking, but then settles down. I think she's dreaming, hopefully about nothing bad.

When I look up, Rem is gone. I expected that, honestly, but I thought him capable of some manner of parting shot.

"Is everything all right in here, Richard?" Simaron comes to my side, kneels by Casey. "Is she hurt?"

"No, asleep. I was...just working some things out. We should get back home. We've got a big day coming up. Might as well be rested and ready for it, right?" My arms are around him before I think twice, and I hold Simaron close to me. The world has become a little darker for me, and I need a light to guide my way.

Chapter Thirty
Yellow Ledbetter

"If only Kendrick were alive, he would prevent this lunacy."

I am in the backseat of a carriage, pulled by four of Tolon Wood's finest stallions, on loan from the stables of the forest god himself. The flags of the duchy are flying from the sides, the coachman dressed formally. Her Grace, Duchess Cadwyn, is seated across from me in her solstice gown, rich in verdant greens to show her connection to the Sunleaves. Her husband, His Grace, Duke Madoc, a svelte-looking sidhe with pale green skin, black hair, luminous green eyes, and dressed in subdued colors, is seated next to her. A purely political marriage, they both know it. A trophy husband, if you want to be blunt about it. No children, unless you count me, and we aren't, not in this scenario.

Granted, the fact that Duke Madoc has been ogling me for the last thirty minutes hardly inspires confidence in his desire to produce heirs. What can I say? Some of us are encouraged to prefer same-sex, and some of us preferred it all along.

"Well, I had to be in the tournament anyway, right?" I try a roguish grin, one that usually works in my films, but my mother obviously isn't working off a script. "Anyway, Dad hated Tremaine too. Or at least he certainly would have, if he knew what he was about."

"Do you realize the position you are putting me in? The damage you are risking not only to yourself, but me?"

"This your way of saying you don't have any faith in me?" There's a pause, and Uncle Madoc chooses this moment to find something outside the window incredibly interesting and worthy of his complete and undivided attention. I wish Sim were here, but he's being driven to the arena by Sir Gaius. I would assume that things are just about as comfortable in that car as they are in this carriage. "I can do it, okay?"

"Ricky, you didn't think this through—"

"You know, I've been hearing that since this all started and—"

"And now this time you will listen! You have no contingencies, no alliances to fall back on, no oaths or boons or favors you can call into play. You should never enter into an arrangement like this without complete knowledge that you will be successful no matter the outcome."

Play the game, essentially.

"Tremaine agreed to the same deal. I don't hear you chewing his ass out."

"Richard!" Madoc's eyes are on me, fixed in a glare. "You will mind your language when speaking to your betters. Especially when speaking to your mother."

The carriage moves in dead silence for a few seconds until he almost gleefully smirks at her. My mother stares at him in shock. "Oh come now, Cadwyn, it doesn't take a seer to figure it out. Put some breasts on the boy and he's you at that age. And don't admonish him too badly. No one in the court truly believed your little coup with the forest god was going to pay off as well as it did."

"Madoc?" Her voice is stumbling to regain its composure. I imagine a figure skater who just bounced her ass off the ice and tries to skate on like nothing happened. "I'm..."

He takes her hand and nods once. "Be at ease, my wife. I can keep a secret as well as you. Honestly? It's a relief there's an heir. I've been able to concentrate on...other pursuits." Uncle Madoc winks at her with an almost leer, and she shakes her head, a bit of color filling her pale face. He then turns toward me. "And you, Richard, should listen to your mother. Tremaine didn't agree to a duel, he goaded you into one, I'll bet. The duke is an excellent swordsman. I'm sure he sees you as no threat. And this way, he can take everything he wants from you without any public scandal whatsoever. Well-played on his part."

"Unless I win." I don't sound as sure of that as I did when I woke up this morning in Sim's arms, gently nibbling on his ear. Gods, to have that every morning...

"I assure you, Richard, that 'unless' has never entered Tremaine's mind. Your reputation is well known in court, especially your, ah...chosen career? This is expected to be a rout, my..." He chuckles lightly. "Well, now that the cat's out of the bag, I would suppose I'm your stepfather, yes? Regardless, the odds favoring you are quite long."

"They're taking *bets*?"

"Only among the commoners, but I know for a fact several nobles have placed wagers through intermediaries. Sovereign to sovereign is on him killing you within the first three minutes." He leans in conspiratorially. "I hear tell the Queen Herself placed quite a hefty wager with the Crown Prince."

The Crown Prince of the Fae isn't as impressive a title as it sounds. Technically, the Crown Prince is the heir to the throne, but the Queen has borne many sons, all of whom try to kill each other off. Her Majesty has made no effort to stop them or shown any intention of stepping down. The current Crown

Prince only became so a few months ago, after the previous heir was found dead and rotting at Sunset Grove.

Madoc gets a light in his eyes as he continues, "And their bets were *not* similar. The terms are unknown, as well as who the wagers are on, but all the talk in court has been choosing sides."

I blink. "You're kidding."

"You've chosen to make a spectacle, Ricky." Cadwyn's voice has recovered from its stumble, regained its poise. "A viscount against a duke? On one of our most sacred days, before the assembled court? You could set a precedent, cause many comfortable in their power to become worried, make those upset with their station seek to improve it through violent means. We cannot afford another era of bloodshed rearranging titles and lands and ending Houses. There are simply not enough of us."

"So even if I win, I could screw up everything." The dread weight starts to sink in.

Cadwyn shakes her head. "You should've come to me, with everything. Given time we could have handled this civilly, Ricky."

"No, you don't know what he's doing, what he's *really* doing. Someone has to stop him, and if protocol gets screwed up, then to hell with protocol. Someone needs to do what's *right*." I take my mother's hand. "Please. Trust me. I need to do this. This isn't revenge anymore. He's hurt so many, please." I swallow hard. "Tell me you'll support me."

Madoc bursts out with laughter, my mother giving him a fierce glare that does nothing to quell him. After a few seconds he wipes his eyes with a finger.

"Oh, Richard, that was priceless." I scrunch up my face in confusion, because I don't really see the humor here. "Trust me, stepson, your mother supports you fully."

"Madoc, please." She looks out the window, her face covered by her hand.

"Oh come now, Cadwyn, you weren't even subtle about it. Sir Gaius placed a wager of five *hundred* sovereigns on young Richard here, and unless you plan to accuse your captain of the guard of stealing half the duchy's treasury, it's rather obvious who arranged it."

She turns to face him, her face a strained banner. "*Five hundred?* He told me he emptied the coffers."

Madoc smiles merrily. "Of course he did, my bride." He then looks out the window again. "After all, I'd already bet the other half." He winks in my direction. "Do try to swing for the head, stepson. I get nine-to-one if you kill him."

Considering where I work, and the class of the people who I work with, I'm aware of many things that would normally be considered beneath a nobleman's notice when it comes to the culture of the City. The first and foremost of these things is professional sports. For the longest time I believed that City was under attack from all manner of creatures such as dragons and tigers and wolves, until I was made aware that the City has a football and basketball franchise.

There's a definite attraction to it, I suppose, getting caught up in the mob mentality, losing your individual voice to become part of the raucous chorus that can only speak in emotional highs and lows, in rage and ecstasy.

I also became aware of the morbid fascination with injuries, secretly wishing that opponents would stumble and fall and, of course, be fine as long as their recovery took the rest of the season. I suppose that's where we Fae get it, the strange thirst for violence that only the tournaments can quench. Whether we're in the arena, fighting for our lives or simply in the stands investing our cheers in one side or the other, we want to see blood, and at the end of the day, we're exhausted. Father once told me that the tournaments are the closest we will ever come to embracing the Nightmare.

Knowing what I know now, if I'm to lend Rem any credence, it will only make the scene all the more chilling. An opportunity to free our demons, to let them nearly emerge. What sort will I be facing out there?

The arena is the very same one where the aforementioned basketball franchise puts on its show. Luckily, we're in the off-season so the building is open to be rented out for the right price and influence, and we Fae can be quite good at influence when we need to be. There's plenty of security outside when the carriage arrives, making sure that only a certain class of people are allowed through the doors. To the humans this is probably some exclusive charity event, considering how many beautiful people are arriving in limos.

No decoration outside, though. No banners welcoming anyone. Despite the attention we're bound to attract, it doesn't mean we're going to advertise.

"Count Stone!" A valet helps me out of the carriage. He's dressed in formal attire, wearing the colors of the Summersword House, a royal servant. Despite my title, I'll be expected to give his requests the same weight as those of Her Majesty's. "If you'll please follow me?"

I nod deferentially and then bow deeply to my mother, to my uncle, well, stepfather. We're outside the carriage now, appearances must be kept. Cadwyn is struggling to keep calm, and I know she wants to do something, anything to show her love, as the next time she sees me, it could be my death. Not wanting to prolong the moment any longer and make it even more difficult for her, I turn to follow the valet. "Has my second arrived?"

"He has, Your Excellency. Your sword and armor await you." There's a slight pause as we pass security with little more than a nod from the two guards, and we cross into the building, the grand lobby looking so out of place considering what's going by. You hardly expect to walk by a gift shop and a place that sells eight-dollar corn dogs an hour before a duel to the death. We move toward more nondescript doors that lead into the less-pretty innards of the arena. No one about, save the guards. "Her Majesty requested I give her regards, Count Stone."

I stop dead. "Excuse me?"

The valet turns, looking at me oddly. "Is there a problem, Count Stone?"

"The Queen *Herself* sent regards...to me?" Holy shit...

The valet arches a brow. "You would take issue, Count Stone?"

"No!" I regain my composure, kind of. "No, no, not at all. I'm honored, please send my warmest regards in return, and my deepest thanks. I am humbled that she would think of me."

His arched brow drops. "But of course." He then continues his escort, and I follow.

Perhaps I should tell you just how big a deal that is.

The Queen, well, doesn't give a shit about the fringe. The Benedict Shores matter little to the Kingdom of Rainbows. Destry Bay on the other hand, does. That Her Royal Majesty would send regards to a lowly pissant like me? And that those regards were *not* ironically accompanied by a dagger in my back?

"I realize it's not any of my business, but..."

"No, Count Stone." A slight smile on his face. "Her Majesty

felt her regards to Destry Bay would be simply assumed, so she elected not to formally send them. Since this is your first participation in the tournament, however, she felt it only civil to send regards."

And that is just about the biggest possible middle finger the throne could give to Duke Tremaine. She sent regards to me. She *didn't* send regards to my opponent. Oh, to see his face. However, I fear Her Majesty only aggravated the situation. I would guess that the last thing you want to do is make an abusive person feel angry and humiliated, and this will easily do both.

"Again, please send my thanks." Nothing I can do about it though. I can't exactly tell the Queen to extend him that courtesy. That would only make the situation worse for me, as telling the Queen how to do her job would be an insult.

I'm taken to the visitors' locker room, the walls painted in the home team's colors of green and gold. My armor is on a stand, polished to a mirror sheen, my sword on a small table that would normally hold the pregame buffet, I'd wager. Simaron is seated on a bench, wearing studded leather armor, dyed a deep slate gray. His saber is leaning against the bench next to him.

The valet stops at the doorway. "Will you be requiring anything, Your Excellency?" It feels odd to hear that in the same room as Sim and not hear it from him. I shake my head and the valet leaves the room, closing the doors behind him. We are, for the moment, alone.

"Any trouble getting here, Sim?"

Simaron shrugs slightly, standing, stretching, the leather tight against his body and messing with my concentration. "I received quite a talking to from Sir Gaius about my conduct, but the trip was otherwise uneventful." He walks over to me.

"You'll need to get into your armor, sir."

"You don't need to call me sir, Sim. We're alone."

His eyes meet mine. "I could be dead before this day is out, sir." He smiles weakly. "And you will have led me to it." Sim brushes his fingers along my face. "Still, I cannot imagine any place I would rather be. Knowing that you go out to face Tremaine, and what you are risking, and that it is all for me, I cannot imagine not fighting at your side." I lean into his touch, his fingertips calloused, but warm. "I could think of far worse fates than dying alongside the man I love."

"I don't plan on us dying."

"I am aware of this." Another smile crosses his face and I feel ten pounds lighter. "Still, such impending events tend to inspire emotional honesty in humans, and as you are steadfast in making me accept, I am human as well as Fae." He leans in closer, his lips brushing against mine. "How long have you loved me, Richard?"

"I think since... I don't know. I started to know a few days ago, after I was doing that film and you got me the apples and..." Right about when the flame of the sword went out. "And I love you, Simaron Arthur Gray." I feel like I'll float away if he doesn't hold on to me.

"And you need to disrobe, my love."

My eyes go wide, until I chuckle slightly. "Right, right." I remove my jacket, gloves, shirt, start on my boots. "I forgot, it takes a little while to get that armor on."

"Indeed, Richard." His fingers are working my pants open. "About a half hour, if everything's to be affixed properly. Which, of course, leaves us some time to spare." Simaron then gives me a smirk. "This will proceed more quickly, Richard, if you help me out of my armor as well."

It takes a few seconds to register, but when I feel his lips press to mine my head tilts of its own accord, my eyes close and I start to realize that even Sigil doesn't quite have words to describe what I'm feeling. Though we're enclosed in the locker room, at this moment I know that the sky is cloudless above, that the darkness is only temporary, that there are indeed things worth saving, worth dying for, and that what Simaron and I have is unique and sets us apart while making us part of something greater than ourselves, that unites us all. There's a lot more, but like I said, I'm at a lack of words to describe it. If you've experienced it yourself, maybe you'll nod your head along, and if you haven't, don't worry, you will, and you'll know when it happens.

What follows is…

I've been with Simaron before, this much is obvious, apparent, all that. I know his body as well as he knows mine. There's nothing new or adventurous about what we're doing, other than the fact that Simaron himself is taking the lead this time, showing me that he wants me as well, and maybe that's what makes the difference. I could describe it, how we hold each other, arms and legs wrapping about the other tightly, the warmth we share, the way he feels in me, and I in him. It doesn't feel any different, at least physically. I'm just as vocal when I climax and he is just as free with his kisses when he reaches the end.

But I don't want to do it with anyone else now.

It's not a possessive thing. I don't feel he's my property. (Since he's my knight, protocol would suggest he kind of is.) He hasn't really ruined me for all other men. It's another thing I can't quite put into words, or I'd have to lean on song lyrics that have started making sense, that old one about how birds suddenly appear. Because of Simaron, I now know there's so much more going on outside myself and my own little world that he can show me, teach me to see, and that there's so much in my world he doesn't know of yet, that I want to show to him.

Is this what it means?

In all of those stories and songs and poems and movies and paintings that our kind have endeavored to inspire for so long, but never truly understood?

Is this what it truly means to make love?

Chapter Thirty-One
Severed Hand

It's only been a few days since I've worn it at my side, but it's more than a little odd to have my sword again, to know that I can draw it, wield it. I'd always thought of it as a simple heirloom before, albeit one with a nifty trick to it and an interesting story. Still, I never gave it any more importance than a symbol of office. It was just a heavy thing to carry to formal events so everyone would see how important I was. When I drew it, I smiled with no small amount of self-satisfaction at the sight of that azure flame. It let me know that I was, in fact, special. Better.

Ye gods, what world was I living in?

"The challenger, His Excellency, Count Pembroke Kendrick Llewellyn Richard Firemane, Lord of the House of Stone, Knight of the Realm, Viscount of the Benedict Shores, and Custodian of the Azure Blade!"

Oh yeah, the world where I can be killed in full view of six hundred witnesses over some asshole's slighted honor.

"It will be fine, my lord." Must be nice to have the confidence that Simaron has. Then again, he doesn't have to face Tremaine, just my wife. "How far am I permitted to defend myself, sir?" The tone in his voice seems a bit odd until I look across the hardwood court and see Jen.

A bastard sword, hand-and-a-half it's also called, is slung over her back, her body clad in heavy chain, tinged green, emblazoned with the crest of the Duchy of Destry Bay. Her hands are in gauntlets, dull metal shinguards, a shorter blade at her side. She's wearing a helmet, the visor down, more than likely to hide the scar that marks her as an Oathbreaker.

She draws both blades and flourishes them.

Holy. Shit. My wife is a deceptively strong badass. Wielding a hand-and-a-half sword requires an impressive amount of muscle, but a long sword in the off hand? Humans would call it impossible. But that's Fae for you, I guess; to hell with realism.

"Sir?"

"She's wielding a bastard sword."

"I can see that, sir."

"One-handed."

"It would appear so, sir."

I look at Simaron, my eyes wide, feeling true worry sinking in. "She'll kill you."

And he smiles, actually smiles, and takes a genteel bow before drawing his saber. "I do not need to defeat her, my love, merely remain just beyond her reach until you have obtained a yield from Duke Tremaine. However, should Her Excellency be forced to press the issue, how far am I allowed to defend myself?"

Meaning, if it comes down to it, who will I choose?

"Do everything you can to avoid mortal wounds, but..." Oh gods. "If she makes it her or you..." I can't finish that sentence. I feel his hand on my shoulder.

"I will do everything in my power to prevent that from happening, sir." He then motions off toward Tremaine.

"The challenged, His Grace, Duke Bran Owain Gavin Tremaine Duskstar, Lord of the House of Storms, Knight of the Realm, Slayer of the Dagger's Line, Guardian of the Dying Wood, Duke of Destry Bay, and Wielder of the Adamant Heart!" Raucous applause greets the duke, of course. Easy when you're well favored in the betting odds, not to mention that duke is higher than viscount, much higher, and for most Fae that's all the reason they need. The underdog is not respected among my people.

Well, that and Tremaine didn't parade a knighted half-blood into the arena on one of the Fae's most revered holidays and act completely blasé about the whole thing. Just because I'm forward-thinking doesn't mean my fellow aristocrats are going to be.

A fanfare sounds from the luxury boxes, and immediately everyone in the arena turns their attention to them. They're a bit far off, but I can see a female figure with long flowing ebon hair, her skin nearly white, her gown black, probably plucked from the dream of a local designer. I sink to one knee faster than even Simaron can, my head bowed low. I know that everyone in the arena is doing the same. She needs no fancy introduction, no listing of titles or accomplishments or honors. I simply know, as all other Fae do, in my mind, heart and blood, who she is.

Her Majesty, the Queen.

Did I mention she sent me her regards, by the way?

I mean, it's not like she does that for everyone, you know. Big deal, and maybe it could mean a few things for—

"Duke Tremaine, you may draw your blade first."

Her voice carries, even from all that distance, having weight and authority. I doubt I could resist if I wanted to. And I kind of want to. I still don't know what's going to happen here.

"With greatest and deepest honor, Your Majesty." Tremaine rises from his position and pulls the Adamant Heart from its scabbard, the blade gleaming under the house lights, the enchanted steel a deep bloody red, looking constantly wet. It's said that the Adamant Heart cannot be bent or broken, that it's forged of the same mythical metal that makes up its name, that the Emperor himself made it thirst for blood.

Her Royal Majesty then turns her attention to me.

"Count Stone, if you please."

Moment of truth.

Every time before that my fingers have closed around the grip of my blade, I've felt reassured, confident. When I tug at the sword to inch it out of its scabbard, there's a bit of resistance at first. As the blade emerges into the light, I can feel the dead silence in the arena as it does not, in fact, ignite with a glorious azure flame. The muffled comments start next, a building roar. I half-expect Rem to suddenly appear and admonish me, or give me some support, or *something*. It would be appropriate, after all.

I look at the blade and lift it high, closing my eyes for a few seconds. The words come easy, sliding through my throat, shaped by my tongue and vibrations of my vocal chords, emerging as song. I don't even know which song it is, it's just what I'm feeling, what Simaron helped me feel. I think of the sword itself as an empty staff, the Sigil filling it with the glowing notes of my heart and my soul.

Surprised sounds echo through the arena afterward, and I open my eyes to find a silver fire blazing brightly, proudly.

"Impostor!" Tremaine has leveled his blade on me. "That isn't the blade he agreed to use for this duel. He must forfeit immediately." I can see his eyes... Fear? The audience is shouting, so much rage coursing through the air over bets, arrangements, wagers. Simaron remains still, so does Jen. Cadwyn is off in her own box, her face placid. I think she knows, now, what I truly am.

"Tremaine." The arena goes silent in a heartbeat. Her Majesty tilts her head in what looks like amusement. "I believe it is not your prerogative to decide a winner." I feel her eyes on me. "Count Stone, is this your family's blade?"

"It is, Your Majesty."

"And you can explain this...change in your blade's disposition?"

"I can, Your Majesty." I don't continue, not until she tells me to. It's not to withhold information, it's that you don't bore Her Royal Majesty with details unless she fucking asks for them, thank you very much.

"Then please do, Count Stone."

"The blade will alight with azure fire for any Fae, Your Majesty." Quite a few gasps there. Her Majesty appears unmoved. "However, if one has been fully accepted by the House of Stone, then one may call the blade by its true name and it will show its favor." I am telling the truth here. Rem approves of me, I know the blade's name, and it will show its favor, hopefully, if I live through the day. The silver fire is all me, but I'm not confessing to that unless I'm asked.

"I see." A curt nod, and that's it. "I cannot find reason why this duel cannot proceed, Tremaine. I'm certain that the Adamant Heart would have little trouble facing what you feel is an impostor's blade." Ouch.

He's getting angry, which isn't good. I know they say a calm mind prevails in battle, but this is a Fae we're talking about. All he has to do is let himself go to the Nightmare and...

Tremaine turns to Jen. "The viscount has insulted us all with his choice for a second. Kill the tainted one. Make it bloody." He then practically shoves her out in front of him, which...is *not* done. Seconds don't start the fight. I proceed forward, sword raised, and motion with my hand for Sim to stay behind me. Already the crowd is stirring up its bloodlust. I can feel the heat of it churning in me as well, the subtle pull to let go, and all the strength I'll need will be there to cleave that fucker in twain. All I have to do is—

No. No, I need to handle this.

"You send out your *second* to fight your duel?" Because clearly the right move is to underline the fact that he was asleep when they taught Dueling 101. Ye gods, I'm just asking to get killed. Wait, wait, wait... Maybe that might work.

Getting him mad, not the getting-myself-killed part.

I remember Simaron's mother teaching me to sing, the difference between the "head voice" and the "chest voice", how to project. I make sure to put my full voice forward. "Afraid to fight someone from the *fringe*, Tremaine? I was right, you are a little *bitch.*"

A laugh. From the crowd.

It's a snicker, contagious, breaking the mood slightly, culling the bloodlust by degrees as it starts to spread.

"And using the Adamant Heart." I start circling, staying away from Jen and Tremaine, still in full voice. "It is an impressive blade, though. Long, straight, inflexible, never failing when it's needed to perform..." I smile big for the crowd. "Considering you have no heirs, I'll bet that's the only thing you own with those qualities!"

The snickering becomes full laughter, echoing through the arena. I can hear repeated demands from Tremaine for silence. I take a moment to bow, elegantly, to the Queen's box. I'm leaving a huge opening, here. I know this. But I want it to seem that the Queen supports me over him, whether it's actually true or not.

I'm surprised Jen hasn't come after me, to be honest.

"My lord, what are you *doing*?" Simaron is behind me, his voice agitated.

"Rattling him, Sim." I do have a plan, I'm sure. I just don't quite know what it is yet.

"He'll fall to the Nightmare, sir."

From the look of the duke, it appears that he's well on his way to that. He's wildly gesticulating at the crowd, demanding quiet. I mock his gestures, ratcheting up the laughter even more. They think me a fringer? County trash? A mere fool? Fine, I'll play the role to the damned hilt.

"Sir!" I look toward Tremaine long enough to see that he is, in fact, rushing me, holding the Adamant Heart one-handed. I shove Sim backward and dive to the left, rolling, thankful that my momentum can get me back into a somewhat upright position. My armor isn't made for agility, after all. I see Tremaine rush by, and I swing the sword after him, the silver flame that sheathes the blade splashing visibly as the flat of the sword slaps the duke in the ass.

In case you're wondering why I didn't cut his head off, he was running away from me when I swung. The best I could hope for was contact. The sword probably would've bounced off his armor anyway. Best to keep up with playing the fool for the crowd. It works, the laughter building into a roar, the bloodlust of the crowd ebbing away, clearing my head. I blow a kiss to the assembled Fae and take my guard as Tremaine turns to face me.

He's rattled now, definitely.

Tremaine swings the blade, and I block it, locking our blades, our strength pitted against the other, my face close to his.

"I will kill you." His voice is an almost growl, his eyes red. *Literally* red, and growing darker by the second. The Nightmare is taking him, slow but sure.

"Doing a fine job of it so far!" It's all I can do to keep him back. Ye gods he's strong. I drop my voice low, almost a whisper. "Why so much difficulty, Tremaine? I'm just county trash, aren't I? Can't you claim victory over a mere actor? Then again, it appears the only fight you *can* win is with a defenseless woman." I then spit, hard, right in his eyes, and shift my weight, pivoting to my right, releasing the locked swords, letting his full strength barrel forward while he's temporarily blinded, right over my extended leg.

He trips and bobbles his steps for a second before crashing onto his chest, the roar of laughter almost deafening now.

Another roar. But not from the crowd. From him. I back away slowly, my sword up. Jen is still...standing there. What the hell? You'd think she'd have attacked by now.

He stands, his eyes...

Black.

That... That's not...

Oh shit, what did I do?

"Sir?" Sim is beside me, his sword raised at Tremaine.

"I see." I gently push him to my left, away from Jen. "Flank." He nods quickly and circles as Tremaine starts trembling, then screaming, waves of rage coming off him and coursing through me. This... This isn't the Nightmare.

The laughter has died in the audience, bloodlust not taking its place. No, this is fear. Ye gods, what's happening to him?

I hear crunching sounds, sounds of pain, anger coming from Tremaine as his armor starts to shift about, his skin darkening into a sickening violet, blood streaming down his forehead as...

As horns begin to grow outward.

I hear a scream from the crowd, which multiplies all too quickly, the crowd starting to rush the exits. To hell with me, I guess.

Tremaine gains height, his armor bursting its bindings, only the sword remaining in his hands as he slams it hard into the floor, splintering the hardwood. I stagger backwards, my body locking its muscles in terror. No. No. No. I have to get a handle on this.

"Sim, run. Get out of here. Take Jen and go!" I can't leave the arena. I'm bound by vow to not leave until either Tremaine or I have drawn final breath. That...thing... It's still Tremaine, whatever sort of Nightmare he's lost himself to...

The Nightmare. I taught you all how to ride it, to make its strength your own, but some of you, you became lost to it but you would fight so well, even the gods themselves, even other Ra'Keth would fear you. The demons. They were Fae.

Holy shit.

Tremaine has become a demon.

"Sim, run!" Desperation tinges my voice. It's a noble sacrifice, right? Dying to save the one you love? I'm sure they'll tell nice stories about me at my funeral. Simaron damned well better mention my prowess in the bedroom several times as well. In my eulogy.

"I will not abandon you." He takes a guarded stance, his steps tentative. "My vows to you do not end with minor inconveniences such as this, sir."

And Tremaine rushes me. I ready myself, feeling vibrations through the earth as his heavy feet stomp on the wood, leaving cracks behind. He swings the Adamant Heart with speed and ease. I'm sure he doesn't even know what's happened to him. All he probably knows right now is that he's been humiliated and I'm the reason.

The Heart comes down and I barely knock it away in time, preserving the ongoing existence of my left arm. Holy shit, that *stung.* I manage to keep my grip on the blade and attempt a riposte, and connect with the strike, the blade slicing cleanly into his forearm...

And leaving a pretty superficial wound. Apparently silver flame doesn't have the same preternatural sharpness as the azure fire of family shame. I look up at him, into his abyssal eyes, and shrug almost comically, tittering with high anxiety.

The response is a backhand that sends me airborne. I land hard on my back, skidding across the three-point line. My chest is a crumpled tangle of pain, more than likely caused by the massive dent in my breastplate. Good thing Dad's not here to see this, he'd be pissed.

I hear a short grunt of pain from the demon as I wearily raise my head, and see Sim stick Tremaine in the leg, a short slash across the hamstring, but unfortunately not connecting all that well. Tremaine brings the Adamant Heart down on him and Sim sidesteps, trying to swat away the blade, but only receives a broken saber as a result. The impact of the sword is still lessened, though, and Simaron is knocked back, an angry gash cutting through his armor, a spray of...of...blood coming from...from him and...

"*No!*" I force myself to my feet. I can feel the Nightmare thrashing in my heart. It could be so easy. I could unleash all the rage and slice through him clean for...

No. Sim isn't dead yet. I can't give in.

The demon chuckles darkly as I stumble toward him. Jen is on the sideline, cowering.

Cowering? She's supposed to be a Demonbane! What the fuck?

I raise the blade, the damage to my armor lessening my mobility. I feel like a giant bruise but I can't give up. I have to do this alone. Is this how it was for you, Dad? Will this scene be engraved on the fuller of the Azure Blade—

Right, it's not actually the Azure Blade, it's...

It clicks into place as Tremaine raises the sword, preparing to swing.

You've been calling it by the wrong name for millennia now.

The sword has another name, its true name.

I wanted a blade sharp enough to cleave a raindrop in twain without splattering it. And I succeeded in forging it.

And it is only that sharp to those who call it by its name.

"*Rain Cutter.*"

The Adamant Heart comes down.

Rain Cutter slashes up.

Soundlessly, effortlessly, my blade slides through the sword thought unbreakable.

The blade of the Adamant Heart clatters to the hardwood somewhere behind me.

Holy shit, did I really just do that?

The Adamant Heart has a blade only dagger length now. I take a second just to adjust to the shock of it. Ye gods, I really just did that and—

I see a quick flash of metal, hear a soft whistle as Tremaine brings his truncated blade down.

And I drop my sword.

I hear it hit the hardwood and I didn't drop it, what the hell? Why does my arm...hurt?

I look down, and just before Tremaine connects his fist with my face, I see my sword, Rain Cutter, lying on the half-court emblem of the basketball team.

With my right hand still holding it.

Even as I'm in the air, the cracking sound of my jaw breaking still echoing in my ears, all I can think is...

Why is my hand on the floor?

I lift my head slowly, my vision a blur. Something wraps tightly around my right wrist, the warmth like a strange bubble there. Why isn't my hand moving?

A large shape lumbers toward me and my body is dragged backward, slowly. I hear grunts of exhaustion behind me, mixed with pain. "Do not leave me, Richard. Please."

Sim?

I can't make words. What emerges is a pained gurgle as my chest labors to draw in breath.

"I love you too, Richard." Arms draw me close as the demon comes into slow focus, raising his blade. Sim and I will die together, at least. I can think of worse fates. I can certainly think of better ones though.

Tremaine roars in satisfaction above us, preparing to stab us both with the remnant of the Adamant Heart.

"*Rain Cutter.*"

No, it's the Adamant Heart. I'm pretty sure.

I hear a soft whistle of wind, and Tremaine stands stock still and then gurgles softly...

His torso slides off the rest of his body, spilling black blood onto the hardwood as the bottom half of him topples over, revealing Jen standing behind him. She flicks the blade, the demon's blood splattering the wood to her right, and she comes to Sim and I, laying the sword beside me.

I try to thank her, but it doesn't emerge.

"Thank you, my lady." Sim provides the words on our behalf.

She lifts her helmet off and...

And Duchess Catrin turns her head to spit on the corpse of her husband.

"No, Sir Simaron, Count Stone. The gratitude is mine."

Chapter Thirty-Two
Love, Reign O'er Me

I vaguely remember blacking out sometime after the battle, and when I awoke, I was rather certain that I had ascended to the afterlife, simply on the virtue of the wounds I'd sustained. After you suffer wounds like that, you expect to wake up, if you wake up at all, in a hospital bed with all manner of tubes sticking out of you. I wake up in my own bed, the stereo playing through one of my bootlegs. The air smells slightly of cinnamon and sage.

My head feels like it's made of wood and stuffed full of cotton. My chest still feels like a horse is sitting on me. And yes, there's pain. A bit of it, but all in that "manageable" zone you can tough out if you really put your mind to it. Thing is, I've been through hell. I don't want to put my mind to it. Those humans have figured out all manner of opiates, and I personally wouldn't mind seeing what they've come up with for this sort of situation.

I start to lift the covers off my chest to survey the damage when the most apparent injury makes itself known—my right hand doesn't grip the covers. All that's there is a heavy mass of clean bandages that cover my wrist. I stare at it for some time, in pure disbelief, my left hand waving back and forth through the empty air where my right hand should be.

“Oh fuck...” My voice is rough, gravelly. I can move my jaw, though it feels like all my joints are rusted shut. I run my tongue along my teeth and feel plenty of broken edges, all of them loose. I’ll get another set of teeth, just like my broken ribs will mend, and probably already have. Dream-food does that for us, like I mentioned. But no amount of it will restore my hand.

“I suspected you would awaken the moment I left the room. The seer told me that a narcissus does not bloom whilst one gazes on it. It made little sense until now.” The voice breaks my trance, and I look up to see Sim, shirtless, his chest wrapped in bandages as well. His steps are slow, deliberate, his face clearly showing effort to fight off pain. He sits on the bed next to me, on the left side, taking my hand. “I was confident you would recover.” He does sound confident in that, evident by his smile.

“Good to know one of us was convinced of my survival.”

“Of course. Stories such as this cannot end with the hero dying.”

I try to laugh, but it comes out as half-sputters of breath.

“You really believe that?”

“I had to, Richard.” He squeezes my hand tightly. “I needed to. If you were not to survive, I do not believe I could have...” Simaron exhales, glancing away a moment. “It is no matter. You are alive, I am alive, although we did not escape unscathed.” He motions to his chest. “I have been told I will carry a reminder of the late Duke Tremaine for the rest of my days.” His face softens as his gaze falls on my right...arm. “I apologize, Richard. I did not mean to belittle...”

“Hey, chicks dig scars.” I attempt a wry smirk. “By that logic they must really go for amputees, right?”

“Richard.” He rests his hand on my wrist. I keep my smile going, but his eyes tell me it’s okay, I can let go.

And then I cry. I’m in Simaron’s arms, my head buried in

his chest, wetting his bandages with my tears. It certainly could have been worse, I know this. The humans have made remarkable progress in prosthetics. With a few weeks I'll be as skilled with my left hand as I was with my right. I'm Fae, it'll all be as easy as it needs to be for me. Simaron will love me and does love me, no matter how much of me is left. I know all of this.

But it's still my hand. It needs at least a few minutes of mourning.

Simaron is there to give me all the minutes I need.

I emerge from my sorrow some time later, all cried out, my curiosity starting to win over my loss. "So...do I remember right? Was Duchess Catrin there at the end?"

"Yes, Richard. It appears she invoked her authority over Countess Stone and ordered her to attend to Tremaine's goblins as opposed to fighting in the duel. As Her Excellency swore her fealty to Duchess Catrin, and given her personal connection to her, she obeyed. I would suppose Her Grace felt a Demonbane would be more effective against goblins than she. Apparently, Her Grace wished to have her late husband's duel be as difficult as possible. A clever ruse, it surprises me what dishonesties a Fae can accomplish by simply standing mute rather than correcting a false assumption." I'm sure Duchess Cadwyn would probably blow his mind, then.

Sim leans back on the bed, resting me against his chest, making no mention of whether he can handle it or not.

"What about Jen?"

"Countess Stone is dealing with the nobility for the moment. As you have been recovering from your injuries, she has been handling the day-to-day matters of the House. You will be interested to hear that the Duchy of Destry Bay has offered a formal alliance between it and the Benedict Shores.

The treaty is waiting on word of your recovery. Considering the damage that Tremaine did to the duchy's reputation…"

"I would be doing them a favor. I'll go over it when I'm feeling a bit better. How are things at the commune?" I then furrow my brow. "Gods, how long have I been out, anyway?"

"Five days."

I blink several times, but I really shouldn't be all that surprised. Simaron runs his fingers along my side while he continues.

"I have not been able to check in personally, but quite a few perishables have been sent by courier. I would suspect that all is well there." He strokes his head over my chest comfortingly. "I fear our time together alone will not be too much longer, Richard. You have a few visitors anxiously awaiting news of your health. It would be cruel to deny them much further, but…" He kisses me, gently. "I admit I am tempted to be selfish for a moment longer, call you by your given name, as a lover should, be more than your knight. I fear you have been a corruptive influence on me, my love."

I smirk. "About damned time." I lean up to kiss him again.

"It would appear that I am interrupting. Should I wait outside, Count Stone?" I know that voice. I look toward the door and…

"Your Majesty!" Both Simaron and I say it at the same time. Simaron nearly tumbles off the bed, falling onto bended knee. Me, well, I bow my head, that's pretty much all I can do. I don't avert my eyes, to do so would be an insult to her as Fae perfection is to be awed at, not ignored.

Her Royal Majesty, the Queen, is wearing a silk dress, flowing, almost sheer, like it's made of moonbeams, but then again it might be. Her hair is swept back, wavy, her face deceptively plain, looking effortlessly beautiful with no assistance. The weight of her authority is like a hand of the gods pressing down on the room itself.

"An excellent bout, Count Stone." She almost floats to the foot of my bed, her fingers gracefully trailing along the footboard. "It is a pity that I had to cancel all wagers placed, as the duel was between you and Duke Tremaine, not the creature who slew him. Your arrangement with Tremaine was also rendered null. Duchess Catrin has informed me though, that she seeks no recompense for the conduct of your..." Her gaze falls on Simaron. "Knight." She looks to me again. "I was not aware that viscounts could raise those of his kind to knighthood, Count Stone."

Oh shit. Oh shit, shit, shit.

I have only a few seconds to answer before this gets very bad. "I thought it fitting, Your Majesty, given his exemplary service to my House and county, as well as his bravery and valor."

She shakes her head once. "I apologize, Count Stone, but it is not the place of viscounts to decide such things." She beckons Simaron over, and he gingerly makes his way to her and kneels before her. "Your name."

I see him swallow hard. "Simaron Arthur Gray, Your Majesty."

"You are devoted to your lord?"

"Yes, Your Majesty."

"And his county?"

"Yes, Your Majesty." She sees my anxiety that my broken body won't let me hide.

"And your kingdom?" Her attention returns to Sim. "Does your devotion and loyalty extend to that as well?" And then that attention falls back on me. "You do understand, Count Stone, that it would not bode well for me to have one of my viscounts with his own twin-blooded knight, as well as a community of twin-bloods on his land, all of whom would swear loyalty to him." She turns to Simaron. "It would be best for all involved if your loyalty was to the kingdom as well, Simaron Arthur Gray."

He nods quickly. "Yes, Your Majesty." She then places her hand on his forehead.

"Then I dub thee Sir Simaron Gray, Knight of the Realm, and appoint you as my liaison to the twin-blooded people. As the majority of the twin-bloods live within Count Stone's holdings, I believe it prudent to station you here and work closely with him." He gazes up at her in awe. A twin-blooded knight, initiated by the Queen Herself. While this is hardly equal treatment for his people, it's a formal recognition of their existence. It's definitely a place to start. Also, with the Queen calling them twin-bloods, everyone else will have to as well. "Now, please give me a moment alone with Count Stone."

"I..." He glances to me, and I don't do anything, don't nod, nothing that would imply that I hold sway over him. He takes the hint. "Yes, Your Majesty." Simaron makes his exit, but probably is waiting just outside with the rest of my visitors. The door opens and I see my mother, my stepfather, several other Fae I recognize. When the door closes, the Queen turns back to me.

"Firstly, I must decree that everything we are about to speak of remains secret. There is no secret you will be able to trade that will be worth this. Do you understand?" I can only nod in assent. "Tell me of the sword, Count Stone."

I take a deep breath, which yes, kind of hurts a little. "It's called Rain Cutter, not the Azure Blade. It only burned blue to show my House's disapproval of whoever drew it. When you know the blade's true name, and call it by that name, well, if the sword accepts you it can cut through anything. Even the Adamant Heart, apparently."

"Intriguing, but you've made no mention of it burning with a silver flame. You told me that the silver flame was a sign of your House's acceptance, do you remember?"

Oh shit. She doesn't look angry, but this is a Fae Queen. Beautiful and terrible as the dawn, all that. You can't get a read on her.

"The House's acceptance doesn't have to do with the sword. I was able to make the flame because I proved myself to my ancestor."

"Mercia?" she asks, but she knows the answer.

"No."

"Then who?"

"Rem, a Ra'Keth." I swallow hard again. "The Ra'Keth who founded the House of Stone."

"And how did you gain his acceptance?" She doesn't sound at all surprised or shocked.

"Long story short? I became mystic." I bow my head low. That is grounds for a death sentence if the stories are true, and why wouldn't they be?

"Are you aware, Count Stone, what it means when a member of the Sunleaf line is revealed to be mystic?"

I exhale hard. "We aren't Sunleaves anymore?"

She nods once. And my world starts to crumble apart. I'm still a Firemane. And I'm still a Stone. That's got to mean something, right?

"What is the royal line called, Count Stone?"

I blink at her. "You're a Summersword, Your Majesty."

"Indeed." She places her hand where my hand used be, her

fingertips brushing my wrist. "Though the royal line goes through the Sunleaves. You and I do share blood, however distantly." My arm is feeling oddly warm. "But, to be a Summersword, the crown must choose you, choose your line. Much like proving oneself to one's House." I can feel tendrils of pain knotting up in my wrist. "But one cannot rule the Fae, keep a living dream alive in a changing world without being in balance with it." Ye gods, it hurts so much. Please make it stop. I can't say anything though. Either her authority or the pain is keeping my lips sealed. I hear a tearing sound, feel heat, something wet on my wrist. "One must accept the touch of humanity. If we are to be their dreams, we must do no less. To rule the Fae, one must have the approval of one's Fae forebears..." My body trembles almost violently with pain spasms, and then calms, so quickly calms, my hands clenching tightly and... Hands? "And our Ra'Keth ancestors."

She removes her hand from me, and while it's covered in my blood, my hand is there. It's...really there. I flutter my fingers a few seconds, expecting it to vanish at any moment. "Is it...?"

"Your recovery will take several days longer, but yes, you have regained what you lost."

"How?"

She smiles gently, and it all comes clear.

"You're...mystic?"

"To be a Summersword, Count Stone, the crown demands no less." She rises from my bed and walks toward the door. Before I can say anything more, she holds up her hand to me. "No thanks are required. It is the least I can do..." She stops at the door. "For one of my heirs." She opens the door and closes it behind her before I can react. I feel the weight of the decree silencing my words. I can't tell anyone...

I'm...one of the heirs to the throne?

Holy shit did my life just get a lot more complicated. The Crown Prince is still the Heir with a capital H, but I'm in the running now. Simaron comes in seconds later, his face showing concern, but I offer a weak smile to let him know that everything is all right and beckon him over with my right hand. He rushes to my side, covering my face with kisses before he sets to wiping my hand clean of blood. He doesn't ask how or why, he accepts or guesses correctly that I can't talk about it.

I have to be thankful that it's a secret between me and Her Royal Majesty, at least for the moment. Now I have assassination attempts to look forward to, as well as nobles seeking favor, noblewomen looking to carry my heirs, and probably a thousand other things I won't see coming.

And here I thought I'd earned some of those salad days of yore that the bard was always yammering about.

"Duchess Cadwyn is waiting to see you, Richard."

I nod once, and he moves away to let her in, but I pull him back into a long deep kiss. "I suspect Duke Madoc is sore about his bet. If it had held up, he'd have forty-five hundred sovereigns. Let them wait a little longer. I've got a few days on this recovery."

"Are you upset about the Queen's plan for me?"

I shake my head once.

"Richard, it eventually will be difficult. While everything is placed well at present, my loyalty is now to the Summerswords and the throne itself. I will have to discern some way to continue my devotion to you while staying loyal to the throne." And I smile. I smile big. "Richard, please, we must consider the possibilities of the future."

I pull him close to me for another kiss and feel his warmth against me. The world and all of its responsibilities and dangers are waiting for me just beyond my bedroom door, but I'll have Sim to stand beside me, whether I end up slain by a demon or crowned King of the Fae. Maybe I don't know where the road will lead, but I know I'll walk it with open eyes, and I won't walk it alone, and in the end, that's all you can really ask for. The rest?

"Simaron, my love, I believe the future is going to take care of itself."

About the Author

Vaughn R. Demont is a writer trying to beat the odds and be a career writer. Gay, poor, and living in the subarctic tundra of Central New York, Vaughn likes to think of himself as a quintessential Scorpio. He received his Bachelor of Arts in Creative Writing from Oswego State University, and his Master of Fine Arts in Creative Writing from Goddard College. He has published several novelettes and novellas. *House of Stone* is his first published novel.

To learn more about Vaughn R. Demont, please visit http://vaughn-r-demont.livejournal.com. Send an email to Vaughn at vaughndemont@yahoo.com.

Deep runs the world of magic—and desire.

Tatterdemalion

© 2010 *Anah Crow and Dianne Fox*

Foundations of Magic, Book 1

Lindsay Carrington is a prisoner of his life—first in the mundane world, then in the military testing facility where his parents sent him to have his magic dissected, studied and "fixed". When he finally escapes, freedom comes at great cost. The man who rescues him from near death in a dark alley is far from a savior. He's a feral mage nearly as broken as Lindsay himself.

Dane knows better than to argue with the wind that summoned him to Lindsay's rescue, but playing nursemaid isn't the role he envisioned for himself in the battle to end the human campaign to control his people. In spite of his resistance, he is bound to the delicate, skittish mage who unwittingly harbors one of the greatest magical powers ever known.

Lindsay desperately hides his growing desire, sure that Dane could never reciprocate. Yet Dane lays his life on the line to protect him, restoring the one thing Lindsay thought was gone forever: hope.

But true freedom to live—and to love—will elude Lindsay until he can regain his magic and win Dane's complete devotion. And survive long enough to do both.

Warning: Contains graphic language, violence and explicit erotic content.

One warrior, one sorcerer,
and a legacy that will change their lives forever...

The Lost Son

© 2010 Mychael Black

Secrets of Socendor, Book 1

In the world of Socendor, humans are forbidden from using magic and elves keep their distance.

Kalen Ysindroc has risen far from his humble beginnings as a blacksmith's adopted son. Now the king's general, he investigates reports of magic-wielding half-human, half-elven *lithings* sighted along the kingdom's borders. It would be a lonely life, if not for the company of his best friend and long-time elven lover, Micheil Theirauf, the king's sorcerer.

An attempt on Kalen's life makes it clear to Micheil that there's more afoot than random breaks in the land's defenses. His lover is plagued by dreams no human should endure, and Micheil's probe into Kalen's subconscious reveals a past neither of them expected. And a future Kalen can't escape.

Suddenly, everything Kalen never knew about his life is laid bare. A father possessed of terrible magical power. A half-brother who could be the family Kalen never had—or the catalyst that will rip Micheil out of his life forever...

Warning: Explicit gay sex (on a horse, even!), men in armor, swords (not just THAT kind!), sorcery, betrayal, and at least one conniving ghost.

CPSIA information can be obtained at www.ICGtesting.com
229241LV00001B/53/P

9 781609 280918